THE RED KING OF HELSINKI

LIES, SPIES AND GYMNASTICS

HELENA HALME

Helena
HALME

The
RED KING
of Helsinki

1

Iain watched on the snow-covered jetty as a small tugboat slowly piloted HMS *Newcastle* into Helsinki South Harbour, frozen but for a jagged shipping lane cutting between thick sheets of ice. He'd been following the gradually expanding navigation lights for over an hour while the faint winter sun rose above the Gulf of Finland.

The snowfall had made the day's copy of *Helsingin Sanomat* folded under his arm limp. Iain shivered as he placed the paper inside his thick winter coat and pulled the collar further up around his ears. A glance at his watch showed 08:06. They were on time at least. He stamped his feet. The Finns say the coldest winds blow from Siberia, and this morning Iain understood what they meant. Even the weather from the mighty Soviet Union was a bully to its small neighbour.

Finally the ship docked and Iain climbed onboard. He nodded at a Sub Lieutenant, who bounced down the gangway and told Iain to follow him. He looked like a child, with a freshly scrubbed pink face, and at the last minute Iain remembered not to salute him. He kept forgetting he was a civilian now. But the ship, with its musty smell, a combination of salty seawater and diesel oil, made him feel at home. 'Good passage?'

'Yes Sir,' replied the officer, showing Iain into a small cabin.

The Colonel was bent over a tiny desk in the corner, his back to Iain.

'Welcome to Helsinki, Sir,' Iain said. Again the desire to stand to attention overtook him, and he half lifted his hand, but placed it down before it reached the side of his head.

'Ah, Collins. You look cold and wet. Is it really that bad out there?'

Iain ignored this jibe and looked around the cabin. It was a small space, but a luxury for any officer onboard. There was a small porthole, 'heads' and crisp white linen on the bunk. The Colonel nodded towards a chair and Iain sat down.

'Well?' the Colonel said. His cheeks had broken veins and in the harsh overhead light of the cabin he looked old and weary.

'Sir, page five, bottom right-hand corner.' Iain handed the Colonel the damp *Helsingin Sanomat*. The short article was buried amongst domestic news.

'A woman, aged 29, was found dead on Tehtaankatu late yesterday morning. It has been confirmed as the body of a Soviet citizen, employed as a temporary administrative assistant at the Embassy. According to the official source the woman died of natural causes.'

The Colonel considered the page. Iain watched his eyes as he scanned the print and spotted the small, insignificant notice. After a brief moment, he handed the paper back to Iain without saying a word. He crossed his hands over his considerable belly and leant back in his chair. Iain wondered if the Colonel's Finnish was sufficient for him to understand the meaning of the words.

'Don't know if it's significant, but brought it along in case.'

'Hmm, well done,' the Colonel said.

'I wasn't sure if I should have contacted the paper?'

'No, of course not. We'll look into it.' The Colonel looked at his hands, then up at Iain, 'How's the surveillance going?'

'Well, Sir.'

There was a silence and Iain wondered if he was supposed to make a move to leave the cabin and the Colonel. But the Colonel handed Iain a green folder.

'Try to find out more about this man, Jukka Linnonmaa. He's just come back from Moscow and we need to know how active he is. He might get in the way.'

Iain opened the file.

'Take it home and read it. There's the address, wife's name, any family connections, that sort of thing. Have a little look at his place, see where he goes.'

'Yes Sir,' Iain said.

'You'll soon get the hang of it. Report back to me daily.'

The Colonel got up, and Iain followed his example.

'And Collins,' The Colonel said when Iain was at the door, 'try not to come onboard too often – once more to welcome us into town on behalf of the British Council, and perhaps when we leave to wave us goodbye, is the norm.'

'Yes, Sir,' Iain said. The Sub Lieutenant had reappeared outside the cabin.

'Goodbye, Sir,' the young officer said and saluted Iain as he made his way back down the gangway.

The city was quiet – only the noise of the tram trundling down from Ullanlinna broke the downy silence that the freshly fallen snow had created. Iain sighed and stuffed the folder inside his coat. With hands deep in the pockets, he walked briskly up the South Esplanade. People were hurrying to work, huddled against the cold wind. It was already ten o'clock and still not full daylight. The Esplanade Park looked grey. The bare trees were heavy with last night's snowfall. Only a narrow path in the middle of the park had been cleared and sanded. He wondered if the sun was going to show itself today. It was February. At least the days were slowly growing longer, though in this kind of morning twilight, midnight sun seemed impossible.

Iain wondered what the hell he thought he was doing. Had it not been for the money, he'd never have accepted a job like this. But he now realised he'd also fallen for the flattery. The Colonel had been complementary when they met in a stuffy office at the British Embassy in Helsinki. Iain had never been inside the Embassy before. It was a beautiful white house on a leafy street in Ullanlinna. Had it not been so cold, Iain would have walked there, up the hill from the Council. But it had been a dull January morning, with a bitter northerly wind. So Iain rode the tram up three stops from Erottaja to Puistotie. The meeting was arranged to discuss the forthcoming British naval visit to Helsinki. Iain assumed he'd be told to arrange the appropriate, low-key publicity in the Finnish press. He'd wondered if the visit was organised to silence the reports running in the Western press about planned Finnish joint military exercises with the Soviet Union. Even the long-standing President Kekkonen, who was rarely directly quoted in the press these days, had given a televised interview just before Christmas to counter the press reports. Political and military neutrality was taken very seriously in Finland.

The Colonel had offered him a drink, 'Whisky and soda?'

It was barely eleven o'clock.

'So, how long have you been in Helsinki?' the Colonel had sat down heavily opposite Iain.

'Just over five months.'

'Your wife was born in Finland?'

'Yes.' Iain looked down at his hands and added, 'ex-wife.'

'I see.'

There was a brief silence. Iain had studied the Colonel closely on that first meeting. Mrs Cooper at the Council had hinted he was an important man in Helsinki. His build was heavy and he was in his late forties, or perhaps early fifties. His fair hair was thinning at the top. He wore half-moon glasses and was softly spoken, with the kind of low, commanding voice you'd expect from an Army officer.

A voice that would carry far on the parade ground.

He was studying a black file.

'Now then,' he began, 'you're ex-Navy, fairly recently retired?'

'Six months February.'

'Her Majesty must be sorely missing you already,' the Colonel looked up and smiled, 'we could use more officers like you.'

Iain had felt his cheeks redden. When he resigned, no one had asked him to stay. The Colonel was reading from his file. First Iain felt the flattery, then something else. Like a noose tightening around his neck. What was this all about?

'You ex-wife, she would have no family or friends in Helsinki?'

'Of course she does,' Iain said, his voice rising when he didn't want it to. Didn't the Colonel know, or hadn't he bothered to find out, that most people in Finland had a relative – aunt, uncle or brother – who had moved to Helsinki in search of work?

The Colonel sighed and looked down at his hands, 'Your Finnish language skills are quite unique.'

Everyone, particularly Virpi's parents, had been stunned Iain mastered the language – which they'd told him was the most difficult to learn after Chinese – so quickly.

'It's love,' Iain had joked, squeezing Virpi closer to himself. The embarrassed silence following the comment reminded him how private and serious the Finns were. That was in the early days, on his first visit to see her parents near Joensuu.

When he left, and the break-up was obvious, Virpi had wanted to stay in their end-of-terrace house in Old Portsmouth, which Iain had painted pink in happier times. The house had become too small for the two of them. As long as Iain was away at sea for long parts of the year, Virpi was happy. She couldn't cope with Iain at home. After six months of constant rows, Iain jumped at the chance of a job in Whitehall, only to regret it weeks later. He should have stuck it out in Portsmouth, worked on his marriage. But Iain had never been a match for Virpi, her determined voice, deadly looks and icy conviction. So instead he'd moved on and taken the job in Helsinki. In search of what? Escaping what?

'Thank you,' Iain said and smiled at the Colonel.

The Colonel made it all sound so easy, yet honourable. And Helsinki was so much more expensive than Iain had remembered. He couldn't understand how one could live on the measly British Council pay in one of the most expensive cities in the world. Had he been earmarked from the start? No, Iain couldn't believe that. The Colonel told him they'd found out by chance he was ex-Navy.

'Handy for the Official Secrets Act,' the Colonel had said, then continued, 'What I'm getting at, old boy is...', the

Colonel glanced at Iain over the top of his glasses. The leather chair squeaked as he moved his leg on top of the other.

'I understand. You're right. No one from my past knows I'm in Helsinki,' Iain said. And he was right. In the six months he'd spent in the small Finnish capital he'd not bumped into any of Virpi's relatives or friends. Iain smiled. Perhaps they'd seen him first and were avoiding him. Or they didn't expect to see him there without Virpi. Just as well, he thought.

The Finns liked to think Helsinki was a big city. Iain assumed that in a country with a population smaller than London's, the largest centre would seem substantial to its inhabitants.

Hurrying along the sanded Esplanade to return to the warmth of his office at the British Council, Iain nearly collided with a woman in high-heeled boots. First he thought it was Maija. She had the same direct gaze, and the same colour eyes. Her fitted coat tied neatly around the waist reminded him of Maija too. He nodded to the woman and smiled. She hurried past him, not returning his smile. Iain was reminded of one of Virpi's anecdotes about Finland.

'In winter only drunks, lunatics and foreigners smile at strangers. And none of them can be trusted.'

Waiting for the traffic lights just outside the Council building to turn green, Iain decided he'd give Maija a call. He thought of her soft round breasts, her uncomplicated attitude to sex. As long as he remembered not to smile to strangers, life was uncomplicated here in Finland. No ex-wife, no long-lost naval friends reminiscing about the good old times, which never were so very good. So why did he complicate it by doing a job for MI6 of all things? Was he bored by his job at The British Council? Most days he sat in his office, on the fourth floor of a stone office building in the centre of the city, reviewing papers, planning cultural events. Not much different from driving a desk in Whitehall. Except there were no pubs, no English beer, no banter. Just drunks on street corners; even at well below zero temperatures they were there, singing to themselves, or shouting abuse at passers-by. Then there was his twice-weekly English night class at the Workers' Institute, where he'd met Maija three months ago. She had sat at the front, her blue eyes watching him intently. After class she'd hung back and Iain felt like a school teacher, embarking on an illicit affair with a teenage student. Except Maija was by no means a teenager. She was divorced, like him, but unlike him had a seventeen-year-old daughter. That had scared him a bit, a complication he didn't need. They used his small flat on Laivurinkatu, only a few streets away from Maija. Though it was up the hill to get home from her place, it could not be more convenient. Iain smiled. There was something about Finnish women that he still couldn't resist, even after the divorce from Virpi. The blue eyes, the pale skin, the easy nakedness. This time, though, there wasn't going to be a marriage. He wasn't that stupid. His divorce from Virpi had come through just over a year ago.

Iain decided to skip the creaky old lift and walk up the stairs. He needed the exercise. On the fourth floor he was hopelessly out of breath. Surely spies were supposed to be fit? He smiled at the absurdity of the thought. Who did he think he was, James Bond?

Mrs Cooper greeted him with a quick, efficient smile. She smoothed down her skirt and opened the door to the stuffy offices. It always smelled of old books and the air hung heavy with dust. A man in a brown jacket sat reading a book in a corner where a few low-slung chairs were arranged around a table. Iain nodded to him and thought how rare it was to see the Council actually used as the library it partly was meant to be. He walked past the rows of ceiling-height bookshelves and opened the door to his office. His vast steel desk was covered with a pile of newspapers and a few letters. Iain sat down and sighed. The only good thing about his office was that it overlooked the Esplanade Park. Although on a grey day like today it might have been better not to be able to see out into the cold street.

Iain considered the green folder for a moment. Did receiving this file from the Colonel mean that he had an additional brief? Did he get it because his work had been satisfactory? Or just because he was already involved? Perhaps MI6 was short-staffed in Helsinki. That wouldn't surprise him, though the Colonel had said this place was one of the most active Cold War cities.

The file contained only three type-written pages. Jukka Linnonmaa, 42 married to Beta (born Segerstram) for 19 years. They had a daughter, Anni. Iain noticed they lived just a few streets from Maija, on Tehtaankatu 48. There was a bunch of keys. Mr Linnonmaa's career had taken him from Helsinki University, via Vaalimaa border station to Stockholm, Paris, London and lastly Moscow. He was fluent in Swedish, French and Russian. Beta's profession was housewife, though she too studied French at the University of Helsinki. Iain ran down the list of Mr Linnonmaa's titles and made a note of his present one, Special Counsellor, as well as the address at the Department of External Economic Affairs where he'd worked since September last year. So

he'd been back in Helsinki for just over five months.
Though brief, the file was comprehensive. There was even a
picture of the family. It was taken in a traditional pose in
front of a vast Christmas tree lit with candles. Iain looked
closely at the faces. This was not a poor family. Mrs Linnonmaa's smile was warm, though a little put upon. She was
seated next to a serious looking blonde girl with long hair
tied up in a bow. Mr Linnonmaa was standing behind his
wife, with his hand on her shoulder. Iain turned the picture
and noted the date, 24 December 1974. When he closed the
file a piece of paper dropped out. It was a hand-written note
dated 'September 1978, Anni Linnonmaa enters Helsinki
Lyceum.'

2

Pia had never met a real life Russian before. Not that she would dare to call the blonde man standing next to the headmistress that to his face. Pia wondered if the word was really banned in Finland. You weren't allowed to use that word for the country, although everybody did, secretly. Even the right-wing Mrs Härmänmaa, or the Old Crow as everybody called her because of her harking voice, never spoke badly of the Soviet Union. She stood a little apart from the man and watched him suspiciously. When she first introduced him, she'd tried to smile, forcing the corners of her mouth up.

'Mr Kovtun has come from the Soviet Embassy to talk to you this morning.'

Pia smiled and turned her head towards her best friend Anni, who was sitting in the desk next to hers. But Anni was facing the front, with her back straight. Usually, she'd rest her elbow on the desk and let her long blonde hair fall on her face. It was a trick. That way the Old Crow could not see what she was whispering to Pia. Today Anni actually seemed interested in what Mrs Härmänmaa was saying.

Sitting like that, she looked even taller than usual, with her arms crossed under her breasts. Anni was really slim. While Pia was always on a diet, Anni didn't need to cut down on her eating – she had whatever she wanted and still wore jeans the size of a child's. And she was the most popular girl in the school. She had the best body and the coolest clothes. Today she was wearing her dark-blue Levi's with platform boots. Pia sighed and turned her head back towards the Old Crow.

Mrs Härmänmaa checked her watch and cleared her throat.

'Class 6 A, please be quiet.' She turned towards the Russian man and pulled her lips wide in another attempt at a smile. As usual her lipstick had bled into the corners of her mouth. 'Mr Kovtun from the Soviet International Friendship Town Committee has come to the school today with some very exciting news.'

At that moment the door to the classroom opened and Miss Joutila burst in.

'Sorry, I'm late, Mrs Härmänmaa.'

Everyone laughed.

The Old Crow cast her evil brown-eyed spell over the room and it became quiet again. Pia held her breath. She was so close to a full giggling fit she didn't even dare to look at Heikki at the back of the class, who'd laughed the loudest.

Instead, Pia started daydreaming about last Friday's *Vanhainpäivät* party. Even though *Vanhainpäivät* was a school party, and the punch was supposed to be alcohol-free, it was the best ever. When the two teachers were out of sight, Heikki had poured a bottle of *Koskenkorva* vodka into the mix. Half of the punch had gone by the time the Old Crow noticed. By then it was too late, everyone was way past it. But she didn't stop the music. Anni said it was so everyone would sober up before going home drunk – that way, the parents wouldn't complain to the school.

Pia had worn her new blue satin shirt and trousers. She'd used heated rollers on her hair and must have looked good, because Heikki told her he fancied her, and they snogged for ages in the cloakroom on top of a pile of overcoats. He pushed his tongue inside her mouth and kept trying to get his hand inside her blouse. Once he touched Pia's right nipple and it felt really good. But she stopped him because she was afraid someone might come in. When they got up, he pressed his hand between her legs and said, 'I want that, Pia, you make me crazy wanting that.' His breath was hot and his voice hoarse. Pia giggled and pulled herself away. He moved his hand to her bottom and squeezed it. 'Nice arse too,' he said. Pia turned her face to him and gave him her best smouldering look. His eyes were dark on her and his fair hair was tousled. Pia straightened herself up and walked out into the darkened gym hall. Everyone was dancing to a slow number. Pia turned around to take hold of Heikki's arm. She wanted to join the couples on the floor, but Heikki had disappeared. Pia had looked all over for him, but he must have been smoking at the back of the school building. She didn't see him for the rest of the evening.

Pia forced herself to listen to the Old Crow. The Russian looked very tall next to the short and fat headmistress. He had straw-blond hair, which he'd combed back from his angular face. He didn't look very friendly, though he did smile at Miss Joutila. Perhaps the PE teacher knew the Russian. Why was she here anyway? It was a Monday morning and the class was supposed to have Finnish with the Old Crow first thing.

'As I was saying,' the Old Crow gave Miss Joutila, who again was wearing trousers at least two sizes too small for her, a quick nod, 'we have some exciting news. As you all know, the cities of Moscow and Helsinki are twinned, cementing the friendship, mutual understanding and co-operation between our two great countries. This year, 1979, we are celebrating the 25th anniversary of this great association. As part of these celebrations, we are proud to be taking part in a gymnastics competition between Moscow Girls' Lyceum and Helsinki Lyceum. Please, Mr Kovtun, perhaps you would like to tell us some more.'

Suddenly Pia grew serious. She listened intently as the Russian spoke in his broken Finnish.

'From our great school in city Moscow, five girls will come to you. We will have a Friendship Trophy competition of gymnastics. The best will win!'

That's all he said and then he started clapping.

Old Crow nodded to the class and put her hands together. Everyone clapped.

'What are we clapping for?' Pia whispered to Anni, but she didn't hear her.

The Crow spoke again.

'Five girls, from all the age groups at the school, will be selected to take part in the competition. Five schools from Helsinki and five schools from Moscow will take part. Helsinki Lyceum will compete in the group gymnastic section. There'll be one girl from the Sixth Form. As the Upper Sixth are in the middle of their Baccalaureate revision, it's been decided that the oldest girl, and therefore the Head Girl of the team, will be selected from the Lower Sixth. I don't have to remind you what a responsible position this is. All those who wish to be considered should go and see Miss Joutila.'

Pia made a quick calculation. There were a couple of girls in the Upper Sixth, who – if Pia was honest – were slightly better than her. Anni was good. She was supple and could bend her body to amazing positions on the mats. But Pia didn't think she was really that much into the sport. Please, don't let her want to take part. Then of course there was Sasha. Pia glanced over her shoulder. Sasha gave her a sideways smile, a sneer really. She was sitting next to Heikki, as usual, leaning towards him, while playing with the curls on her permed, coloured hair.

Miss Joutila said something to the horrible Russian. He was looking directly at Pia. Pia smiled. Whatever, she thought, as long as I'm in that competition I'll suck up to any Commie Russian they want me to.

After both Miss Joutila and the Russian had left the classroom, the Old Crow started handing out the week's essay titles. Pia leant over to Anni, 'I'm definitely going to go for it!'

'What?' Anni's pale blue eyes were wide. She seemed upset, even angry.

'What's the matter?'

'Bloody Commie,' Anni whispered. She picked up her pen and started writing.

Pia didn't understand what her friend was on about. Of course all Finns, at least the patriotic ones, hated the Russians. If the Soviet Union hadn't been attacked by the Germans in the Second World War, it would have invaded Finland. The country would be behind the Iron Curtain now, like Estonia and Hungary, instead of being neutral. Pia's grandmother told her that when the tanks rolled into Czechoslovakia in the sixties, it was only because of President Kekkonen that the Soviets left Finland alone. So now President Kekkonen and the rest of the country had to keep the Russian neighbour sweet.

Surely that's exactly what Mrs Härmänmaa was doing too?

Why was Anni getting so upset up about it?

At break time, Anni said, 'Why do you want to be involved in some Communist gymnastics competition?'

'Because I want to win.'

Anni wasn't looking at Pia, but was walking resolutely towards the tuck shop. Pia felt in her jeans pockets for any coins but knew she would find nothing. She hadn't had her allowance for two weeks now and it was getting embarrassing borrowing money all the time. Her mother would be paid tomorrow. The smell of freshly baked apple doughnuts became stronger as they got nearer the stall. It was only half past ten but Pia was starving.

Queuing up, Heikki stood next to Pia and Anni. Heikki said, 'You two gorgeous birds don't mind if I join you, do you?'

There were looks from the smaller kids down the line.

'Yeah, sure, you just want to jump the queue,' Pia said, her eyes on him. Heikki Tuomila was the best-looking guy in the school with his fair hair and broad shoulders. Today he wore a duck-egg blue shirt. His thumbs rested inside the back pockets of his faded jeans. Pia looked down the line but to her relief Sasha was nowhere to be seen.

'So you'll go for the competition, then?' Heikki asked Pia. He was standing so close she could smell his aftershave. The kids were following her every move, eavesdropping on their conversation. 'Might do,' she said.

Anni looked at her, 'What are you having?'

'Nothing,'

'You want cash?'

Pia lifted her eyes to her and said, 'No, it's OK.'

'Two apple doughnuts,' Anni said to the woman in a bright pink housecoat. She gave her the money and picked up the brown paper bag. The smell was unbearable. Then she took one doughnut out and gave it, wrapped around a paper napkin, to Pia. Anni was a real friend.

'Thanks,' Pia said.

Anni was the reason Pia had become one of the inside gang. Before she moved to the school, Pia had been a nobody. Anni's parents were rich, her father was a diplomat and she'd lived all over the world. The family were only staying put in Helsinki for Anni's education. She was planning to go to university in London or Paris. She lived in a huge old flat, with a bay window and a crystal chandelier in the salon. Sometimes when both Anni and Pia had a free period, they'd go and have lunch there. Anni's kitchen overlooked a private leafy courtyard, with a lawn in the middle and benches. A secret garden in the middle of the city. Pia had never seen all the rooms in the flat. Anni told her there was a massive attic with windows, but that no one ever went there.

Anni's father looked like an absent-minded professor, always in a worn-out cardigan, carrying books and papers. But he'd smile and say hello to Pia. She wished her own father was around more, though for years it had been only her and her mother in the little flat on Kasarminkatu.

Pia saw her father once or twice a year when he came over from Malmö in Southern Sweden to stay with Grandmother. The summer weeks by the lake with her dad were the best. They swam, fished and had a sauna nearly every night. Her dad called Pia his little sauna baby. He told her she'd only been two days old when she was taken into Grandmother's dark, wood-fired sauna. 'You never cried a bit, just laughed when the heat touched your little body.' He squeezed Pia close to him. In the winter, just before Christmas, they had less time, but then he brought her nice presents. He bought them in Stockholm on his way through. Last Christmas he even went to Hennes and Mauritz to buy really fashionable clothes. He said the shop assistants helped him, although Pia suspected it was his new wife, whom she'd never met, that had chosen so well for her. Pia didn't mind. She wished her father and his new wife could live a little closer to Helsinki. But he said his work at the car factory in Malmö couldn't be moved. Once when Pia was younger, she'd asked if they didn't need car mechanics in Finland. Her father laughed but didn't answer the question. Of course, now Pia understood about the unemployment situation in Finland. Sometimes she wondered if the Old Crow ever talked about anything else while she nagged about the importance of a good education.

Walking between Heikki and Anni along the glass-fronted corridor towards the lockers, Pia stopped. Miss Joutila and the Russian were standing in the middle of the schoolyard. It was snowing lightly, and the Russian was wearing a black fur hat, making him stand even taller. Mrs Joutila also had a hat on, a woollen crochet beret. Pia shook her head, how unfashionable could the woman get? Miss Joutila and the man were laughing together. Something about how they stood so close together made Pia think they knew each other very well.

'She's a bit of a dark horse, eh,' Pia said.

Heikki said nothing. He was munching on his doughnut.

Anni moved closer to the glass and said, 'Traitor.'

'What?' Pia didn't think she'd heard her friend right. What had got into her today?

Miss Joutila and the Russian walked to the gym hall by the side door. Pia decided this was her moment. She stuffed the rest of her doughnut into her mouth and said, 'See you later.'

Pia was sure Miss Joutila would take the Russian to her little office next to the changing rooms. From the side door, a steel staircase took you up to the gym hall. Pia opened the heavy door and took off her boots. The red-faced caretaker was always telling the pupils off for walking on the polished wooden floor with their outdoor shoes.

Pia looked at the blue mats rolled to the side of the hall and at the climbing ropes tied together in the corner of the room. She felt at home here. She wished she could do a few front rolls on the blue mats instead of having to walk by them. She imagined a hall full of people, all cheering as she preformed her programme to perfection, each hand stand and each roll more gracious and controlled than the one before. She'd attempt a set of three or four back flips. Surely there'd be enough time to practise. She'd ask Miss Joutila.

When Pia reached Miss Joutila's office, she heard voices.

'You chosen the girl, yes?'

'I...'

'You take one with long brown hair.' The Russian man's voice was loud and clear. As if he was issuing instructions to an army.

The gym teacher was quiet, or perhaps Pia didn't hear her answer.

'What her name?' the Russian said.

'Mäkelä, Pia Mäkelä'

Pia stopped breathing. Her heart was beating so hard, she was afraid that Miss Joutila and the Russian would hear it. Quickly she tiptoed out of the hall, ran past the mats and put her boots back on. She skipped down the steel staircase, then realised how childish it must look and forced herself to walk normally back to the school building.

After the English lesson, Sasha came over to Pia.

'You're going for it then?'

'Going for what?'

Sasha Roche laughed so that the mock blonde curls on her head shook. She was much shorter than Pia, but the hair made her head look twice its size. The whole effect was ridiculous. But her parents were rich. She had a swimming pool in her house and held the most amazing parties. So everyone wanted to be her friend.

Including Heikki.

'Pia, take my advice. Forget about the Friendship Trophy. You know there are at least two people better on the mats than you. Anni isn't going to take part. Her right-wing Nazi parents wouldn't allow it. So that leaves me. So sorry, but we have to think what's best for the Lyceum. We wouldn't want to lose at the 25th Friendship Trophy, now would we?'

Sasha left Pia standing by her desk. She was glad she hadn't said anything about what she'd overheard the Russian say to Miss Joutila. She would enjoy seeing Sasha's face much more when the team, with Pia as the head gymnast, was announced in assembly.

What Sasha had said about Anni played on Pia's mind as she sat on the tram on her way home. The number ten was full to bursting. Pia had managed to get a seat but as it approached the centre of the city more and more people came onboard. She had to give her seat to an older lady wearing a huge overcoat and laden with shopping bags. The woman didn't even say thank you, just slid into the seat as if it was her right. Pia held onto a pole and thought that Anni's father didn't look like a Nazi. What was Sasha talking about? Pia hadn't seen Anni since she'd left her and Heikki in the school corridor. Finnish was the only lesson they had together on Mondays. Even their lunch breaks clashed.

Pia stepped off the tram and instead of walking up to Kasarminkatu, she turned left towards Tehtaankatu and Anni's home. She couldn't wait to tell Anni her news. The street was dark, and as the echoes of the tram disappeared behind her, Pia felt a shiver run down her spine. She quickened her step.

All the lights in Anni's house were out. Pia stood on the pavement opposite for a while, looking at the large windows. The block was a very old one, 'Jugenstil', Pia had heard Mrs Härmänmaa once brag to Miss Joutila, '... a fabulous example of Finnish Art Nouveau.'

It was a beautiful house. Only four storeys high, with an attic on the top floor. It looked just as Pia imagined a Parisian building, with decorative golden window frames. The roof was slate, with smaller sash windows. Pia looked at the darkened third floor. Anni's parents weren't sitting in the dining room or the salon. Pia walked around the corner. Anni's bedroom was dark too, with the curtains drawn and no light on inside. Pia moved to the other side of the street and stood under a large elm to get a better view. It was cold. She put her hands in the pockets of the white down jacket her father had bought in the autumn.

Pia gazed up at Anni's flat. Even the bay window was dark. They had a small lamp there, on a dark mahogany table with two antique chairs either side. It was usually

switched on, with the curtains tied back with heavy gold
tassels. Now all the curtains were drawn. It looked like
Anni's parents were away. Pia walked back to the front door
and pressed the intercom button. She stood and waited for a
few minutes. Perhaps someone else living in the block
would come home and let her in. But the street was quiet.

Opposite Anni's beautiful building stood the vast Soviet
Embassy. It was a modern, grey, three-storey structure,
surrounded by a high steel fence and large gardens. The
fence was topped by barbed wire. To keep people out or in?
All the windows in the building were lit up. Pia hadn't seen
many people enter or leave the building when she'd been to
visit Anni. Sometimes the large steel gates opened and a
dark car with blacked-out windows drove in or out. Otherwise the vast three-storey building and the gardens
surrounding it seemed void of people.

Pia hurried back down Tehtaankatu. As she turned into
Kasarminkatu, her own street, a man in dark clothing nearly
knocked her over. 'Oi, watch it!' Pia shouted, but the man
didn't even look at her. Pia stopped dead. She'd recognised
him from that morning.

The Russian, Mr Kovtun, was running as fast as he could
on the slippery street towards the tram stop.

3
___

Leena Joutila sat at her desk, smoking a cigarette. She should be getting ready for her next class, but she didn't move from her seat. She tapped the fingers of her free hand against the heavy black telephone receiver on her desk. She thought about Vladsislas, or Vadi, as he had asked her to call him. How long had it been since Leena had last been this infatuated? She didn't usually allow herself this kind of teenage behaviour, but Vadi was different. As soon as Leena heard his voice, or saw his eyes, she felt her armpits dampen, her breath quicken. He was also the first foreign man Leena had ever fallen for. Not that her love life had been that exciting. Leena pursed her mouth and smiled. Well, at least she would have something to tell the young girls who at that very moment were doing everything but what they'd been told to in the gym hall. As if they'd be interested. What the girls didn't understand was how much Leena could help them if they allowed her to. Instead they didn't listen, thought they knew everything already. Instead they were obnoxious, unruly and loud. Always giggling, always making faces behind her back. Oh, Leena was so tired of the Lyceum. Tired of Mrs Härmänmaa, who seemed to think Leena had no idea how to do her job. The Head should remember that Leena, at forty-four, had two years' seniority to her.

Vadi was tall, blond and muscular. She saw how his arms flexed through the tight-fitting shirt as he clapped at the end of the performance in Moscow. The pupils at the Soviet school had been immaculately behaved at all times. They were so orderly during the gymnastics display Leena had attended at the end of the visit, it had left her breathless. Afterwards she and Vadi had shared a drink in the bar of the vast hotel where Leena was staying. Vladsislas' Finnish was charmingly disjointed, but flirtatious. At the end of the evening he told her she was beautiful.

Leena didn't worry about first or second date rules. She was grown-up after all and didn't need to play games. She invited Vadi to her room and after a couple of vodkas Leena found herself amongst tangled sheets, admiring Vadi's lean body.

Back in Helsinki, Vadi called her the next day. Leena was flattered. She cooked him a meal in her small flat in Töölö and bought *Koskenkorva* vodka for him. She even drank some to keep Vadi company. The liquor made her heady. When Vadi made his move, she was glad she'd put clean sheets on her bed. Afterwards he told her about his daughter. Leena had noticed the long-limbed, brown-haired girl was the star of the Moscow school team.

'My daughter, she very beautiful. And talented. But so, so sad,'

'Why?'

'She cannot go home.'

'Oh,' Leena was puzzled. Why was he telling her all this? 'Where is home?'

Vadi looked at Leena as if she had asked him to share his most intimate secret.

'Minsk.'

'And her mother?'

Vadi waved his hand, 'No good.'

'Oh.' Leena didn't know what to say next. 'What's her name?'

'Alyona. Beautiful name, no?'

'Yes.' Again Leena struggled to know what the man was getting at.

'They keep her jail, yes?' Vadi looked at Leena.

'Prisoner?'

'Yes, yes, because she so good at jumping.' Here Vadi made an arch with his arms like a ballet dancer.

Leena smiled.

Vadi fixed his dark eyes on her and continued with a serious face. Leena straightened her mouth.

'But it terrible. Not enough food, very, very hard work. And school cold – you notice, yes?'

'Yes.' Leena was surprised at the man's critical tone. In Moscow, Vadi had seemed a typical Soviet official, towing the party line. He hadn't said a word about the lack of proper drink or food at the hotel, nor about the poorly-fitting costumes the girls wore during the performance. He'd hardly seemed to notice that the hall was cold, even though their breath steamed in the chilly space as they exchanged compliments on the girls' performance. Had he been watched in Moscow? Leena didn't say anything for a while. Vadi got out of bed. He had such a wonderful physique; no doubt where the girl got hers from. He pulled on his white trunks and trousers and poured himself more vodka.

'So I want to help her,' Vadi took Leena's face into his strong hands, 'and I ask you help too, yes?

It was now three days since he'd last been to the flat. Leena missed his strong body next to hers. Was it wrong of her to enjoy sex with him so much? He seemed to know instinctively how to touch her. She felt her cheeks redden when she thought of the power with which he entered her. Was she getting obsessed? She shrugged at the thought. Of course she wasn't. She was a modern, single woman with a lover, that's all. If only there weren't all these complications. If only Vadi hadn't told her about his problems. On that first time in Helsinki, she'd tried to control her emotions, but couldn't help promising she'd do everything she could to help.

Leena inhaled deeply on her cigarette. How would it all end? To have a chance to win the Friendship Trophy was wonderful. But the level of achievement at the Moscow Girls' School was far beyond that of Helsinki Lyceum. None of the girls in Leena's school spent enough time training. How could they possibly win? Especially with Pia Mäkelä. Vadi had insisted that Pia had looked the most upright and enthusiastic, and that he'd spotted real talent in her at Christmas.

'Sometimes, my beautiful educator of young Finnish minds, you not see who is best, eh?' he told Leena. Sitting on the side of her desk, Vadi had looked Leena deep into her eyes and kissed her. 'But me, I can!'

The glory it would bring the Lyceum, and Leena, was unimaginable. But if this was her reward for helping Vadi, the victory would be tinged with shame. Vadi and his daughter were a good cause. Leena would have helped them even if he didn't occasionally share her bed.

Finishing her cigarette, she heard the girls' prattle coming from the changing rooms. She had to go soon. Then she heard a sharp scream. Leena sighed and dropped her cigarette out of the small window high up on the wall. She tried to waft the smoke out into the cold air, but gave up. She'd lock the door and no one would know. She could always say Mr Kovtun had been smoking there.

At home Pia was greeted with the smell of cooking. She walked into the kitchen and saw her mother bent over a pot. She had rollers in her hair and was wearing a dressing gown.

'What's going on?'

'Disaster!' her mother said.

Pia could smell burning.

'We've got a dinner guest! And the pork is ruined!'

Pia's mother had an English boyfriend. Pia called him Admiral Jones. She'd forgotten what his real name was. He worked at some English library in the centre of town and Maija had met him at English language classes. She laughed when she told Pia the story. The Admiral was trying to explain the silent "k" in "knock" and "knife" when their eyes met. They'd sat for at least five minutes just gazing into each other's eyes. The class around them shifted uncomfortably in their seats. Eventually someone in the back coughed and the Admiral returned to the front of the class. Afterwards he'd asked Pia's mother out.

The doorbell rang.

'Pia, please can you get that?' Her mother hurried past Pia into the hall and then the lounge, which was really

Maija's bedroom, with a sofa that turned into a bed. She sat at her little dressing table, Grandmother's old one, in the corner. She looked into the mirror, her eyes wide.

'I need to do a couple of things,' she said turning to look at Pia, smiling, 'If it's the Admiral, could you just push the door shut and sit him in the kitchen. I won't be long.'

'Ah, it's the young lady of the house,' the Admiral said, in English. Pia took a step back and let him into the long narrow corridor. Then she walked into the kitchen and said, 'My mother won't be a minute, you can wait here.'

The Admiral wore a tie and a navy blazer with gold buttons. He was really slim and tall, with black wavy hair, combed to one side of his head.

'How was school today?' The Admiral sat down at the table. He attempted Finnish this time. His silk tie was red with yellow spots, showing under the blazer. It was the middle of February and he didn't look like he was wearing enough clothes for a winter evening. Pia and her mother had laughed about that; he always looked cold with red cheeks and ears.

Pia turned around at the door and looked at him, 'Fine,' she said.

'You have many friends?'

From the kitchen window Pia saw it was snowing again. Large, flat flecks of white were slowly floating past and settling on the rooftop of the block on the other side of Kasarminkatu. She looked at the Admiral. Why was he interested in her all of a sudden?

'No,' she lied and went back to her bedroom.

During dinner the Admiral talked and talked in his funny Finnish, mixing in some English, and making bad jokes all the time. Pia looked at her mum, thin and beautiful in her black velvet dress. She didn't look thirty-five at all. The Admiral kept asking Pia questions.

'How are you doing at school? Top of your class?'

'No,' Pia said, trying not to look at his mouth. He was struggling with a piece of meat, burnt and overcooked to a pulp. It was dill stew, Pia's absolute least favourite.

'Is it a good school?' he said, turning to Pia's mother, his eyes on her cleavage.

Her mother made a little wriggle, showing him more of herself. Pia looked away.

'Yes, it's the best school in Helsinki, probably Finland,' her mother said. 'Would you like some more salad,' she smiled and reached across Pia for the bowl.

'Lot of Embassy people, yes?' The Admiral had his eyes on Pia, ignoring the salad.

'Yes,' Pia said and wondered what's it to him?

'Hmm,' he said and took the salad bowl out of her mother's hand. Then smiling at her said, 'This is wonderful food' – he slipped into English – 'darling Maija'.

The English flattery worked on mum. She blushed and bent her head down in a shy smile. Pia scraped the last of the meat off her plate and into her mouth.

'How many years do you have left?' the Admiral asked.

'Just the two, she's in lower sixth,' her mother replied before Pia had a chance. It was as if she wasn't in the room.

'And there are only two classes, a very difficult school to get into!' Pia's mother continued.

'Ah, very good,' the Admiral said, smiling at Pia.

Pia had had enough.

'I forgot to tell you, I'm going to be in a gymnastic competition!' Pia said to her mother.

'Really?' Her mother looked at the Admiral's full plate; he hadn't eaten much of it at all.

'Yeah, this Russian,' Pia glanced at the Admiral, 'I mean a man from the Soviet Union came to the school and announced it. Then I heard them talk about me – they've chosen me to take part! Even though I am good – I mean I am very good – Anni and Sasha are good too, so I was really surprised...'

The Admiral dropped his fork.

Pia's mother moved her eyes from the Admiral to Pia. 'Slow down – what did you say?'

Maija listened in silence as Pia told her the story of the gym teacher knowing this Soviet official, and how she'd – accidentally – overheard them discussing her.

'I mean, it's not absolutely sure yet. It'll be announced tomorrow.' She looked at her mother's worried face. 'It's fantastic. You know how much I love gymnastics! This is a great chance.'

Maija smiled. She leant over the table and patted Pia's hand, 'Well done, good girl.' But Pia knew she wasn't happy, for some reason.

'Who did you say this Soviet man was?' the Admiral asked.

Pia hadn't told them his name.

'Kovtun, I think.'

The Admiral stared at her.

The Colonel gave Iain a long, severe look, 'Collins, looking after civilians is a little different.'

'Sir?'

They were sitting in the darkened Council building with only Iain's desk lamp for light. Iain was behind his desk and the Colonel sat opposite him. It was past midnight. The city behind him was quiet. Even the trams had stopped running.

In the semi-darkness his dull office had taken on a menacing air.

The Colonel shifted in his seat. 'For one thing, you need to keep the girl's mother out of this.'

'Of course.'

'I know you're new to the Agency, but...' the Colonel considered Iain for a fraction of a second and continued, 'When you quiz Pia you need to make sure she doesn't talk to her mother.'

'How?' It seemed impossible to control two people when you weren't with them all the time. Did the Colonel want him to move in with the two women?

The Colonel stared at Iain for a moment too long. Iain felt he was being incredibly stupid.

'For Goodness sake!' the Colonel said under his breath. 'OK, a young girl like that could be involved in anything. All you have to do is convince the mother that she's gone a bit wayward. You become the mother's confidant and supporter through the difficult times with her daughter. She doesn't believe anything the daughter tells her and so forth.'

Iain's first thought was, how the hell was he to come between mother and daughter? He cleared his throat. 'Wayward?'

The Colonel inhaled deeply. After a long silence he said, slowly, as if speaking to a child, 'Use the old trick of drugs.' Seeing Iain's grave face, he resumed a normal tone of voice. 'Everybody with a teenage child is terrified they're high these days, I know I am.' The Colonel paused for a moment, looking at Iain. 'You're lucky not to have these kinds of worries. Bloody children, nothing but trouble! Anyway, take money from the mother's purse when she's not looking. Hint that it was the daughter needing it for drugs. It works every time.'

4

The date of the competition was announced in assembly the next day. It would be less than a week away on Monday. The Old Crow addressed the back of the vast hall.

'We haven't been given much time to prepare, but I am sure the chosen girls will give the best performance of their lives. Remember, you are not only representing your school, the Helsinki Lyceum, but also the city of Helsinki and your fatherland, Finland.'

Nobody seemed to be interested. The Crow had to clear her throat several times to be heard. She scanned the room with her brown eyes full of threat. The restlessness in the vast assembly hall subsided. Pia was sitting right behind Sasha. Next to her was an empty seat, which she'd reserved for Anni. But she was late and would miss the whole of the announcement. At last came what Pia had been waiting for.

'And now, I'll pass you onto Miss Joutila who will announce the team.'

When Miss Joutila read out Pia's name first, she saw

Sasha jerk her head towards the left, as if she wanted to look at Pia but stopped herself at the last second.

After assembly, Pia walked past the lockers in the hallway towards the central staircase. She scanned the hall for any sign of Anni. She'd have to slink into the line of pupils making their way to lesson if she didn't want the Old Crow to know that she missed assembly. But there was no sign of Anni. A few people patted Pia's back as they passed her. Heikki was waiting at the top of the stairs. He stood with his feet apart, with his hands in the pockets of his jeans.

'Meet me at the smoking place after class,' Heikki whispered into her ear. Pia's heart started pounding. It was so loud she was afraid Heikki would hear it. She nodded. Someone pushed her from behind and she saw the Old Crow had appeared behind them. Heikki and Pia entered the classroom side by side and everyone stared. Pia didn't look at the people in the room, but hurried to her desk. As she flung her bag down to the floor, she saw Anni's empty desk. Where was she? Usually, if she was bunking off school she'd call Pia to ask if she wanted to join her. They'd spend the day in town, walking around Stockmann's department store looking at all the clothes and shoes they couldn't afford. Or at least Pia couldn't afford. Anni must be ill. Pia decided to go and see her after school.

The Old Crow started handing out sheets on some grammatical point or other, 'You must all listen very carefully. This is the most common mistake you all make, and making it during the exam will deduct valuable points from your essay.' Pia sighed and tried to concentrate on the writing on the sheet. But all she could think about was the Friendship Trophy. Why had the Russian wanted her to take

part and not Sasha or Anni? They were both good on the
mats. Because of Sasha's size, it seemed to come easy to her.
Pia was forever cursing her long legs. They took so much
more effort to control. How did he know which girls were
good? Had Miss Joutila told him? And how did Miss Joutila
know a Russian from the Soviet Embassy?

Whatever, Pia wasn't going to let Miss Joutila and the
school down. She was going to train hard. She wouldn't have
any dinner tonight. She would lose at least two kilos before
the competition.

That would show Sasha.

'Pia!' The Crow called, after the most boring Finnish
class ever. 'You are to go and see Miss Joutila in her office.'
Pia looked at her watch. Miss Joutila would have to wait
until next break.

Pupils weren't allowed to enter the area behind the Lyceum.
But to have their break-time ciggies the smokers climbed
through a massive hole in the chicken wire fence. When it
was cold like today, they huddled under a large pine tree,
and the smoke rose straight up to the large, lower branches.
The ground was covered with cigarette butts. Pia had only
been to the place a couple of times, because she didn't
smoke. She'd tried it once, but inhaling made her feel sick.
She didn't mind the smell of it, though, especially when it
was on Heikki.

When Pia got to the tree, Heikki was already there,
smoking and talking with Sasha. Because of the Old Crow
she'd got there before Pia. Sasha was standing close to
Heikki, her down coat touching the sleeve of Heikki's jacket.

'Pia, come here, hon,' Heikki said. He was blowing
smoke rings. When Pia was next to him, he put his arm

around her. Pia held Sasha's gaze. Nobody said anything for a while. Heikki dropped his cigarette and put it out with his boot, kissed Pia lightly on the lips and said, 'We're off – see you Sash.'

That showed her, Pia thought, as they walked around to the back of the school. Pia had never before dared to come here. A small path led all around the school building. On the other side was marshland, with the occasional birch tree. The bare trunks looked sad and lonely, sticking out of the white snow like ghostly skeletons. They walked past several low windows. Pia recognised the biology labs and the home economics classroom with its row of stoves and ovens and kitchen cupboards. Heikki peered through each window before they passed it.

'In case some old cow is sitting and spying on us,' he said and looked back at Pia.

After the classrooms there was a wide bit of the red brick wall with no windows. This is where Heikki stopped and turned Pia's back against the wall. Pia could taste the cigarettes in Heikki's breath. His lips were as soft as they had been the night of the party. There was a strange sensation in the pit of her stomach. She wanted to melt into him. Heikki's tongue became more persistent, getting deeper into her mouth, exploring every bit it could reach. Pia pulled back – she needed air.

'Heikki,' Pia started, but he'd put his hands inside Pia's jacket and started kissing her again. This time he was gentler. Pia was glad he had hold of her waist. She could have fainted out of happiness.

Heikki was moving his hands further up; then he pushed them inside Pia's jumper. His touch felt cold against her bare flesh. With one hand, Heikki undid Pia's bra.

Pia pulled back out of Heikki's grasp. 'Not here!'

Heikki took a step back and put his hands into his jeans pockets. His eyes were dark. 'I need to talk to you about something.'

'What?' Pia was struggling with both of her hands to redo the bra. 'What is it?'

'The Tournament'

'What about it?' Finally she got the hook and the eyelet to meet.

'I don't think you should do it.'

Pia looked at Heikki. His lips were smaller and pinched together, as if he was trying not to breathe. What did Heikki have to do with the Friendship Tournament? Pia was confused. Then she heard the shrill sound of the bell.

'Listen, Pia, don't get involved in this. It's dangerous!' Heikki said. But Pia was already running round the building. Being found smoking (though she hadn't smoked!) would put an end to her gymnastic career at the school. Miss Joutila was dead against smoking. And The Old Crow had told them that being found behind the fence would result in suspension. Being unable to go to school was the last thing Pia needed. It would also mean she'd not see Heikki every day. Pia ducked underneath the windows and finally reached the hole in the chicken wire. Just before they entered the school, Heikki caught Pia's arm and said, 'I mean it Pia, the trophy's not worth it!' His grasp was firm. Even through her thick jacket, it hurt. His face was serious and his eyes dark. Suddenly, he let go and casually walked through the door without looking back.

Leena wasn't herself. She was nervous and worried. Perhaps it was just the time of the year: there was something infinitely depressing about February. The days were short and grey and the nights drew in early in the afternoon. From her office window she saw the snow piled high on both sides of the road. It had turned into a grimy charcoal colour from the traffic fumes. Leena couldn't remember when she last had a glimpse of the sun. She sighed. Perhaps it was the hopelessness of the situation. In spite of Vadi's optimism, Leena could not see how the Lyceum would have any chance of winning the Friendship Trophy. The competition would be a humiliation.

Absentmindedly she scanned the schoolyard. That's when she saw him. A man was standing on the edge of the car park with his hands in his pockets. He didn't look like he belonged there. He looked foreign and cold. His crop of thick black hair was uncovered. Who was he and what was he dong there in the middle of the day, watching the school building?

A knock on the door interrupted her thoughts.

'You wanted to see me, Miss?'

Pia stood in the doorway, leaning against the frame.

'Stand up straight, girl, and come in.' Leena turned to face Pia Mäkelä. Would she, as Vadi had assured her, prove to be the most talented gymnast at the school? She had the same build as Vadi's daughter, though she was slightly heavier. Could she lose a few kilos and be trained up in time? Leena doubted it. Yet she had agreed to the selection. In truth she had done so rashly. She now regretted her weakness in the face of Vadi's persuasiveness. Though what did it matter? It certainly wouldn't matter for him. But Leena couldn't help being ambitious. She couldn't just think of the future and not give a damn about the Lyceum. She was too used to doing the best she could for these ungrateful girls. And she was too used to being independent. She'd been on her own for years. Unmarried at the age of forty-four, how could she suddenly put her trust in a man? Put her future in his hands? Yet that's exactly what she had done. And now here she was, the result of this foolish trust, standing in front of her, with false hope in her eyes.

'Pia, you heard the announcement.'

'Yes, Miss, thank you.'

'We have a lot of work to do and very little time. You realise that?'

'Yes'

'Starting from tomorrow, you will come to training at 12.30 without fail. We will also do a day-long session on Saturdays as normal. The Tournament is this coming Monday. The smaller girls will also be there. It will be hard work. Are you up to it?'

'Yes, I am.' The girl sounded confident. She'd been listening to Leena with a serious face, nodding in agreement to everything Leena said. Perhaps she would come good after all. Leena stood up and showed Pia out of the office. She went up to the window again and peered out. What she saw startled her and suddenly chilled her. She pulled her cardigan closer over her body and her arms tightly around her waist as she watched the man walk up to Pia Mäkelä. It was obvious the two knew each other, though Pia seemed to behave as insolently towards the man as she usually did towards all the staff at the school. How would Pia know a foreign man? Couldn't be her father, surely? Leena hurried to the telephone. She dialled the number of the Soviet Embassy.

'What you phone here? I told you not phone here!' Vadi said in his soft, broken Finnish. Leena blushed. She had behaved childishly and now he would get in trouble.

She couldn't remember being told not to phone the Embassy.

'Sorry, it's just...'

'What?' Vadi said impatiently.

'I've seen something.'

There was silence at the other end.

Leena went home via the K-shop on the corner of Töölöntori. She was going to cook Vadi a borscht soup. She'd found a Russian recipe book in the school library. The raw beetroot would take a while to cook, so she flung her coat on the bed and headed for the alcoved kitchen. At the end of the small space was a window overlooking the inner courtyard. On Saturday mornings she often saw carpets being beaten on the mattoteline, a structure designed just for the task. Puffs of dust would go up from stripey, brightly coloured mats as a woman in a housecoat took a cane beater to the woven fabric. Now the courtyard was empty, the ground, the structure and the dustbins covered with a layer of snow. The light had almost faded, at only three-thirty. Briefly Leena wondered why the caretaker hadn't cleared a path to the bins. Perhaps the tired-looking man was hung over again, she thought. As she chopped the vegetables, Leena shuddered at the thought of having to talk to him. He was no older than Leena, but years of alcohol abuse had made his face the dull colour of brick. His hands were shaky and his body wiry. Unlike Vadi! How clever she'd been to suggest a meeting in her flat to discuss the Friendship Tour-nament and her observations at the school. Leena knew that once Vadi was inside, and she'd given him vodka followed by a hot bowl of soup and some good bread, he'd not be able to leave. He'd stay. Once again she'd feel his strong, muscular body against her own, his thighs against hers, his hardness inside her, his arms pinning her against the bed as he exploded powerfully. Watching him reach climax was as good as reaching orgasm herself. She never minded that she had to take care of herself after he'd left.

Vadi was wearing a long black coat Leena hadn't seen before. He had a large briefcase in his hand as he pushed past her into the flat.

'So, tell me everything,' Vadi said as he flung his coat onto her bed and sat down. Leena noticed he was wearing a suit, with trousers that seemed too short for him. They made his feet look even larger.

'Come, I have no time!' Vadi flashed his eyes at Leena.

'Would you like a drink?'

'Ah, you women, why not!' Now there was a smile. Leena hurried into the kitchen and poured a large glass for Vadi and a small one for herself from the bottle of *Koskenkorva* she kept for his visits. Vadi emptied his glass in one go and made Leena tell, again, what she had seen from the window of the sports hall. For a while he sat quietly, silently indicating the need for a refill. When Leena offered the borscht, he shook his head and told her to be quiet. Leena sighed and emptied her glass. The vodka burned her throat, but by the time it reached her chest, she felt more relaxed and happy to be watching Vadi's fingers run through his hair. She must make him stay.

'I could ask the girl, Pia Mäkelä, who she was talking to?' Leena said.

'Njet, but you know where she lives, yes?' The dark eyes watched Leena intently.

'We keep addresses of all the pupils at the Lyceum.'

'Can we get it now?'

'No, the school is closed.'

'Ah, Leena, this very important, very, very important.'

'Who is this man? A Soviet spy?'

'You must have keys to school, yes?'

Leena was quiet. She didn't keep any keys, they were for Mrs Härmänmaa only, but she might be able to get to the school via the sports hall. But what if someone found out? What if the Head or another teacher were working late? Leena had never worked late at the school, she didn't have to mark papers or prepare for exams. Then she suddenly remembered.

'I know where she lives!' she said, smiling at Vadi. 'I know exactly where she lives! I'd forgotten. Last year I delivered her grades to her when half the school was ill with the Asian flu. Bad diet and no exercise, of course, in her case, as in many of the cases, but there you are, some people never learn.' Leena looked up to see Vadi putting his coat back on. 'Come, Leena, come now, quickly!'

5

I t was embarrassing seeing the Admiral wait for her outside the gym hall at school, in full view of everybody. He waved his hand, gesturing for Pia to come to him when she was hurrying for her next class. She was late.

The Admiral told her to meet him at something called the British Council after school. He gave Pia detailed instructions on how to find it. When Pia didn't say anything, the Admiral took hold of Pia's arm and whispered, 'We need to talk about the Tournament.'

'Why?'

The Admiral looked uncomfortable.

'There is something I need to tell you.'

'What, why can't you tell me now?'

'It's complicated. C'mon Pia, it's only for half an hour or so. It may be in your interest. You want to win, don't you?'

Pia thought for a moment, 'Does Mum know you're here?'

The Admiral was staring at her. But he didn't say anything, just shrugged his shoulders. All of a sudden everybody's interested in the Friendship Tournament. But the Admiral was right. She did want to win. 'OK,' Pia answered.

You need to ask in English, 'I want to borrow an English book to improve my language grades.' The Admiral hurried off, waving his arm. 'See you later, Pia'.

Pia had never been to the British Council. After school she took the tram straight to Erottaja in the centre of Helsinki. When she stepped out of the lift on the fourth floor, as the Admiral instructed her to, a woman behind a wooden counter said, 'Can I help you?' in English. She had on a brown jacket over a cream blouse. Her hair was pinned up. She looked at Pia over her gold-rimmed glasses which had long chains attached to them. She took off the glasses and let them fall onto her chest. A green brooch rattled from the contact with the glasses, and she looked briefly at the two objects and then adjusted herself.

Pia hesitated for a bit – seeing the high shelves of books reaching far behind her, she blurted, 'I want to borrow an English book to improve my language grades.'

'I see,' the woman said and walked around the counter. 'Follow me.'

Pia felt very shabby walking behind the smartly dressed woman whose jacket was part of a suit, the narrow skirt hugging her wide hips. Pia had on her white jeans, which were a bit dirty because she'd had no time to wash them. Her white down jacket, a Christmas present from her father, was becoming a little grey too. Her corduroy school bag had a hole in one corner.

'You put too many books in there, surely you don't need all of that just for one day?' her mother had said just that morning when Pia told her she needed a new one. As usual it was money that was the problem, so she hadn't said anything more to Maija, just shrugged her shoulders.

The woman took Pia through a large room with shelves and shelves of books. There were no other people about, and when the woman opened a door at the end of the room, Pia began to feel uncomfortable. She didn't know anything about the Admiral. Perhaps she should turn around and run out of the building? The woman stopped and let Pia continue towards a desk at the end of the room, where two men were sitting with their heads bowed. Behind them was a large window, where Pia could see the treetops of the Esplanade Park.

The men looked up as she approached. 'Thank you, Mrs Cooper,' one of them said in English. Pia couldn't make out their faces very well because the light from the window was shadowing their features, but when one of them stood up, Pia saw it was the Admiral. She was relieved; at least she'd got to the right place. He was wearing a dark suit with a pink shirt and blue tie. Pia looked back to the closed door that the woman had disappeared through, and felt uneasy again.

'Pia, sit down with us,' the Admiral said, in English, taking hold of her arm, 'there is someone I want you to meet.' Pia said nothing, just looked at his hand on her arm. The fingers were long and bony, and the grip he had on her was too strong.

'It's OK, Pia, don't be afraid,' he said.

'Speak Finnish,' Pia said, looking squarely at his face. The Admiral widened his eyes, lifted his eyebrows and let go of Pia's arm. He mumbled something to the other man and he laughed. Pia wondered what the hell she was doing and decided not to sit down. Would she be able to run quicker than the men? How many doors had she been led through?

'Pia, all we want to do is talk with you,' said the Admiral, this time in Finnish. 'There is no danger here.'

The other man was sitting back in his chair watching Pia as the Admiral spoke. He was dressed just like the Admiral, but instead of a pink shirt he was wearing a light blue one. Their ties looked the same too.

'Pia, this is Colonel Williams.' The Admiral had switched back to English again.

'How do you do, young lady.' The man reached out his hand. It was warm and much softer than the Admiral's. His face looked kinder too – it was round and had fewer lines on it. He had very blue eyes, peering out from behind a pair of small glasses, and almost no hair, just a rim of pale wisps around and above his ears. When he smiled, his mouth reached from ear to ear, just like a clown's.

'Now, the Colonel does not speak any Finnish so I will have to translate. Perhaps we can try to speak English?' The Admiral was looking at Pia without smiling.

'OK,' Pia said.

'Can I take your coat first?' The Admiral got up and stretched his hand out.

'Now,' the Admiral said, sitting down again. He put his hands on the table palms down and continued, 'This Tournament. We want to know everything you know about it.'

'Why should I tell you?'

'Because you know we can help.'

'Help with what?' Pia looked over to the Colonel. He was watching Pia and listening carefully to everything she said.

'Help Anni.'

'Is she in trouble? Where is she?' Suddenly Pia couldn't breathe.

'She may be, we don't know. But you must trust us. Trust me,' The Admiral put his hand on Pia's. She quickly pulled it away and put both of her hands on her lap. The Admiral said nothing but leant back in his chair. He glanced quickly at the Colonel, who nodded.

'OK, Pia, I will go first. It's not Anni who's in trouble. It's her father. But because of him, she may be affected too.'

No one spoke for a long time. A loud clock was ticking somewhere in the background. She glanced at the new watch that Grandmother had given her for her birthday. It was ten past five. It would be dark outside and her mother would be home by now. During the weekdays Pia had promised to be home by six o'clock, if she wasn't going out. Maija kept forgetting that she was an adult.

'Please, Pia, tell us what you know of the Linnonmaa family.' The Admiral stretched his hand towards Pia on the table, leaning his body over. His face was so close to hers, she could see the black and grey stubble on his chin and cheeks.

'Anni is my best friend.'

Both of the men nodded.

'And her father is a diplomat and they live...'

'We know all this,' the Admiral said interrupting. 'We need to know what happened at school yesterday. The announcement about the Gymnastics Competition, the Soviet official, everything.'

'Yes, yes' the Colonel said impatiently, glancing at his watch.

'Anni was behaving really oddly on Monday...' Pia looked up at the two men. The Colonel nodded as if for her to go on, so Pia told them all about the Russian, how Anni had reacted to it and how she'd not been to school today.

'We were supposed to go out last night and I phoned Anni but there was no answer.'

When she'd finished there was a long silence. The

Admiral was staring at the empty table in front of him. He was pulling the skin of his chin into small folds with his thumb and forefinger, then letting go and starting over again. The door behind Pia opened and the woman walked quickly towards the Admiral. She whispered something into his ear and then both of them looked at the Colonel.

'I'm afraid I must go.' Both the men stood up and the Colonel took Pia's hand. 'Goodbye, you've been very helpful.'

'You must go now.' The woman took hold of Pia's arm. She handed her the down jacket.

And then Pia was standing in the cold, dark street outside. It occurred to her that she hadn't asked any questions, or had any answers to what was going on with Anni or what kind of trouble her father was in. Or how the Admiral knew Anni's family. And there was no mention of how talking to the Admiral would help her win the Tournament. Pia shivered and started walking towards the Esplanade Park, when she felt a hand on her shoulder. Pia jumped and turned around.

'Heikki!' her voice sounded too high, it was such a shock seeing him. Besides he still had his hand on Pia's shoulder. He looked very serious.

'What were you doing up there?' he said.

Pia looked back at the unassuming building, then back at Heikki. He was wearing the same tight jeans and leather jacket he always wore. He still had his school bag hanging off his shoulder. He'd obviously not been at home. Had he been following Pia all the way from school? His eyes were grave, but his mouth, this close to, looked full. His lips were moist as if he'd just licked them. His jaw, the bit of his face that she always thought about last thing at night, had faint

_..ie on it. Then he pulled her closer to him and bent his head towards hers.

Pia would never tire of kissing Heikki. It was as if he wanted to suck all air out of her and when he let go, she felt breathless. Then he did it again. The second time it was longer, and Pia felt less like fainting, more as if she was sinking into a warm, soft lake at the end of a hot summer's day. When he let go this time Pia had her eyes closed. When she opened them she saw him smiling at her.

'Have you got any money?'

'Yes,' Pia said. For a change she did have some. Her mother had been unusually generous yesterday and had given her a whole twenty marks note.

'Give it to me,' Heikki said when Pia pulled the note out of her pocket. He looked at her and smiled again and said, 'I'll pay you back.' He took hold of Pia's arm and led her through the park to the newly opened ice cream bar and café called Happy Days. Everybody at school had been talking about it, especially Sasha, who had, of course, been there on the day it opened. Next time she bragged about it, Pia could just casually say, 'Oh yeah, it's a cool place, isn't it?'

'Oh, you've been have you?' Sasha would say incredulously.

Everybody knew how little money Pia and Maija had. The last thing they'd be spending her mother's earnings on was overpriced coffee and ice cream. 'Yeah, Heikki took me there.' Pia would say and walk away. Pia smiled at the look Sasha would have on her face.

Sitting opposite Heikki, sharing a banana split, Pia felt prickly all over. Was this their first date? Pia didn't dare ask. She watched him eat most of the ice cream, but it didn't matter, she wasn't at all hungry. Instead, she looked around. The place was a bit like a Russian tearoom she'd seen in films, from before the Revolution, with glass walls that arched halfway up the ceiling. There were large palms all over the vast room, and round tables, with French-looking decorative chairs. It was very full of noisy people. Pia felt as if she was abroad somewhere and not in the middle of cold, dull Helsinki at all. Then she remembered her mother.

'I've got to go.'

'Oh,' Heikki said. He'd just taken another mouthful of ice cream. Pia waited for him to suck at the cold stuff in his mouth and giggled. He swallowed noisily and said, 'Don't go yet, I need to talk to you.'

Now he was serious again. He put the spoon down, leaving an untouched ball of chocolate ice cream on the plate in between them. He looked at it longingly, and lifted his eyes to Pia.

'You never told me what you were doing up at the Council?'

'The Council?'

Heikki looked long and hard at her, and shrugged his square shoulders. He glanced at a table of loud boys and girls, people they didn't know. Pia had been in love with Heikki for as long as she could remember, or at least since the beginning of last year. Pia couldn't believe she was finally here on a date with him. She wasn't going to spoil it with talk of the Admiral.

'I don't know what Council you're talking about – I've just been to the dentist up there.'

6

Iain looked up at the chilly air hanging above the tops of the bare trees of the South Esplanade. He stamped his feet against the pavement. His black boots were slippery on the icy Helsinki streets. He was glad that Maija had insisted he should buy a new, warmer overcoat. It was made of grey felt-like material, and Maija had added a dark, burgundy-coloured scarf and warmly lined gloves to his purchases when they were shopping at Stockmann's. 'These will keep you from getting frostbitten,' she'd said and squeezed his arm. Maija couldn't understand why he was so reluctant to acquire the items of clothing, but Iain resented having to spend his own money on winter clothes. MI6 would have to reimburse him. Not that he'd had time to talk to the Colonel about his clothing worries; there were operational issues to worry about. His time ashore was always an issue, as he was officially naval personnel. To be seen at the Council would give a clear indication of the Colonel's 'other duties'. Though Iain supposed everyone, at least on their side, knew what he was really up to.

Maija had taken Iain shopping after they'd met for

lunch. Her concern for his welfare had stung after what he'd just done, but Iain reminded himself that he was working for his country and must, as the Colonel had said, put his personal feelings aside.

The bank where Maija worked had been bigger than Iain expected. Rows of cashiers sat on either side of a grand hall. In the middle were large pillars against which grew tall green houseplants. Maija hadn't seen him at first. Iain had to ask a woman at the first desk, which turned out to be Foreign Exchange. The spectacled woman had nodded to the far end of the hall, where Iain spotted Maija's dark head bent over some paperwork.

'Oh, lunch?' she'd said, looking at her wrist watch.

Iain had sensed the eyes of the cashiers on him as he talked to Maija. 'I thought we'd try The Old Baker's on Mannerheim Street. I hear it's very good.' Iain had hoped taking Maija to an English-style pub would divert her attention from the impromptu nature of his suggestion.

The place had turned out to be nothing like an English pub, apart from it being fairly dark, even in the middle of the day. The dimness suited his task, though.

The conversation with Maija had been the difficult part. Taking a five hundred mark note from her handbag had been easy. He'd done it while she was in the lavatory. That had been what convinced her in the end. She'd found the money was missing when they were sitting in a café drinking coffee after the shopping. On his way back to the office that afternoon he'd felt strangely deflated. Was it this easy to control people's lives?

Iain watched Pia cross the Esplanade Park with a lanky boy who was wearing a short leather jacket and jeans. They

entered the coffee place and Iain sighed. He looked at his
watch. It was three minutes to six and he knew this wasn't
going to be a short wait. The wind was getting up, the Arctic
chill tightening around his body. He considered his options:
the drunken act, brisk walks around the block or
surveillance inside the café. Though the last one was the
most comfortable option, it was too risky. Pia was a smart
and observant girl. She'd notice him straightaway, however
dewy-eyed she was about that boy.

Seeing a well-dressed couple, huddled close to one
another, walking towards him along the pavement, Iain
started to sway, catching the woman's eye.

'Hey,' Iain shouted in a blurred voice, and he faked a loss
of balance with the effort of waving his hand.

The woman looked alarmed and nudged the man.
Immediately they changed the course of their stride and
went to cross the street instead. Briefly, Iain had seen a look
of wary recognition, 'Not another drunk!'

After the couple disappeared down the park, no one
came close enough for Iain to have to re-enact his drunken
role. But he was frozen and needed to pee badly. He cursed
his lack of foresight in not visiting the lavatory at the
Council premises. Now he'd have to wait until he saw Pia
was safely at home, and then walk the two blocks to his own
rented flat. He thought of Maija, how worried she'd be
because Pia wasn't home yet. Now her concerns would be
raised even further. His, or rather the Colonel's, plan was
working.

Just then the door of the café opened and Pia and the
lanky boy came out. They kissed slowly, long enough for
Iain to check his watch again. Twenty-seven minutes past
six. Pia and the boy held hands for another few minutes and
then Pia turned abruptly and started walking directly

towards Iain. It was fully dark now and Iain was glad for the lights in the Esplanade and Pia's white jacket. He stepped backwards deeper into the shadow of the porch and watched Pia cross the street and ascend an almost empty tram. It left an echo from its squeaky brakes behind as it turned the corner and trundled up Erottaja.

Something about the near-empty tram disturbed Iain, and he knew he should have run to join Pia, but his need to pee was making him misjudge things. He hurried to the Happy Days Café. Coming out moments later, relieved, he decided to get out of the cold and go back home. He'd check Pia's lights were on. He could make up some excuse or other to telephone Maija. Surely tonight would still be quiet, he thought, and ran to an approaching tram. When the tram was passing the corner of the Council, he caught sight of the leather jacket and jeans he'd seen before. He cursed and pulled at the cord. The next stop was not until the top of Erottaja. By the time he'd ran down the slippery street to the Council, the boy had disappeared. Iain dug his keys out of his trouser pocket and gently opened the heavy glass door to the Council building. He held onto it before it swung shut, letting it gently close without a sound. He waited. Iain had spoken to the Colonel about the need for a night guard at the Council. This was, as he now knew, the nerve centre of the British operations in Helsinki, and not one single person was here to look after it at night!

'Now, that would be like putting an advert into the *Helsingin Sanomat*, "KGB officers please note that MI6 can be found at the following premises." ' Iain remembered how the Colonel had laughed heartily at his own joke, nearly choking on his beer and the open sandwich he was balancing between his fingers.

The Council hallway smelt of floor polish. Iain stood

silently listening to the sound of the empty building. He could see the swirly shapes the female cleaner had left behind with her threatening-looking machine. Apart from the glow of the street lamps outside, there were no lights inside the hall, or on any of the floors that Iain could see. He stretched his neck round to peer further up the stairwell. There was absolutely no point in even considering the lift, but by tiptoeing with his back to the wall, Iain could see the carriage was on the 4th floor. He sighed heavily, knowing it was bad news. The boy was involved too.

Iain walked quietly out of the building. Outside, he double-locked the heavy glass door from the outside, and hurried along the South Esplanade towards the South Harbour. There was nothing for it; the Colonel would have to be informed about this.

'Collins what are you doing here?' The Colonel said. His face looked flushed. He was in the middle of his supper.

'The boy, Miss Mäkelä's boyfriend, is inside the Council,' Iain said.

'How do you know?' the Colonel was staring at Iain.

'Saw him enter.'

'And?' The Colonel was fidgeting in his chair opposite, still holding a knife and fork in each hand. Iain told him the whole story. He raised his eyebrows when Iain mentioned being inside the Happy Days Café. 'Sir, if I'd followed my original instructions and pursued Pia, I wouldn't have spotted him at all,' Iain said.

'I'll send a couple of men to the Council.'

'Thank you, Sir.'

The Colonel put his knife and fork down and took a file

out of his desk. 'Since you're here, I've got another little job for you.'

Iain was puzzled. Surely he had enough to do?

'A little trip will do you good,' he said and handed Iain the folder. 'I'll speak with the inspector over there. Shouldn't be a problem for you.'

Iain listened carefully as the Colonel explained what he wanted Iain to do. Then the Colonel got up, and Iain followed his example.

'Well done, Collins,' the Colonel said. For what, Iain wondered.

Suddenly he remembered.

'The tram!' Iain said and jumped up, past a startled Colonel. He made his farewells and began running towards the nearest tram stop.

7

M aija sat at the kitchen table looking out of the window to the dark streets below. She heard a tram run past in the distance, its wheels echoing against the old blocks of flats in Ullanlinna. She hoped she'd see Pia's white jacket turn the corner of the house opposite. She'd timed it. It usually took Pia four minutes to reach home from the stop. The clock on the wall opposite said five to seven – only twelve minutes had passed. Maija sighed. What if Iain was right and Pia was in trouble? She couldn't believe her daughter would get involved like Iain said. But five hundred marks had disappeared from her purse. On the other hand, Pia had looked genuinely surprised when she'd confronted her last night. Was she telling the truth? Iain had said that drug users get desperate. Or maybe Pia's friends are in trouble and she was protecting someone. Perhaps Iain was overreacting. In London drug use must be commonplace among the young, but surely not in Helsinki? Particularly not at the Lyceum! The school was ranked the best in the country, and Maija had worked hard to get Pia there.

There was a slim chance Pia had gone by Anni's instead of coming straight home from school. Maija would have to phone her parents. They were well to do Embassy people. It would be embarrassing. All the other kids in the Lyceum were from wealthy families, they had everything they could want. Did that really include drugs? But Maija had been determined that her daughter get a good education. It was her only chance. In the bank where Maija worked, she'd watched young university-educated girls come in and bypass her on the career ladder. The personnel manager, Miss Kourtamo, had told Maija there was no point in applying for managerial posts. 'Your degree is not in a relevant subject, I'm afraid, Maija.' There was pity in the pale-blue eyes behind the rimless glasses. 'But we are very happy with your work as a cashier,' she'd said, closing Maija's file. Maija could feel her cheeks burn even now at the shameful memory of it. The woman had talked down to her. Yet the bank was better than going back to her former career. Anything but that.

As well as the drugs, there was the Soviet Gymnastic Competition. How would Maija be able to stop Pia taking part? She was ambitious, which was good. But Maija knew the Russians could not be trusted. She could not stop Pia without telling her everything. It was too soon for that.

She sighed and dialled Anni's number.

There was no answer.

'Sorry to have bothered you,' Maija said and replaced the receiver.

Maija wondered if she should call Iain. She could see he was fond of the girl, but it was still difficult to burden a man with the demands of rearing somebody else's child. Especially a teenager. Iain was kind, and loving, but would this prove too much for him? Maija didn't want to frighten him. It was enough that he'd warned Maija.

Maija put her coat on. She couldn't sit at home doing nothing. Iain was right. Pia must be involved with drugs.

Pia sat in the tram, recalling Heikki's kisses on her lips, the taste of the ice cream he'd eaten in her mouth, oblivious to the dreary blocks of flats and the cold and dark streets floating past. She hummed Love me Tender, a soppy song Mum turned the radio up for. It wasn't often you heard foreign songs, especially American ones, on Finnish radio, so when the occasional old one came on it stuck in your head for days afterwards. Pia kept reminding herself of everything Heikki had done and said, how he'd looked at her after their long kiss outside on the pavement. Pia had felt his trousers bulging and knew he wanted her. When would there be another party at Sasha's house, where they could be alone? She must try harder to be friends with her.

Pia was so engrossed in her thoughts that she hadn't noticed the man sitting right behind her, until he reached out and put a hand on her shoulder. She jumped up and tried to turn around but the man's hand got hold of her neck. Her eyes darted to and fro. There was no one else on the tram.

'Be good girl, Pia. Sit still.'

Pia tried to let out a scream, but it was more like a mouse's squeak. Pia smelled the man's warm, sour breath, as he whispered hoarsely into her ear, 'No sound.' His hand squeezed tightly on her neck. She didn't move or say a word. Her mind raced. How did the man know her name? The tram turned the corner of Tehtaankatu and he pressed the bell with his free hand. The driver looked briefly at them through the mirror. Pia wished she'd winced or made a face, done something to alarm him, but it was too late, he was concentrating on slowing down for Anni's stop. The hand let go of Pia's neck and the man said, 'You get out with me.'

Pia got up and tried to look at the man's face. But he held tightly onto her neck and she was unable to turn her head. He said out loud, 'C'mon, girl!' Then to the tram driver, who was staring at them with a passive look, '...Daughters!'

'Goodnight,' the tram driver said, without smiling.

As Pia stepped out of the tram, the man gripped her arm, pushing it high up behind Pia's back. He steered Pia towards the top of Tehtaankatu, towards Anni's flat. It hurt. 'Be quiet and follow me,' the man said. Ahead of them, coming from Kasarminkatu, the direction of her own flat, Pia saw a woman, waving her arms, running down the road, as if to stop the tram from moving away. The man quickly let go of Pia's arm – the woman with the brown Ulster and curly hair escaping from the fur hat was her mother.

'Pia!' screamed her mother.

'Mum!' Pia shouted. She started running towards Maija.

As she ran, Pia looked down Tehtaankatu and up the hill to Laivurintie – the man was gone. When she reached her mother, she looked breathless and angry.

'Where the hell have you been, young girl!'

Pia looked into her eyes. They were as dark as the streets surrounding them. Her mother had never sworn at Pia before.

'Well?' her mother demanded, standing in front of Pia, suddenly taller, making her feel five years old.

'Mum, please, let's just go home. There was a man...' Pia was shivering with the cold and fear. The foreign man could come back at any time. He might have just gone to get some help, an accomplice.

Pia's mother gave Pia a long hard stare, 'Yes, who was he? A drug dealer?'

'No, I didn't know him! He gripped me, if you hadn't come, I don't know what might have happened. Please, he might be back any minute!'

Her mother stared at her. 'What have you got yourself involved with?'

'Please Mum!'

Pia's mother took hold of her wrist as if Pia was a child and started walking down the road. Pia felt tears well inside her.

Her mother dragged Pia along the street. Pia felt cold inside her down jacket. What was wrong with her mother? Why was she talking about drug dealers? Her mother was walking so fast, they were nearly running.

'Mum, you're hurting me!' Maija let go of her. If only Pia had asked Heikki to come home with her. He would have hit the foreign man in the face, and afterwards they could have sat in her room and talked while her mother watched TV in the living room. Besides, Pia was sure her mother would not have acted so strangely in front of Heikki.

The snow fell faster, and everything looked as if it was covered in cotton wool. Maija walked in front of Pia without saying a word. Pia glanced behind them – the Russian man could turn up at any minute and do something horrible to her mother. Pia didn't understand any of it.

Her mother opened the heavy outer door to the block of flats.

Pia said, 'I want to tell you everything.'

Maija turned to look at Pia with her dark and angry eyes

and said, 'We'll speak when we're inside the flat. I don't want the whole world to hear what you've been up to!'

Pia couldn't understand why her mother was so angry. It wasn't even eight o'clock. Hardly late for a grown-up daughter to come home, she thought.

Inside the flat, Maija acted like a KGB officer. She took Pia's coat off, looked into all the pockets, sniffed her breath and examined her eyes. 'You smell of cigarettes, or smoking, or whatever it is you've taken,' she said.

Heikki's smoking, Pia thought. 'I went to Happy Days and everyone smoked there.'

Pia's mother gave her an incredulous stare and told Pia to go and sit down at the kitchen table. Her hands shook as she filled the coffee machine.

'I know everything, Pia.'

Pia stared at her mother. Underneath her coat she was wearing a cotton tracksuit the colour of baby's vomit. She'd tucked the trouser bottoms inside woollen socks. The outfit made her look old.

'Iain told me about the drugs!' she said and put a hand over her mouth, to muffle a cry. Iain? Thought Pia. What's happened to the Admiral?

'Iain, is it now?' Pia said. 'Whatever the Admiral has told you, he's lying. I have no idea what you are talking about. None of us take that stuff. It's for kids who don't know better!'

But Maija didn't listen. She whispered, 'Pia, I know it's my fault. Oh, Pia! But I can only do so much on my own.' She turned around and her shoulders started shaking. The only sounds in the room were Pia's mother's sniffles and the gurgles of the machine, dripping black drops of coffee into the glass jug.

'Who are you going to believe, your own daughter or your fancy English boyfriend, who by the way...'

'What about him?' Her mother was now hysterical, screaming the words.

'Oh nothing,' Pia said. For Anni's sake she must not tell her mother about the British Council. Pia couldn't understand what the Admiral was playing at. Or had her mother got the wrong idea?

'Iain said he had contacts, and that he knew that if not you, then some of your friends are taking drugs. And then the money went missing!'

'The money?'

'Last night I had two five hundred mark notes in my purse and now I only have one.'

'And you think I took it,' Pia whispered. She was hurt. Why was her mother being so stupid?

'From now on you are not to go out in the evenings. And I forbid you to take part in that Russian Competition!'

'Forbid me? You're crazy!' Pia had had enough, 'Believe what you like,' she said and went into her room. She turned the key in the lock and lay on her bed crying. Silently. She didn't want her mother to hear. Let her wail and cry like an old Saami woman. If she wanted to believe the worst of Pia, it was her problem. What had got into her? And what did she have against the Friendship Tournament? Or did she just say that to be nasty? Why had the Admiral, or Iain, told her such lies? Typical that she would flip just as Pia needed her. Hadn't she seen how close she had been to being abducted by some man? Pia shuddered and felt a dread in her chest. Who was the man with the stinking breath and what did he want with her?

Maija knocked on the door. She shouted Pia's name, but soon stopped. Pia knew her mother wouldn't want the neighbours to hear them fight.

Iain saw the lights on inside Maija's flat. He considered whether he could make an unannounced visit late at night without arousing suspicions. He saw Maija reach and close the curtains, so sheer that you could see right through them. Maija seemed to be waving her arms about. But Iain could not make out if anyone was in the room with her. Lights came on in the room next to the kitchen, but the Venetian blinds were closed.

Iain stood for a long while hidden in the porch of the block of flats opposite Maija's, watching for any more movement behind the kitchen curtains. He glanced at his watch; four minutes to nine. The lights in the kitchen went out and he could see a woman's faint silhouette leaving the room. Iain decided to use the phone box by the Johannes Church.

'I think they're both at home.'

'You think?' Iain heard the sarcasm in the Colonel's voice.

'Well, I can't believe Maija would go to bed without her daughter at home, Sir. Or do you wish me to make an approach? Might seem highly suspicious.'

The Colonel was quiet for a moment. The phone box smelled of urine. Iain wanted desperately to go back to his flat and get into a warm, clean bed instead of standing in the bitter Helsinki night, feeling unappreciated.

'Alright, Collins, but tomorrow morning, before you leave, I want you there in the same spot to confirm that the girl is inside. Catch sight of her before she goes to school and report back to me.'

'Yes, sir.'

'And Collins – that boy, the girl's boyfriend. No sight of him at the Council.'

'Oh,' said Iain. He had definitely seen him go in. And he'd locked the door after himself. 'Must have heard your men and slipped out.'

'Or heard you and fled before we got there.' The Colonel said dryly. 'But don't concern yourself with him. I've got a pair of eyes following the lad's every move now.'

Iain decided to walk home. He made his way back to Kasarminkatu for one last look at Maija's windows, before he headed south towards his street. When he turned the corner, he saw a blond man, without a hat, walking a few paces in front of him. The ankle-length black leather coat made him look sinister and out of place. Iain ducked into a porch. The man walked along the snow-covered Kasarminkatu. He seemed in no hurry, despite the Helsinki chill. The man stopped outside Maija's block of flats, looked up to the building opposite him and took a swig out of a hip flask. Iain recognised him immediately: Vladsislas Kovtun.

8

———

Pia and Maija didn't speak to each other the next morning. Over breakfast they sat silently eating bread and cheese. Pia was glad her mother had decided to keep her mad accusations to herself and relived when she heard the front door close. But she was also sad. Her anger towards her mother had evaporated during the long, sleepless night. Why did her mother have to be so stupid to think that Pia would get involved with drugs? But she was like that. Once she got something into her head, however trivial, she wouldn't believe anybody. Pia remembered when she insisted that Bobby in Dallas was really called Jimmy. Pia had argued and argued, getting more and more angry, until they'd next seen the programme. Her mother had really been embarrassed then! If only she'd known how frightened Pia was now, not being able to sleep, and thinking about the man all night long. How had her mother missed the whole incident last night?

Pia watched from the kitchen window as Maija, with her head bent against the cold wind, walked briskly towards the tram stop. The night had brought more snow. Pia had heard the snow ploughs working since before dawn.

Some mornings Maija and Pia took the tram into town together. Pia got to school early, but she didn't mind. It was nice to talk to her mother on the tram, instead of watching the same miserable people every day. Pia wished she'd gone with her mother after all. Now she'd have to face the tram on her own. What if the Russian was outside, waiting for her?

Pia ate more rye bread and drank black coffee. The dishes from the night before were still in the sink. Her mother had also left her own dirty breakfast things at the table for Pia to clear up. But she couldn't move a muscle. She was so tired. The block of flats was quiet. The only noise was the humming of the engine outside, as the snow plough moved slowly past the building, its orange warning lights flickering against the grey dawn. Pia wanted to climb back into bed. She could see the wind lifting snow from the top of the piles the plough had created either side of the street. Spirals of white flew upwards as the wind took hold of the newly fallen flakes.

Should she bunk off school today? No, she needed to train with Miss Joutila. And there was a chance Anni would be back. Plus she didn't want to miss seeing Heikki. She would tell him about the man and ask him to protect her. Pia thought of his lips. Would he hold her hand as they walked into the classroom this morning? Or would Heikki think that wasn't cool? She decided to call Anni. It was only half past eight, she might still be at home. Pia let the phone ring for a long time, in case Anni was far away from the hall, in the depths of that large apartment. But there was no answer.

Pia put her feet into the fur-lined boots her father gave

her last Christmas and added a long scarf with multi-coloured stripes. She'd be warm enough. After one final look in the hall mirror, Pia ran down the stairs and into the snowy street outside.

Heikki was waiting for her at the top of the stairs leading to the entrance of the Lyceum. He stood with his feet apart, his hands in the pockets of his short jacket. He wasn't wearing a hat either, and Pia was glad she'd left hers at home. She knew her mother would complain about it later.

'Alright, hon?' Heikki said, and took Pia's hand.

'Yeah, cool,' she said, feeling breathless at the touch of his warm, strong fingers. They walked hand in hand through the front door, past the smaller kids, who looked at them in awe, then past the lockers, where Pia saw Sasha taking off her ankle-length Puffa coat. Sasha turned and immediately saw their hands. Pia flicked her hair back and tilted her head towards Heikki's shoulder. As they walked towards the staircase, Pia turned back and scanned the entrance, but there was no sign of Anni. Heikki gave her a light kiss on her mouth as they parted at the top of the stairs.

When the Swedish teacher, a slight woman with wispy blonde hair done up in a complicated hair-do, took the register and called out Anni's name, Pia looked at the empty desk next to her.

For the rest of the day, Pia didn't share any lessons with Anni or Heikki. Her lunchtime was taken up by a gruelling session on the mats, for which she felt totally useless. All through the session she kept wondering how she was going to be able to do well at the tournament. Miss Joutila made her do the whole competition routine twice, so by the time she'd got to the canteen, Heikki was leaving and just waved to her. Pia cursed Wednesdays. Before, they'd meant a lovely long afternoon, with two free periods at the end of the day, when she and Anni would go either into the Rixi Bar or to her flat for the afternoon. Now she tried to concoct a reason for staying at school for another two hours, by which time Heikki's maths class would be over. She needed to talk to him properly. But he'd know she'd been waiting at school, all that time for him. And going to the Rixi Bar on her own was out of the question too.

Why was Anni not at school? Why were the Admiral and the other man so interested in Anni and her parents? Pia shook her head. She mustn't let her overactive imagination get the better of her. Whatever was going on with Anni's father and the Admiral, surely it had nothing to do with Anni. She was probably down with flu and would eventually come back to school. The preliminary exams were in three months' time in May.

'In the two years of the sixth form, there simply isn't enough time to go through the curriculum, so it is very important not to miss any lessons at all.'

Pia frowned as she remembered the Old Crow's regular lecture on the looming baccalaureate exams. Surely Anni's parents wanted her to do well. Even though Anni was so much brighter than anyone in the class, the Old Crow had warned her, 'Only hard work pays off in the end!' That had been one of the few times the Old Crow had come even close to telling Anni off. Not like Pia, who had to suffer the Old Crow's lectures and death beams every day. And she had so much to tell Anni! What would she say when she heard she and Heikki were now officially going out. Not to mention how publicly Heikki held her hand at school. How at the smoking place he'd put his arm around Pia, right under Sasha's nose. Pia needed to talk to Anni now.

Tehtaankatu was quiet in the early afternoon. The Embassy was lit up as usual, but there was no one about. Pia leant against the front door of Anni's block, and was surprised when it gave way. Someone must have left it ajar. As Pia walked into the hallway, she heard the lock click as the heavy door shut behind her. Everything in the hallway looked normal. The spiral staircase, with its windows over-looking the inner courtyard, made the dark space seem lighter even in the afternoon. Pia felt foolish. What if there was a simple, rational explanation to Anni's absence from school. Anni probably just had a bit of a cold and now Pia was skulking around asking after her. As if she couldn't do without her friend. But Pia felt sure things were not right. Why would a real British colonel say Anni was in danger if that was not the case? Pia pressed the bell to Anni's flat. She moved away from the door to avoid being seen through the spy-hole, and leant against the wall. She listened. There seemed to be no noise or movement inside the flat. Stepping in front of the heavy-looking door, she tried the bell again. This time the door opened immediately. A man in a black coat with thick blond hair and piercing blue eyes opened the door. Mr Kovtun! Pia wanted to flee, but her feet seemed glued to the spot.

'Ah, Pia,' he said in his foreign accent, and grabbed her.

'No!' Pia shrieked.

The heavy door closed behind her and the man took her past the hall with its gilded mirror and table with the tele-phone into the kitchen at the far end, where light was filtering through the windows, revealing specs of dust in the air.

The Russian turned to face Pia, grabbed her hands and tied them together while Pia tried to kick out. The man only smiled at her and tutted, 'A wildcat? Powerful legs, eh, like a good little gymnast!' The man was very strong.

He placed a black tape over her mouth and led Pia into a small back room, which Pia knew had once been a servant's bedroom. There was just a single bed in the corner, covered with a lace bedspread. Heavy curtains at the small window made it hard for Pia to see the hunched-up figures sitting on the floor. When her eyes adjusted she saw Anni. The man pushed her down next to her friend in the corner.

'You promise, hush, yes?' Kovtun put one gloved finger over his lips and nodded to Pia. Her heart was beating so hard she was shaking. She wanted to nod, but no movement came.

'Please, Pia, you must promise,' Anni whispered, touching Pia's arm. Pia hadn't noticed Anni's arms were free. She looked at the man and nodded.

The ripping of the tape hurt, but Pia suppressed the scream. The man stood before them and now Pia could see that the other figure sitting on the floor, next to Anni, with his back to the wall, was her father. Kovtun stood in front of them, staring at Pia, with his arms folded. Just inside his coat, a shiny object was tucked into his pants. It was a gun! Pia felt sick. She swallowed hard and fought the nausea. 'You sit and wait,' he said. 'Quiet and good girls and boys, yes?'

With that, he disappeared into the kitchen. Pia heard a cabinet being opened and a glass being filled with something. Then there were voices and the sound of clinking glasses.

Suddenly Pia's father started shuffling towards her. He crawled past Anni and came to kneel in front of Pia.

'Pia, you must not say anything. It is very important.'

Pia was staring at the diplomat. His arms were tied behind his back and she saw that he had dry blood at the corner of his mouth. Seeing Pia's look, he wiped his mouth against the shoulder of his jacket and carried on, 'You shouldn't be here. This is a mistake. We'll get help soon, so just be brave and say nothing at all.'

Pia nodded and Anni's father shuffled back to lean against the wall.

'Pia, are you OK?' Anni whispered.

Pia didn't dare to speak. She felt close to tears but didn't want to appear a sissy.

'It's OK. We can speak a bit when they're on the vodka.' Anni's eyes were kind and bright. Pia didn't see any signs of blood on her. 'Soon they'll come and take your ropes off – they did mine almost straightaway. Dad told me not to fight them, so they're being really good to us.'

'Who are they?'

'KGB'

'KGB!' Pia said, but Anni put her hand over Pia's mouth.

'Not too loud!'

'Sorry,' Pia mouthed. 'But Mr Kovtun came to the school? He can't be...can he? What do they want with you – me?' she said in a low voice.

Anni didn't answer. Instead she looked over to her father who was shaking his head.

'I don't know,' Anni said looking down at her hands.

Pia knew Anni was lying, but she forgave her because she knew her father had made her do it. Anni would tell her everything when her father wasn't there.

· · ·

The Russian smelled even more of alcohol when he came to fetch Pia. Her knees gave way and he called out into the kitchen for his comrade. He was a much smaller man with short, dark hair and a square jaw. They spoke Russian to each other while they carried Pia. They placed her roughly into a kitchen chair and Kovtun spoke.

'Pia, you want to go home, yes?'

Pia nodded. She was so scared she was sure she wouldn't be able to say a word. What did they want with her anyway? She had an unreal feeling that this was not happening, that someone was playing a joke on her. Or that she was having a bad dream and would wake up any moment. She wanted her mother.

'So, just tell me what you did at the British Council yesterday and we can let you go home to materi.' He drew out the last Russian word.

Pia was thinking feverishly. So the Russian was following her.

'Iain said I could borrow English books there.'

The slap to her face came so quickly Pia didn't have time to react. Afterwards her face burned and she tasted blood. She heard Mr Linnonmaa shout something from the next room. He was speaking in Russian, and he sounded angry. Kovtun shouted something back through the door and then appeared in front of Pia again.

'He tell me not hurt child.' He took hold of Pia's chin and openly viewed her breasts. He let go of her chin and patted her on the cheek. It hurt. Pia felt her stomach tighten, she felt sick. The man moved his hand slowly down her neck and towards Pia's chest. He stopped just below Pia's collar-bone. Pia took a deep breath in. 'But you no child,' the Russian man said. 'You beautiful Finnish woman, eh?' He turned around and said to the other man, 'She not want a broken nose, a bruise on face, eh?' His comrade gave a hoarse cackle. 'She want me to be nice to her. I can be very nice to pretty Finnish girls, you know.' The man winked at Pia. She felt she needed to pee. She started to sob, but the tears hurt her face more.

But then his tone changed, and he shouted, angrily, 'The truth, please, Miss Finland!' His face was so close to Pia's, she could see the dark stubble on his chin.

Pia felt her face grow hot.

'Iain is my mother's friend, and he wanted me to talk to him about, about...'

The Russian man's face looked worn, his eyes bloodshot, 'Yes, yes, you not want a hit in face no more, yes? Speak!'

'About the Friendship Tournament,' Pia whispered.

'Why?' Kovtun asked. His face was so close, Pia was hit by his spittle when he shouted, 'Tell me, why?'

'I don't know. I won't take part, if that's what you want. I just want to go home!' Pia swallowed hard. The reality of the situation was too incredible: the Russian at the school turning out to be a KGB man, now shouting at her, the Colonel asking questions about Anni and her father. Pia couldn't make any sense of it. Tears were running down her cheeks. They hurt and tasted salty on her lips.

The Russian man stood up slowly, holding Pia's gaze as if to see if she was speaking the truth. Then he went over to his friend.

Pia watched the two men speak in Russian in low voices. They were standing at the far end of the kitchen. At the table in front of her were dirty coffee cups, several empty glasses reeking of vodka, an empty bottle of something called Stoli and a saucer full of cigarette butts. It didn't look like Anni's kitchen anymore. Pia's face was aching and her wrists were hurting. She wriggled to try to move the rope around them. That hurt even more. Her movements alerted the men and Kovtun came over to the table again. This time he sat down in front of Pia and, crossing his hands, said slowly, 'We have been watching you and will watch you. So if you tell a lie, we find out.'

Pia sniffled.

The man squeezed Pia's chin and said, 'Now, you a good girl. Tell me all about Iain.' He pronounced the name strangely, as if he was disgusted with it.

'Ok,' Pia said and nodded. She told the man all she knew about her mother's boyfriend. How he worked at the British Council, how he took Pia's mother out to the cinema, how he helped Pia with her English. The Russian listened to her, smiling the whole time. His face made Pia want to scream out, but she tried to keep her voice calm. When Pia had finished, the man leant close again.

'You and your pretty materi live all alone in big flat?'

Pia stared at him.

'You be good gymnast. You listen to Miss Joutila. You go to competition with your school. You keep your nose out of British Council.' The man spoke slowly, as if Pia would have difficulty understanding his words. Suddenly he stood up and kicked the chair leg. Pia toppled over. She screamed. Kovtun bent down and pushed his face into hers. 'Any trouble and your Iain and your materi and you will pay!'

Pia wasn't breathing. She flinched when Kovtun roughly took hold of her arm and lifted her up. The two Russians carried Pia back to the little room.

Pia sat down and let Anni wipe her nose and the tears off her face. Her body felt sore all over. Had she broken anything? She moved her shoulders and flexed her legs. It hurt, but not enough to be broken. She must have dozed off leaning against her friend, because she was startled when the door opened. Kovtun stood in the doorway.

'Up, you, get up!'

He was holding his coat open to show his gun. They were led out of the room one by one. Kovtun took hold of Pia's arm. He smiled at Pia, wagging his finger, 'Remember, pretty gymnast what I say!' His breath felt hot on her face.

Kovtun tied Pia onto the kitchen chair. She was opposite Anni's father, who was holding himself upright and watching Pia intently.

The Russian motioned to his comrade to leave the room. Then he said, in a low voice, to Mr Linnonmaa, 'Mr Diplomat, sorry for trouble! Your friends say we very bad boys!' He laughed. 'But no hard feelings, eh?' he said and winked. He walked out of the flat and shut the door loudly behind him.

Mr Linnonmaa pursed his lips, making a shushing sound. Pia looked at the kitchen. It looked tidy. The table was empty of debris from the KGB men's drinking and smoking. Even the curtains were drawn neatly. Apart from the faint smell of cigarettes and alcohol, it was as if no one had been there at all.

After what seemed an age, Anni's father spoke, 'I'm going to get myself free and then undo your ropes. It's ok.' He looked at both Anni and Pia in turn. They both nodded.

Pia was still too afraid to speak but Anni said, 'Have they gone now?'

'Yes, I should think so,' Mr Linnonmaa said, and turning to Pia, added, 'Are you alright? Did he hurt you?'

'What's going on? What is this all about?' Pia asked. She looked at Anni's father, but he was looking down, neatly putting away the ropes. 'You must telephone your mother, to let her know you are here,' he said, not looking at Pia.

She turned to Anni. 'I think I have the right to know what's going on?'

'Pia, of course you do,' Anni's father said. 'I am sorry you've got involved in this. Neither of you,' he made a wide gesture with his arm, 'should ever have been involved. Looking at Anni, he added, 'What good fortune your mother is away!' Pia noticed his wrists were raw from the tight rope and looked at her own. She, too, had marks but much fainter than Mr Linnonmaa's. How was she going to explain them to her mother? Anni's father looked down at the floor for a moment, and continued, 'I will tell you as much as I know, or as much as I can without putting you in any more danger. The fact is,' his eyes met Pia's, 'you must be very careful. Tell me what happened here with the KGB men?'

Mr Linnonmaa seemed relieved to hear how little Pia had been able to tell the man.

'Good girl.' Anni's father put his hand over Pia's at the kitchen table, 'It took a little longer than it should, but finally the KGB realised they were making a grave mistake holding me hostage. They should have known better!' He was now standing upright, with his chest lifted. Pia could imagine him, giving a speech to a roomful of important people. Anni was looking up at her father proudly.

Just then Pia remembered. 'But I don't understand. He wants me to take part in the tournament, and last night he tried to grab me in the tram. I'm sure it was him.' Pia glanced at Mr Linnonmaa and Anni, 'When I was here the day before yesterday I saw him run past your flat.'

'Really?' Mr Linnonmaa was quiet for a moment. 'Hmm,' he said and again paused. 'Don't worry Pia, he won't bother you anymore.'

'But he said he was going to watch me!'

'Will they come back?' Anni asked.

'No.' Mr Linnonmaa said.

'But now you must call your mother, and then tomorrow you two,' he nodded to Anni, 'will go back to school. It is past eight o'clock already, your mother must be home from work? And remember, you mustn't talk about this to anyone, particularly not to your mother's boyfriend, Pia.'

'Why?'

'Well. Let's just say he doesn't really need to know. The KGB is allergic to the British security forces.'

Pia was stunned into silence, British security forces?

Anni's father added, 'I'm going to telephone your mother and say you had some kind of accident outside. Then I'm going to walk you home.'

'She's going to go crazy. She's got it into her head that I'm on drugs!' Pia said. She was surprised how she just blurted it out.

Anni let out a cry, 'What? But we don't touch that stuff!'

'No, I know, but try telling her.' It was all too much for Pia and she started to cry. Anni came over and put her arms around Pia. 'It's OK, my dad will fix it. Won't you?' she said turning around to look at Mr Linnonmaa. He didn't say anything for a while. He sat down again and drummed the table with his fingers, 'Why does she think you're taking drugs?'

Pia had stopped crying. She thought of what Mr Linnonmaa had said about Iain being one of 'the British security forces'. She wondered if she should tell Mr Linnonmaa how the Admiral seemed to have lied to her mother about the drugs. But, her mother might have completely got it wrong. She decided she'd better not say anything until she'd had a chance to talk to the Admiral.

'Oh, you know, she saw some TV programme,' Pia said.

'I'll see what I can do,' Mr Linnonmaa said and smiled.

Before she opened the door to her flat, Pia took a deep breath. Her gloves covered the marks on her wrists, but Pia knew her face must be red from the slap and puffy from the crying. All her make-up was gone. Pia had cleaned off the last traces in Anni's bathroom. Her mother was sure to notice something was different about her. Her changed appearance would only fuel her mother's belief about the drugs.

'Darling, at last you're home!' Pia's mother took Pia into her arms and hugged her hard. 'Mr Linnonmaa phoned and explained everything. And,' she took Pia's cheeks between her hands and looked her deep into her eyes, 'you needn't feel ashamed!'

Pia took her coat off while her mother whizzed off to the kitchen. She was wearing her blue dressing gown and had rollers in her hair.

'I'm making hot chocolate for you, just like in the old days when you came in from playing in the snow. Then I'll have a look at those hands of yours. Are you bruised anywhere else? I can rub some cream on if you want. Mr Linnonmaa told me all about your accident,' she shouted from the kitchen.

What on earth had Anni's father told her mother? That they'd been playing outside in the snow after school? As if they were kids! Pia shrugged and suddenly felt very tired. At least she didn't have to lie, Pia thought, and flung herself onto her bed.

9

Iain took the overnight ferry to Stockholm. The Colonel had said, 'MI6's budgets are atrocious, so flying is out of the question, I'm afraid'. The argument Iain had put forward for needing to be in Helsinki to keep an eye on Pia or Kovtun had fallen on deaf ears, as had the complaint about losing too much time during HMS *Newcastle*'s visit.

'We've got a week here, we can spare you for a couple of days.' Iain couldn't argue. He didn't know how many other people were on the case. That was something the Colonel had said was best for him not to be worried about. He booked a cabin and paid the extra for a two-berth to himself. The department would have to understand that he wasn't going to travel like a bum.

The day was cold but sunny. By five thirty in the afternoon the sun had long disappeared below the horizon and the huge Silja Line ferry shimmered against the white ice-covered sea and the black sky beyond.

Inside the plush ferry, a pink-coated hostess showed him to the sparse cabin, while looking him up and down.

'Have a good trip,' she said unsmiling. The grey roots of
her jet-black hair and her unpleasant body odour made Iain
shiver as she let him pass through the heavy door. Iain put
his small holdall down and took out the piece of paper on
which he had jotted the name of the Stockholm police
sergeant. Johan Karlsson had sounded almost unfriendly on
the telephone, but that might have been his limited
command of English. Iain hoped it would be sufficient to
translate the file he'd mentioned. But those were tomorrow's
worries. Tonight he'd relax. Have a good meal at the famed
smorgasbord, a few drinks at the bar, even a Finnish tango
in the nightclub.

Iain first noticed the woman in the duty-free shop. Her
lips were painted bright pink, which suited her pale colour-
ing. She was quite short, but slim, with small features and
fragile-looking bones. Iain guessed her age to be around
thirty, perhaps younger. Her large eyes were lined with
black make-up and she looked a little tired. She was oddly
attractive to Iain, who didn't usually like short women. She
bought her full quota of drink. She filled two bags with
vodka, wine and a few beers and carried her heavy shopping
with difficulty. Iain wondered if it was too forward to offer to
help, when she turned into a corridor and descended the
stairs into the cheaper cabins.

Iain only went to the duty-free to see what was on offer.
And to pass the time. Maija had told her that the prices were
amazing. Shame he couldn't tell her he was finally taking
the ferry to Stockholm. She'd told him several times how
pleasant the trip was, how good the food, how cheap the
drinks.

When Iain walked into the nightclub he saw her again.
She'd changed into a black floaty dress and high-heeled
boots. The outfit suited her. The boots were shiny and made

Iain feel a small twinge in his groin. She was sitting at a table alone, surveying the couples gliding on the tiny dance floor. Her legs were crossed and she was swinging the top one to the rhythm of the fast Finnish dance, humppa, the band was playing. A disco ball above the dance floor threw blotchy lights around the room.

'Would you like to dance?'

She lifted her head in surprise. Though Iain crossed the dance floor slowly, he'd obviously not made much of an impression on her. He'd made a mistake. He lowered his hand and straightened his back, ready to turn around and lessen the humiliation of her refusal.

'Oh.' She reached her hand out and touched his. Her small hands were surprisingly strong.

She was a good dancer. By the time they'd reached the floor, a new slower tune was playing. A version of Blue Moon. She asked where Iain was from, and he told her London, to make it simpler. He told her his ex-wife was Finnish and that he was on a business trip. Luckily she didn't ask many questions. He wasn't keen on a complicated discussion. They moved around the floor in silence. The feel of her body made him want to take her to his cabin straight-away. The way she'd let him hold her close made him hope-ful. But he decided to wait. After three songs he took her back to the table and asked if he could join her. She nodded and smiled into his eyes. They had a few drinks and danced two or three more times.

Kerttu was from Eastern Finland, but because there was no work there she had followed an uncle to Stockholm. She'd been in Sweden for only a year, but already she was earning more than she would have done in Finland. She told Iain she struggled with the language. He didn't ask what kind of work she did in Stockholm.

Her mouth tasted of the cigarettes she smoked tentatively at the table. The way she inhaled made Iain think she had only just started. When they danced, her breasts against Iain's chest felt soft and large, while her tiny waist was fragile in his grip.

Iain made his move. They were on the dance floor and had been kissing through most of the slow piece. Kerttu looked into his eyes and nodded. Iain paid at the bar and led Kerttu to his cabin.

Unlike smoking a cigarette, Kerttu had clearly done this before. She was willing and passionate. Afterwards, she asked if she could light a cigarette and Iain nearly laughed at the banality of the situation. But the sight of her full bare breasts in the faint light of the cabin, as she fumbled in her handbag for the lighter, looked so sexy, he could only think how lucky he was. He made love to her again, this time more slowly. She was noisier than before and he came with such power that he decided not to leave such a long time between women in future. After Kerttu had dressed, apologising that she had to work the next day and needed her sleep, Maija's beautiful face came into his mind. He felt no guilt. He hadn't promised Maija anything.

Iain fell asleep immediately and slept deeply without dreaming. He was awakened by the same dark-haired hostess, who, after not getting any response to her knocking, opened the door and peered in.

'Half an hour to harbour.'

Her shrill voice made Iain's head hurt. He'd had too much to drink last night.

Kerttu was already eating at a sea-facing table in the cafeteria. She was wearing a pair of pale-coloured flared jeans with the shiny boots and a tight yellow jumper. Iain tried to kiss her, but she pushed him away.

'I've got my make-up on.'

She had a suitcase next to her, with the two bags of shopping. Iain made a joke about the weary-looking people queuing up for food. Kerttu laughed, but concentrated on her food.

'Let me help you with those. I'll get my things and we'll go out together,' Iain said when he'd finished eating the egg sandwich, which was the only food he could consider having from the counter. His cup of awful black coffee was half-drunk.

Kerttu looked at Iain, then at her hands. Iain hadn't noticed the untidy fingernails last night.

'I...I can't,' she looked at Iain and continued, 'I'm married. My husband is waiting at the jetty.'

They said goodbye and Iain returned to his cabin. Of course it all made sense. Kerttu was a cleaner, the 'uncle' she'd gone after, her husband. He'd been working in a factory outside Stockholm for two years while she was still in Finland. They had no children, but he wanted some. 'I'm sorry, I drank too much,' she said. Iain smiled, then laughed out loud.

'You don't mind, do you?' Kerttu had asked him, her eyes wide with anxiety.

No, he didn't mind, he'd assured her.

The sun was blindingly bright when Iain stepped outside the ferry port in Stockholm. It was noticeably warmer here than in Helsinki. As Iain followed a crowd of people from the ferry walking wearily towards the underground station he noticed the Swedes looked more Western. They wore colourful, fashionable clothes. There were many more foreign faces than in Helsinki. And everyone spoke perfect

English. Even a teenage hippie sitting with his feet up in the ticket booth at the station, with the hems of his frayed jeans on show, spoke to Iain fluently, giving him precise instructions on how to get to Solna.

Solna police station was a small red-brick building in the older part of the Stockholm suburb. It stood a little way from the modern shopping centre, with its new, tall blocks of flats overlooking the low commercial buildings, where Iain's bus had stopped. He'd got directions to the police station by a friendly pizza restaurant owner, speaking English in an Italian accent. After a few minutes' walk, the street turned narrower and the blocks of flats were only four or five storeys high.

Sergeant Karlsson wasn't like the other Swedes. His English was very shaky. He was a young, tall man with angular features, his long fair hair resting on a colourfully patterned tank top. The sleeves of the shirt underneath were slightly too short for his long arms. He gestured for Iain to sit down and settled himself opposite. They were in a small office, with windows overlooking a snow-covered park. Folders and papers were strewn all over a couple of grey filing cabinets.

Sergeant Karlsson held an orange folder. For a moment he said nothing and Iain waited.

'You are interested in the Miss Berglund case?'

'Hmm, yes,' Iain looked at his notes.

Karlsson leant back in his chair and crossed his hands. He surveyed Iain.

'Why?'

At last Iain had found the bit about Miss Berglund in his

notes. The Swedish policeman's pronunciation made the name sound wholly different.

'It's an Embassy matter. We believe she was a British citizen. I thought my colleague had telephoned Inspector Lund?'

'Yes,' Karlsson bent down towards the file again. He lifted his eyes to Iain and continued, 'but there was no UK passport.'

Iain waited, keeping eye contact with the policeman. He was parched and wished that instead of being so difficult, the young man would offer him a coffee.

Finally Karlsson took a deep breath in and handed Iain the folder.

Miss Berglund was beaten to death. The pictures shocked Iain. There were black and blue marks all over her body and her face was smashed up. It was unrecognisable as that of a young woman in her late twenties. The police report was in Swedish, but Iain could see it was dated about a month ago, 22 January 1979.

'Cause of death?'

'Bleeding, like, here,' Karlsson pointed to his belly.

'Internal bleeding? And how was she found?'

'She did not go to work and a friend came to her home.'

There was a brief silence. Karlsson continued, 'She was beaten and also there was sign of sex.'

'Rape?'

Karlsson stared at Iain.

'Had she been forced to have sex?' Iain tried again.

'Aah...we know not. There was, how do you say? Seed inside her.'

'Semen.'

'Yes.'

Iain looked at the pictures again. Poor girl, what sort of person would have done this?

'And did you find out who did it?'

'We think this man,' Karlsson leant over and pulled out a black-and-white picture. It had been taken with an old-fashioned camera and there was white edging to the picture. The man was standing a little way off, leaning on a railing by water. He was wearing a leather coat. Though he wasn't looking into the camera, Iain recognised him immediately. The Colonel had been right.

'Did you catch him?'

Karlsson looked down at his hands, 'No.'

The Swedish policeman explained how all their searches had been futile. No one seemed to know where he'd disappeared to. The work friend knew that Miss Berglund was in love with a foreign man, perhaps from the Soviet Union. She'd met him once, accidentally in the centre of Stockholm. He'd been with Miss Berglund and the three of them had gone for a beer in a bar. The friend thought he was very controlling, and had warned Miss Berglund about the man.

'And there are no other suspects?'

Karlsson shook his head, 'No other boyfriend. Her family come from northern Sweden. She know nobody in Stockholm,' Karlsson added, 'so I think you wrong. She is Swedish, not English.'

'Yes, I'm sorry, mistaken identity,' Iain said, getting up from the chair, 'Thank you anyway.' He shook Karlsson's long, bony hand and left the police station.

Iain spent the rest of the day sightseeing in Stockholm. He went up to the Kaknäs Tower and surveyed the place from above. The city was made up of several islands, connected to the mainland by long bridges. Trains and cars crossed the overpasses, emitting fumes into the crisp, cold air. Several shipping lanes were cut into the frozen sea. Iain thought he must come back to Stockholm in the summer. Perhaps bring Maija. He had lunch in one of the many reasonably priced restaurants near the train station, and finally had a look at the Old Town before heading back to the North Harbour. At the ferry terminal he went into a telephone booth.

'That's very careless,' the Colonel said when Iain told him about the photo.

'Don't think he knew it was taken.'

'Have you got it?'

'No,' Iain hesitated. It hadn't occurred to him to ask for a copy, 'It was difficult as it was, Sir!'

'Alright Collins, have a good return trip.'

10

It took Maija only to the first tram stop to tell Iain about Pia's accident at the Linnonmaas' house. Iain looked at Maija's eager face.

'I'm so relieved that Pia isn't involved in anything, you know, what you thought.' She straightened herself up slightly and looked out of the window. 'Otherwise, I wasn't sure if I'd have been able to come out tonight.'

'I'm so glad,' Iain said. The tram came to a corner and the movement shoved him nearer to Maija. She looked up at him. She looked so fragile. Iain bent down and kissed her mouth. He put his arm around Maija and said, 'She's a good girl, your Pia.'

Maija reached for a hankie in her handbag and blew her nose loudly. Iain took his arm away. He'd never get used to the manners of the Finns, even after marriage to one, it still took him by surprise how natural they found all their bodily functions. For sex, of course, it was liberating. The image of Kerttu's full breasts flashed quickly in front of him. Iain glanced at Maija. He mustn't feel guilty; it was just sex. Iain shook his head, this must not do. Concentrate on the task. He started talking about the film, Heaven Can Wait, they were about to see. Of course, in Britain it had been showing for weeks already, and he'd read the reviews in the papers at the Council. Just the sort of romantic thing Maija would like, he thought.

'So, tell me, what did Pia say she'd done at Anni's?' Iain was taking a chance, asking too much might make Maija suspicious, but he could not think of any other way of getting the information. The Colonel had told Iain about the 'incident' at the Linnonmaas' flat. Iain's new brief was to forget about the Linnonmaas and concentrate on Kovtun and Pia. But how could he when the two seemed intertwined?

'They'd been messing around in the snow outside, you know kids' stuff, really too childish for them, and had fallen sideways onto some rock or other,' Maija said.

'But you said she had marks on her wrists?'

Maija looked sharply at Iain.

'The ropes on the sleigh were around her wrists.'

When they arrived at the Kino there was already a queue for tickets. They heard a commotion, someone shouting ahead of them. Iain leant across to get a better view. He felt Maija's body next to him, also stretching to see. A man in a shabby coat was talking to the ticket seller in a loud voice. The woman behind the glass was shaking her head. She looked frightened. The man was holding a bottle of clear liquid, and waving it at the woman inside the booth. He said something and stuck the bottle in his pocket. A real drunk, Iain thought. The man turned around and Iain could feel Maija freeze. She moved swiftly back in line with the queue. The man had both his hands in the pockets of his jacket. He was standing still, staring at Iain and Maija. People behind him in the queue were nudging him to move and eventually he did, walking slowly past the queue and past Maija and Iain. When he was level with them, he looked at Maija and smiling said, 'Dobryj večer'.

Iain watched the man, who kept his eyes on Maija as long as he could, walk out of the glass door. The queue was moving quickly forward. Iain glanced at Maija. She was facing forward, with her head held high. She hadn't reacted in any way when the man had spoken Russian to her.

'Did you know him?' Iain asked, trying to sound casual.

'Who?'

'The Russian man.'

Everyone in the queue turned to look at Iain. He coughed and looked down at his boots. He'd forgotten Finns didn't use that word.

'Of course not,' Maija said, lifting her eyes to Iain and then looking pointedly at the people around them. Iain nodded and placed his hand around Maija's waist. She was still tense.

When Iain paid for their tickets, he said, 'What did the drunk want?'

The cashier looked at Iain in surprise.

'Come on, the film is about to start,' Maija said anxiously, taking hold of Iain's arm. But Iain wasn't budging. He glanced at the clock above the ticket booth and saw they had plenty of time yet. The woman behind the glass was looking from Maija to Iain. A couple behind Iain in the queue started to shuffle closer to him. Eventually the ticket seller coughed and said, 'Oh, he just wanted to buy a ticket to the cinema with a bottle of vodka. Like many of the Soviet citizens we get here, he had no Finnish marks.'

Just as the film was about to start, Iain made an excuse. 'Sorry Maija, need the loo,' and found a telephone in the foyer of the Kino Theatre. He was glad to see it was empty. Even the lady selling the tickets had left her post.

'We need to talk to the girl again. She's becoming a nuisance, isn't she,' the Colonel said.

Iain had considered telling the Colonel of the little incident with Maija and the Russian, but decided against it. He needed to work out what it meant first.

Back in his seat, next to Maija, Iain put his arm around her. The film had barely begun, but he needed to get back to Maija's flat as soon as possible. He started to cough violently, taking his arm back and reaching for a handkerchief in the pocket of his trousers. A few people around them started to shift uncomfortably in their seats. Iain's throat hurt. Maija whispered, 'Should we leave?'

Iain insisted that, as recompense for missing the film, he should take Maija right back to her flat instead of saying goodbye at the tram stop on Erottaja. Iain thought he might get in to check, and hopefully talk, to Pia about that night's events. In the tram to Kasarminkatu, Iain was thinking how close he was to telling Maija all. She didn't lack intelligence; he feared she'd soon see through the stupid excuses he had to invent to speak to Pia. If only there were fewer days until

the Geordie gunboat sailed back to the UK. Iain didn't know
how long he could keep up this act.

Pia woke to the sound of a door slamming. She was fully
clothed, but covered by a blanket. For a moment she didn't
know where she was. She held her breath and listened for
any noises. She'd been dreaming of being shut in a ship,
sitting amongst crates of machine guns, surrounded by the
faint scuffling of rats and dirt, hiding from the Gestapo. The
hold of the ship smelled musty and all Pia could hear were
the echoes of somebody's heavy boots walking on the deck
above her.

Pia sat up and looked around the room. The street light
cast an orange glow through the Venetian blinds. She put
her bedside lamp on and saw a note had been pushed under
the door.

'I've gone out to the cinema with Iain. Have the tinned
pea soup and rye bread for supper. Mum.'

Pia looked at her watch and saw the red marks on her
arms and suddenly remembered. No wonder she had the
Gestapo dream! Pia didn't want to leave her room in case
someone was lurking behind the sofa in the living room.
She shook her head, determined to ignore the fear. Light,
she thought. That will make everything look normal. Now
the room looked safe, with no hidden corners, just the piles
of clothes on the floor, the school books on the desk,
reminding Pia of the Finnish homework she had to do for
the Old Crow.

She'd been tired at school. In the morning her mother
had said she should take a day off, insisting Pia looked as if
she was sickening for something. Maija was surprised when
she hadn't taken any notice. Apart from training for the

Tournament Pia might as well have stayed at home. Anni had still not been at school, and Heikki, too, had been away. That wasn't unusual, though; he often skipped days. But now, with the two of them going out, Pia had hoped he'd tell her when he was planning to bunk off. She'd felt lonely all day.

First a cup of coffee and then pea soup. It was nearly nine o'clock. She must have slept a good two hours. Pia decided to phone Anni as soon as she could on the pretext of telling her about the Old Crow's homework assignment. Pia hoped she'd be coming to school tomorrow. Without her father present, Anni would tell her what was going on. Pia stepped into the kitchen, putting lights on as she walked through the hall and the living room. She thought about the Admiral's involvement in the British security forces. She'd talk to him, too, she decided, and slowly stirred the thick green soup in the pan. The smell of the salty pork and soft peas filled her nostrils. Suddenly she felt very hungry. She was spooning the soup into a bowl when the phone rang.

Anni, Pia thought, and ran smiling to the phone.

'Hello!'

'Miss Mäkelä?' a man's voice said.

'Umm, no,' Pia said, not really knowing why.

'I speak with Pia Mäkelä?' the voice said. Now she recognised the accent. It was Kovtun. Her voice mustn't tremble, Pia thought, and she said, in her most grown-up manner, 'I'm afraid she's not in.'

Pia was trying to copy her mother when she wanted to get rid of someone. She'd heard her use the voice on the Reader's Digest salespeople, as well as on the Jehovah's Witnesses who came to the door.

There was a long silence.

Pia noticed her hand was shaking. She heard a quick

breath being taken at the other end. Then the Russian hung up. It took Pia a long time to replace the receiver. She double locked the door and placed the chain across, then turned the lights off in the hall and in the kitchen. Crawling to the window, she stood up at the side, looking down at the empty road. The clock ticked in the kitchen. When Pia saw him, she stopped breathing. The man was walking slowly along the street opposite. He went past the flat, then turned around at the corner and came back. He came to a halt right opposite the kitchen window. Pia's mind raced. What was he doing there? Had he followed her home? She looked around and saw she'd forgotten the light in the living room. He could probably see her shadow through the thin cotton curtain. Pia pulled herself back and sat on the floor underneath the window and waited. The faint smell of the pea soup now made her feel sick. She wanted to cry but didn't dare make a sound. What could she do? Mr Linnonmaa had said they'd not trouble her anymore. Should she phone him? Or the police? Perhaps Anni's father could send the police to arrest the Russian. Could the Finnish police do anything with the KGB? Pia doubted it.

After what felt like an age, Pia crawled out of the kitchen and into her room, turning the light and the lamp off. She peered through the bottom of the Venetian blinds, parting them a fraction.

Kovtun was still there, watching the block of flats. He was wearing the long black coat. He touched the edge of his head as in a salute and walked away. It was as if he had been watching her, as if he knew exactly what Pia had been trying to do, first hiding behind the kitchen curtains and then cowering underneath the window. Pia sat down with her back to the wall, trying to control her breathing and stop the trembling of her hands. If only her mother would get home soon, she thought, she'd be with Iain. Iain! Would her mother be in danger going around with Iain? Or maybe he was the best person to protect her. Pia put her head in her hands and tried to think. She needed help. Remembering Heikki's laughing eyes and warm hugs, Pia jumped off the floor and ran to the hall. She'd memorised his number, though she'd never called him before.

Iain saw Vladsislas first. He was standing looking directly at Maija's flat. Maija was holding Iain's arm as they were about to turn into Kasarminkatu, but just in time, Iain took hold of Maija's shoulders, and turned her to face him. They were now standing right at the corner of the road.

'You know how much you mean to me, don't you Maija?'

Maija smiled back at him. Iain had to act quickly; he could not be seen by the Russian. He bent down and kissed Maija on the mouth, then gave her a long embrace. Over Maija's shoulder, Iain saw Vladsislas Kovtun start walking south towards Tehtaankatu. He noticed the Russian's silent salute towards Maija's kitchen window. This was serious. No more evenings out with Maija, unless they were at her place. He let go of Maija and gave her a peck on the cheek. 'You are lovely, Maija,' he said, in English, and hooked Maija's arm to his and started towards the flat, a little faster than he would have liked.

'Thank you,' Maija said and leaned closer to Iain.

When they reached the heavy front door of Maija's block, she turned around and said, 'Would you like to come back for a little while? It's a weekday, but...'

'I'd love to,' Iain said. Thank goodness he didn't have to

invite himself up. Old charm must still be working. The truth was he'd quite taken to Maija and Pia. He regretted playing awful tricks on them. The straightforwardness and simplicity of their life together appealed to Iain in the same way Virpi had. He thought of the first time he'd spent the night with Virpi. The sauna, the lake, the sex, all carried out in the same unassuming way. She'd stripped off in front of him, and asked Iain to do the same, then taking his hand had lead him to the dimly-lit sauna, and poured water onto the hot stones. The steam had made them both disappear for a moment, then, after the stinging on his body had gone, Iain had looked up at Virpi and seen that he'd fallen in love. Those long, pale legs and arms silhouetted against the darkness of the sauna, the blue eyes somehow looking even clearer and bluer. And her skin, how soft it had felt to his touch afterwards.

Finns were socially naïve and strange in many ways, but had a connection with nature that Iain envied. The way they coped with the bitter cold of a Helsinki winter and the intense heat of its summers, and everything else that nature could throw at them, was more than admirable. Iain had seen Maija ski on the frozen sea outside Suomenlinna Island and he had no doubt she swam in the same spot in the summer. It was as if the Finns had invented the sauna to reproduce the same abrupt change of seasons – hot steam room followed by an icy lake and back again. Was the forcefulness of nature imposed upon the Finns what made them so earnest? Iain warned himself to back off. Don't fall in love again. One Finnish woman in one lifetime is enough.

· · ·

The flat was quiet and dark. When Maija went to open the door, the chain was across it. 'Pia!' she shouted through the gap.

Pia looked pale and serious when she undid the chain. Iain had no doubt then that she'd seen Vladsislas Kovtun outside. He took Pia's arm and said, 'Are you OK,' in English.

Pia ignored him and went to hug her mother.

Maija gave Iain a look he could not interpret. Was it anger? Why was the Russian watching Maija's flat? What had Pia stumbled on? What was the 'incident' the Colonel had talked about at the Linnonmaas' place?

Iain needed to talk to the Colonel, but at the same time he needed to know the two women were safe.

Pia was crying in her mother's arms.

'What is the matter?' Maija said. She looked at Iain. 'This is not about drugs is it? You aren't involved in them after all? Mr Linnonmaa assured me that both Anni and you were such good girls, and I trusted him, but...'

'No,' Pia sobbed, 'I've got to tell you mum...'

'No, I'm sure Mr Linnonmaa is right. I was mistaken,' Iain said, interrupting the girl.

'Pia, tell me what the matter is, see if I can help,' he looked at the girl intently. 'Because I'm sure I could, if you need help in your English school work? Perhaps you've had a bad report?' Iain continued to look at Pia, trying to stop her from telling her mother everything.

The Colonel had warned Iain over and over not to get Maija involved.

'The fewer people know about the Russian, the better. Once we're gone and the operation is complete, it will only become embarrassing for the Russians, and then you don't know what the KGB boys will cook up to save face. Neither Pia, nor her mother, must know the full scope.' The

Colonel had removed his glasses and lifted his eyes from a file he'd been reading, 'We must try not to compromise any locals, you know.' As if Iain didn't know that. The Colonel made it all seem so easy. But Iain had not been trained to be a spy.

The doorbell rang.

'Who can that be, at this time of the night?' Maija said.

Iain turned to the door first, 'Let me,' he said. He feared the worst. Had Kovtun gone for reinforcements? Surely he wouldn't ring the bell!

The boy Iain had followed into the British Council was standing at the door. He had a wide grin on his face. His hands were in the pockets of his half-open jacket.

Pia let out a cry, 'Oh, Heikki, it's you!'

'That's cool, what's up, baby?' The boy looked from Pia to her mother, then to Iain. There was not a flicker of recognition. Iain said, in English, 'How do you do, I'm Iain Collins.'

The boy looked at Pia, then took Iain's hand and shook it with a force that took Iain by surprise. Pia shut the door behind the boy and said, coyly, to her mother, 'Mum, this is Heikki Tuomila.'

Maija shook the boy's hand. She hesitated for a moment, then said 'It is rather late, but would you like some coffee?' She made for the kitchen.

Pia took the boy's jacket, and, leading him by the hand, followed her mother. Iain stood in the hall for a moment. He knew he should leave. Had it been a normal scenario, a boyfriend's first introduction to a girl's mother, he would have. However, he could not be sure of the boy's motives, or his involvement. Nor could he be sure Pia wouldn't still tell her mother or the boy everything. He needed the Colonel's advice.

'Maija, could I use your telephone? I know it's late.' He glanced at his watch. It had gone half past nine.

'Of course,' Maija said and disappeared back into the kitchen. Iain could hear Pia giggle. He was glad she'd recovered a little. For now at least. While on the phone, maybe he could keep one ear out to the kitchen. The boy's arrival seemed to have distracted Pia enough. All the same, he needed to warn the Colonel.

'Hello, it's Iain Collins. I'm sorry but I'm not able to make it tomorrow.' Iain paused. The Colonel said nothing. 'But something has come up. I have an old friend who needs my help. He's asked for it quite suddenly.'

'Our old friend from the East?'

'The two will clash.'

There was a silence at the other end.

'Ask the girl to come to the Council to return the books.'

'Yes, I'm afraid this is quite necessary, there is also the one who left without paying. He's now reappeared.'

'The boyfriend? Don't worry about him. I've got someone on his tail,' the Colonel said.

Iain laughed, 'Well, what can I do?'

'You're doing fine, just make sure there's no one outside when you leave and I'll come and see you tomorrow at the Council.'

'Thank you. Goodbye.' Iain replaced the receiver.

When Iain entered the kitchen, Maija, Pia and the boy sat around the small kitchen table, drinking coffee. It never ceased to amaze Iain how long Finns could just sit without speaking to each other. Iain sat next to Maija, who poured him coffee. The silence continued. Every now and then Pia smiled at the boy, but still not a word from anyone.

'Well,' Iain began. Everyone lifted their heads from the coffee cups and looked at him. 'I must go.'

'OK,' Maija stood up.

Iain held his hand out to Heikki, 'Nice to meet you and goodbye.' There was still no change of facial expression from the boy. Iain was relieved.

'And Pia, could you return the English books tomorrow, please? Whenever suits you, I'll be there all day.'

Heikki lifted his eyes at this, and said, 'Can I come too, Mr Collins? I've never been to the British Council.'

11

P ia woke up the next morning and looked down onto the street. A strong wind was blowing wisps of snow over the pavement. A woman, hunched up against the cold, was walking briskly towards the tram stop. Everything looked familiar. Pia began to wonder if she had just imagined being held by the KGB at Anni's flat. Did she really see Kovtun stand on the same pavement last night? She hoped Anni would be at school today. Pia leaned against the Venetian blinds and thought about Heikki. She wrapped her hands around her body. Pia couldn't wait to see him and Anni. After she had spoken with Iain this afternoon everything would get back to normal. The KGB and the English could sort whatever it was they were fighting over amongst themselves.

The steps to the main hall were very slippery. Pia had to follow a line of sand the school caretaker had sprinkled over them in the morning. The soles of Pia's boots were so worn out she had to be very careful. With her head bent, she didn't spot Heikki talking to Sasha until she was almost next to them. They were standing very close to each other. Heikki was speaking in a low voice.

'I know I'm not supposed to get involved, but you haven't exactly been an angel either! ' Heikki poked his finger at Sasha's chest. She nearly lost her balance and then turned her face and saw Pia. Sasha's eyes were black with anger. She moved her eyes from Pia to Heikki, and back, nodding. Heikki turned around and said, 'Hi baby.'

Sasha rolled her eyes and turned on her heels.

Heikki put his arm around Pia's shoulders. She felt the warm sensation in her stomach that she always did when he touched her. He squeezed Pia and gave her a quick kiss. 'See you later in class,' he said, releasing her and waving goodbye.

Sasha was watching them from where the lockers were. Pia ran to her. Her bag was heavy with books this morning and it slowed her, but she reached Sasha just as she was shutting her locker door.

'Oh hello, baby,' Sasha said in a mocking voice.

'What are you up to?' Pia tried to keep the anger out of her voice. It was about time Sasha realised it was she, Pia, who Heikki wanted.

'What do you mean?' Sasha was wearing a new pink angora jumper with a huge round collar over her tight white jeans. She put her hand on her hip and looked Pia up and down. The stacked heels of Sasha's brown boots made her the same height as Pia. She wished she had new clothes to wear. Instead she had on last year's brown cords and her favourite white college shirt. The outfit she'd worn to school nearly every day of the term.

'Sasha, you know Heikki and me are an item now, so

there's no need to keep on trying to get him for yourself,' Pia said.

Sasha laughed, throwing her head back, her blonde curls shaking with the movement. 'You are a silly girl,' she said and left.

Pia threw her bag down on the floor and wished she'd kept her mouth shut for once. She looked around to see who had heard their conversation. A few kids from the lower school were loitering at the far end of the row of lockers. No other sixth formers were around. Pia could have been humiliated in front of everyone. Then she saw what time it was – on top of everything, now she was late for her first class with the Old Crow. She wondered how to avoid Sasha during the lesson. But when she approached the classroom all she could see from the doorway was an empty desk where Anni was supposed to be sitting.

Even Pia's handstands were off kilter, Leena thought, as she watched her team of five gymnasts practise their programme. Only two days to go and Pia stood out like a sore thumb.

Leena sighed.

'Pia Mäkelä, you alone, one more practice of the whole programme!' she shouted from the end of the gym hall. 'Others watch and see what can be improved in Pia's performance!'

Pia walked slowly to the corner of the blue mat and lifted her arms up.

'Wait for the signal!'

Leena let Pia stand there for a few moments. 'Now, take a deep breath in, prepare yourself, and, starting with the front handspring, go!' Leena watched as Pia struggled to keep her balance, pulled her legs down and moved into the front roll, looking like a sack of potatoes. She struggled in the handstand, but at least she kept herself upright. When her legs were pointing up into the air, her feet were together and she stayed still for a fraction of a second. The thumping sound she made as she landed made Leena wince. The girl's bulk seemed magnified on the gym mat. But one must stay professional. Leena put her hands together for a clap to a performance that had Pia panting. The other girls, who'd done a hundred percent better, joined their teacher in showing Pia their appreciation. They clapped enthusiastically.

'Now can anyone tell me what Pia needs to improve most, and how she can achieve this?' Leena looked at the girls. They'd surrounded Pia and were giggling and talking simultaneously. 'Quiet please,' Leena said in as calm a voice as she could muster. 'Please, we only have...'

'Three days in which to become perfect,' Pia said, clearly mocking Leena's voice, but so slightly that she didn't feel she could pick her up on it. The other girls continued to giggle.

'Well, I'm glad you know this. Which is why we must get you up to the level of the others!' Leena looked at the faces of the group of girls: her team that could, Vadi had promised her, win the Friendship Trophy. Leena clapped her hands and told the girls the session was over.

She went into her office and lit a cigarette. She opened a window and let the cold air invade the small space. Turning back, she saw the portrait of the President of the Republic, Urho Kekkonen. It was an old black-and-white picture. The President looked young, but wore the same black-rimmed glasses as he had now at least ten years later. Leena took a deep drag out of her cigarette and wondered whether what she'd agreed to with Vadi was a crime against

Finland. Would President Kekkonen approve? Certainly wanting to win the trophy wasn't wrong, but was helping Vadi?

Heikki was waiting for Pia underneath a street lamp, outside the school gate. She'd decided to bunk off religious studies and home economics. Anyway, she wanted to rest after the training. She needed to conserve her energy. Miss Joutila had made Pia and the other girls go over the programme ten times. Pia made the little ones laugh, as each time they restarted the routine she showed the number on her fingers behind Miss Joutila's back.

Once, when Miss Joutila was correcting the position of her handstand, Pia wondered how involved with Kovtun she was. Pia had two bruises on her thighs and several smaller ones on her arms but Miss Joutila didn't take any notice of them. It wasn't unusual for gymnasts to have bruises. Pia had her fair share, especially as she often tried the more difficult moves. She had covered the marks on her wrists with make-up. She wondered if Miss Joutila knew Kovtun was KGB. What would she say if Pia told her he'd hit and threatened her? What if she talked to Mrs Härmänmaa about Kovtun? Mr Linnonmaa had told her not to talk to anyone about the Russian's other activities. It could harm him – and Anni. That would also put a stop to the whole competition and that was the last thing Pia wanted. Gymnastics was the only thing she was good at. If she won the trophy for her school she could perhaps get a sports scholarship to America, or become a famous gymnast, or dancer. Someone everyone admired. So she said nothing to either Miss Joutila or the Old Crow. Heikki and the Admiral were the only people who could help her now. She was worried about Anni too. Why wasn't she back at school? She'd missed three whole days.

Heikki was smoking a cigarette under the streetlight, in full view of the staff room. His other hand was in his jacket pocket.

'Aren't you afraid you're going to get expelled?' Pia said. She joined her hand with his in the pocket. He put his fingers around hers. His hand was warm. Pia had left her gloves at home that morning and her hands were freezing. It was only half past one, but already getting dark. The white snow seemed to be glowing against the grey sky.

'Nah, it's cool,' Heikki said and kissed Pia on the lips. His nose felt cold against her face. Pia's knees felt weak.

They walked up to the tram stop. Pia matched her steps with his so that she could still keep hold of his hand inside the pocket. Pia squeezed his hand harder and said, 'Thank you for coming with me.'

Heikki kissed the top of Pia's head and said, 'Anything for you, doll.'

The Colonel sat opposite Iain on the musty-smelling top floor of the Council. He'd been quiet for a long time. His chin rested on his thumbs, palms facing each other, slowly letting each finger touch its opposite number in turn.

'The boy said he wants to come to the Council?'

'Yes.'

'And the woman, what's her name again?'

Iain sighed, 'Maija.'

'She says her daughter was playing in the snow? Playing?'

'Yes.' Iain shifted uncomfortably in his light wooden chair. His buttocks would go numb if he was forced to stay put for any longer. He'd been sitting in the office for the best part of the day. First waiting for the Colonel, then sitting opposite him, going over and over the events of the last day. 'Mr Linnonmaa had telephoned her and told her this story. Now she's convinced that Pia is not involved in anything untoward, especially not drugs. I think that cover is blown, Sir.'

'Yes, yes.'

The Colonel was silent again. Iain wondered what he was thinking. Perhaps he was plotting another improbable story to tell Maija. The drug story made Iain look like an idiot. It had also hurt both the women and lost him valuable credibility. Iain watched the Colonel's grey face behind his slowly moving fingers. From now on he would deal with the women in his own way.

What he found out in Stockholm was playing on his mind too.

'I was wondering...this business in Stockholm.'

'Yes?'

Iain hesitated. The Colonel scrutinised him.

'You knew it would be him?'

After a brief silence, the Colonel said, 'Yes.'

So Iain was just sent to confirm what MI6 already knew.

'And the secretary at the Embassy?'

The Colonel bit his bottom lip. He stared at Iain over his glasses.

'Iain,' there was smile, 'I was very glad you spotted that article. Well done.'

The Colonel kept eye contact with Iain. It was uncomfortable, but Iain was determined to get some answers.

Finally the Colonel continued, 'She was Kovtun's secretary.'

Iain didn't say anything. He didn't want to show how shocked he was. Two bodies already, both women. How many more would there be before HMS *Newcastle* sailed?

He glanced at the Colonel, who was now pacing the room. Iain knew he was impatient at having to wait. Iain, on the other hand, seemed lately to spend his life hanging around waiting for things to happen, unable to protect or help anyone. That morning he had followed Pia to school, taken the tram back to the Council and was now again waiting for the Colonel to speak. He presumed there was someone outside the school keeping an eye out for the children. But he couldn't be sure. Iain no longer trusted the Colonel. He suspected an assignment in Helsinki was a low priority in the Colonel's busy working life. As far as Iain could see it was all going terribly wrong. At least he was sure it was taking more of the Colonel's time than had been anticipated in London. Iain couldn't ask, but he kept wondering how they'd come to recruit Kovtun. He was violent – a murderer – and unpredictable. He behaved as if he owned Helsinki. Perhaps that was the key. The Russian had been providing vital information. But was this worth it for the Royal Navy, and to London? Worth all these innocent people getting hurt?

'What about Kovtun?' Iain asked. 'He seems to be keeping an eye on the flat.'

'Yes,' the Colonel said. He walked to the end of the room and peered outside. 'I just think he's getting nervy. Must have seen you go in and out and wants to make sure you're not, you know, messing things up for him.'

This was the limit. Iain knew for certain the Russian

hadn't spotted him once. There was more to it than even the Colonel knew, but Iain couldn't quite put his finger on what.

'Sir,' he said, but before he could continue, the Colonel said, 'At last! They're here!'

Mrs Cooper brought the two youngsters into the room. This time Pia looked more relaxed. She was holding the boy's hand. Iain examined his face. He had open features, fairly attractive, he presumed. His hair was not exactly blond, but sandy coloured and unruly. He looked uncomfortable in his body, as boys of that age often did, not quite used to their long limbs. But his face displayed no unease. He looked straight at Iain, and then nodded towards the Colonel.

'And who's this, another spy?'

Mrs Cooper stopped at the door. The Colonel looked up and put his hand up to her. She left the room, silently closing the door.

'Sit down,' the Colonel said in English, 'I hear you wanted to see what this place was like?'

'Yeah, sure I did.' The boy's English was remarkably good, though his accent was more American than British, but then that was the influence of the television here.

'I have it from good authority that you did in fact make an unannounced visit to our premises two nights ago. Is this true?'

Heikki looked straight at the Colonel. 'I might have done.'

'What were you looking for?'

No answer.

The Colonel leant over the table and put his face very close to the boy's.

'Now young man, people's lives are at stake and we are not playing games here. Do I make myself clear?'

'Heikki, just tell them why you came,' Pia said to the boy in Finnish. He didn't look at her, as if he hadn't heard a word she said. Pia glanced at Iain.

'That's right, Pia, we do not want Heikki to be in danger,' Iain said, also in Finnish. Just in case the boy's English wasn't as good as it appeared.

Heikki looked at both Pia and Iain in turn. Then he faced the Colonel again. His English faltered a little at this point. As Iain understood it, he'd just been curious when he saw Pia coming out of the building. When Iain asked him how he'd got in – and out – of the Council, he grinned and said, 'I like to open locks.' Pia looked shocked.

The Colonel sat back in his chair. He held the boy's gaze. Without moving his head he said, 'We need to talk to Pia alone.'

'No' the boy said. He took hold of Pia's hand again, but she pulled it back.

'It's OK, Heikki, you go on.' Pia said in Finnish. 'I want to talk to Iain and the Colonel alone.'

'The Colonel?'

Pia turned her face away from the boy and Iain suppressed a smile. Heikki looked at each one of them in turn. Mrs Cooper must have been standing outside, waiting and listening, because as soon as Heikki got up the door opened and she led him away.

Pia couldn't believe what she'd just heard. Why hadn't Heikki told her about being in the Council right after their first date at the Happy Days? She bit her lip when she remembered the night before. How, after her mother had left them alone in the kitchen, Heikki had kissed the bruises on her wrists. 'I told you to be careful, silly,' he'd said. Pia had told him absolutely everything. The relief she'd felt at not being alone in the middle of the whole mess had been overwhelming, as was not having to face the two men on her own this afternoon. Especially when she'd tried phoning Anni and her number had been engaged. And then Anni still hadn't showed up at school this morning.

'Where's Anni?' she asked the Colonel in English.

'We don't know,' The Colonel answered. Pia looked over to Iain. His face was stern.

'Pia, what have you told Heikki?'

Pia looked down.

The Colonel sighed. 'In that case can I ask that you tell us everything as well then, please?'

'I don't understand anything,' Pia said. Suddenly tears started running down her cheeks. She thought about the KGB man, Anni, her chance to win the Friendship Trophy. Iain looked at her and eventually Pia calmed down. She told them about being held by Kovtun and what Mr Linnonmaa had said about Iain.

The Colonel listened with a grave face. At times he shot a quick, unfriendly glance at the Admiral. Pia felt almost sorry for him.

When Pia had finished the Colonel sat in silence for a moment.

'Thank you, young lady,' the Colonel said finally. 'You mustn't worry, everything will be alright. Iain will let you know what to do.'

The woman in the tight skirt appeared at the door again and showed the Colonel out. Pia sat with Iain for a while longer. The woman brought them tea with biscuits. Iain started talking to her in Finnish.

'Are you OK?' he said. His eyes looked kind.

'Yes,' Pia lied.

'I know we haven't told you much. But it's for your own good.' Iain reached across and took hold of Pia's hand.

Pia pulled her hand away, 'You told my mum I'm on drugs.'

Iain moved further away from her in his seat.

'I know,' he said, looking down at the floor between his feet.

There was a silence. All Pia could hear was the faint noise of the traffic from the street below them. Iain lifted his eyes to Pia. 'I have no excuse for what I did. All I can say is that it was to protect both you and your mother. You see, the less you know the less danger there is.'

'But it didn't work, did it!' Pia felt a surge of anger. She had been dodging questions about Iain while Kovtun had threatened her and hit her!

'I know, and believe me it wasn't my fault.' Iain hesitated and continued, 'I know it's not fair.'

Pia looked at Iain. He seemed genuine and she couldn't help but trust Iain.

He was speaking again, 'I also think you shouldn't tell Heikki any more than you have. It will only be dangerous to him, too. Same goes for your mother.'

Pia looked at Iain. 'What if I do tell, everything to everybody?'

Iain stared at her.

Suddenly Pia felt strong. She was fed up with playing games. Whatever the British security forces, the KGB and Anni's father were fighting over, it had nothing to do with her! Or Anni! Why should Pia be the piggy in the middle, being told nothing, but still suffering the consequences? She wanted her old life back, be a normal teenager, go to school, be in love with her boyfriend, go out with Anni. Win the Friendship Trophy. She held Iain's gaze.

Iain sighed. He looked around the room and said in a low voice, 'OK, you win. But you must promise not to tell anyone, and I mean anyone at all. Not even your teddy bear.' He was deadly serious and Pia promised. She felt the hairs at the back of her neck stand up.

'Vladsislas Kovtun is about to defect to the West. We are here to help him do that.'

12

The doorbell to Leena's flat rang straight after she'd got home from school. As if whoever it was knew her movements. She put the shopping in the little alcoved kitchen and took off her overcoat. The bell rang again, impatiently. Leena went to answer the door. No doubt it was the unpleasant caretaker with some new house rule or other.

'Vadi!' Leena went to embrace the man, but Vadi pushed her away and walked straight into her living room.

Leena followed him, 'Can I take your coat?'

Vadi paced the room from one end to the other, filling the space with his long black coat and large boots.

'Or a drink, I have *Koskenkorva*?'

'We have problem!' Vadi's eyes were dark. For the first time since meeting him, Leena felt a little afraid of the man. He was passionate – so very passionate – but even when he was telling her off for doing or saying the wrong thing he'd never looked as angry and dangerous as he did now.

'Well, let's just have a tiny, weeny drink and I'm sure...'

Vadi started pacing the room again. Leena slid into the

kitchenette and poured two large glasses of neat vodka. He downed the drink in one and Leena went quickly to fetch the bottle. Vadi poured himself another glassful and said, 'Your girl, Pia, she a big, big problem.'

'Why?'

'She has very bad friends.'

Leena looked at Vadi. He finally sat down in one of her comfy chairs, but was still wearing his overcoat. He leaned back with his long legs apart and looked at her with the kind of intensity that she'd only seen in his eyes when he was undressed.

'She's friends with Anni, you know, the girl whose father is a diplomat, apart from her...'

'No, no, not at school, you stupid woman.'

Leena sat a little more upright in the other of her comfy chairs. There was no need to insult her; that she would not take from any man. She looked down at her hands. 'I will help you, I said I would, but there's no need to be rude.'

Vadi was silent for a while.

'Ah,' Vadi said, and after a while, still looking at Leena, he again said, 'Ah.'

They were both silent for a long while, Leena thinking of how she'd got herself involved in this. She looked at Vadi who also seemed to be deep in thought. He was calmer now. Suddenly Vadi got up and knelt down next to Leena. 'You not stupid, Vladsislas stupid.' He took hold of Leena's chin and kissed her. She closed her eyes. There was a taste of vodka on his velvety lips.

'The man Pia meets, I worried. You know this girl, Pia, she very nice,' Vadi said and looked down at his hands. 'She remind me of my daughter.'

Leena knew how much Vadi loved his daughter. She'd

seen it in Moscow, even if she hadn't known his relationship to her then.

'My very beautiful Alyona,' he said quietly and stood up. Vadi flung his coat onto the bed and settled his large frame in front of Leena, 'This is why I want to protect your gymnast girl!' He stared intently at Leena.

'Oh Vadi,' Leena said.

Vadi took Leena's hand and led her to the bed. He pulled her top and jeans off and entered her swiftly; his black eyes on her the whole of the time.

Afterwards, Leena thought about Vadi's daughter. He'd been very secretive about her mother. Leena didn't know if she was dead, or not around for some other reason. Surely a mother would have a problem with what Vadi planned? She looked at him. Vadi was already out of the bed, pulling on his shirt. She needed to approach the subject gently, from another direction.

'So who is this man Pia is friends with?'

Vadi flashed his eyes at Leena, 'He very, very bad. But Pia with him all the time!'

'But it's OK. She has a mother after all. Her mother won't let her...'

'It no good, no good for girl! No good for Tournament!'

'I don't understand,' Leena said, though she was afraid of questioning Vadi too much.

'He English pig! He want sabotage Tournament!'

Suddenly Leena had an idea, 'Do you want me to talk to him?'

'No!' Vadi came over to the bed and placed Leena's hands between his, 'you must not talk to him!'

'Of course not, I promise.'

'Leena, you must watch this girl, Pia. Make sure she keep away from the man, OK?' Vadi was now looking at her bare breasts, his face less serious. Leena pulled the sheet closer to her body, but leaving enough flesh for Vadi to admire. He bent over and kissed Leena's neck. 'You beautiful Finnish woman,' he said. 'Remember. Keep close to Pia, yes?'

Leena smiled and nodded. She could not resist this man. She watched his muscular back as he got dressed and wondered if she'd dare to approach the subject of the mother of his daughter.

'Vadi,' she began.

'What?' Vadi snapped.

The moment had gone.

Five minutes and Vadi was out the door.

Heikki was waiting for Pia outside the Council entrance. He looked cold. He had his school bag flung across his back and was stamping the ground to keep warm. He looked sheepish. Pia wasn't sure whether she was glad or angry to see him. Iain had confused her. Why would the British want a man like Kovtun? And what did Kovtun have to do with Anni's father? And why was he keeping an eye on Pia? Iain hadn't been able to give her any answers. She'd have to find out what was going on herself.

She walked slowly towards Heikki. It was already dark, but the fresh snow was shimmering against the street lights. Suddenly she felt a shiver. She put her hands in her jacket pockets and looked around. No Russian that she could see. Iain had promised to keep an eye on her from a distance. He'd said he couldn't be seen with her too much, especially if Kovtun was following her. He'd told Pia to be very careful who she spoke to. Pia was afraid for herself but even more afraid for Anni. Pia knew Iain had finally told her all he knew, but had the Colonel? Pia wasn't so sure the Colonel didn't know exactly what was going on between the Russian, her and Anni's family.

Pia was wondering how she could get to talk to the Colonel without Iain knowing about it, when she saw a tram approaching. She wondered briefly whether she should run for it and leave Heikki there. Instead she decided to confront him too.

'Why didn't you tell me you'd been to the Council?'

'Dunno,' Heikki said, kicking at the snow with his boots.

Pia saw they'd still make the tram. She took Heikki's hand. 'Come with me.'

They found two seats together. Pia looked at her watch; it was well past six. Her mum would just have to get used to her being out a bit later. At least she no longer believed the story about the drugs. She looked at Heikki sideways. 'Do you want to help me?'

'Yeah, of course.' Heikki said. He took Pia's hand and added, 'I'm sorry about not telling you...'

Pia had her lips on Heikki's mouth before he could finish the sentence. She slid her arm around the inside of his down jacket. She hadn't spotted anyone remotely Russian in the tram, but you never knew who was listening.

'Mmm, I liked that, but what was it for?' Heikki said when Pia pulled her lips away from his.

'Nothing,' Pia said, looking ahead and smiling. How easy it was to distract men!

When they were at Anni's stop, Pia got up and hurried Heikki out of the tram.

In the cold, Heikki turned around and said, 'What's got into you?'

'C'mon, I want you to come with me.'

Pia started walking down Kasarminkatu and up Tehtaankatu, past the Soviet Embassy. She walked briskly, hoping Heikki was following her. She glanced around; there was no one else on the street.

Heikki caught up with her and asked, 'Where are we going? To get to your place shouldn't we have gone the other direction?'

Pia didn't reply, but looked up at the second floor windows. There were no lights on, just as she suspected. She took hold of Heikki's hand and crossed the street to Anni's block. When they reached Anni's door, Pia pressed a button on top of the intercom.

'That's not Anni's,' Heikki said.

A buzzer sounded and the door opened. She ran through the door, and pulled Heikki inside. 'Shh,' Pia said, walking gingerly up the stone steps. Heikki followed. His boots made such a racket, Pia had to turn around to tell him to stop and listen for any noises in the stairwell.

'Hello, who's there?' a woman's voice came from the top of the stairwell. Pia and Heikki hid behind the stone steps. 'Bloody kids,' the woman said and banged her door shut. Heikki sniggered and Pia had to tell him again to be quiet.

When they reached the second floor Pia put her ear against Anni's door. Then she gestured for Heikki to hide behind the pillar supporting the spiral staircase. She stood flush against the wall, hiding from the spy hole and rang the bell.

No answer.

Pia tried again. Again there was no reply, or movement behind the door. The echoes of the bell rang up and down the three-storey building. Gingerly, Pia lifted the flap of the letterbox and peered inside. She could see the legs of the hall table, but not the mat. She could definitely remember

Anni's parents having a beautiful old red rug running the length of the hall. Though she couldn't see very far through the narrow opening, she knew there was no one inside. She could feel its emptiness.

'I wonder where they all are,' she whispered to Heikki.

'What are we doing here?' Heikki whispered back.

Pia said nothing. She was thinking. They heard a door opening at the other end of the floor. An elderly man in a dark green wool coat and felt hat came out of the door.

'Good evening,' he said.

'Evening,' Pia and Heikki said.

'You won't find anyone there,' the man said, nodding his head towards Anni's door.

'Oh?'

'Left for Moscow yesterday. An urgent assignment, they said.'

'Who said that? Mr Linnonmaa?' Pia asked.

'No, they had two foreign chaps doing the moving for them. Didn't see the Linnonmaas at all, actually. Must have travelled ahead.'

The man stood looking at Pia and Heikki. Suddenly Pia realised he was expecting them to leave the apartment block. She nudged Heikki and smiled to the man. They went down the spiral staircase and out into the cold street.

'Hello!'

Pia heard someone shout from the other side of the street. She watched as Sasha ran towards them.

'Did you tell her to follow us?' she said to Heikki.

Heikki was looking at his feet, 'Of course not.'

Pia could have hit him. Instead she put on a false smile. Sasha stood in front of them, panting.

'What are you doing here?'

Sasha looked from Heikki to Pia. 'It's a free country, isn't it?'

'Hi,' Heikki said feebly.

Pia didn't speak.

'My aunt lives on Tehtaankatu, if you must know. She's just had a baby.'

Pia considered this lie. She knew Sasha lived in a big house in Meilahti, the other side of town. She'd never seen her around Ullanlinna.

'The point is: what are you two doing here, hanging around Anni's apartment?' Sasha looked triumphant.

Heikki gave Pia a sideways glance, and said, 'Oh, you know, we were just having a ciggie, thinking we'd ask Anni to come out.' He put his arm proprietarily around Pia's waist. She smiled, but could not help wondering how Sasha knew where Anni lived. She was glad Heikki hadn't spilled the beans, though.

Sasha looked at them and said, 'Oh.' On tiptoe, she moved closer to Heikki and whispered into his ear, 'Give me a call later.'

Pia was furious. She watched Sasha's pink down jacket turn the corner of Tehtaankatu.

'What was that all about?'

'Dunno.'

'Did she really think I wouldn't hear what she said when I was standing right next to you?'

Heikki didn't reply. Pia wanted to ask if he often spoke to Sasha on the telephone in the evenings, but they had to hurry. Pia knew the Russian would not be far away, and now they'd shown themselves twice outside Anni's house. Pia told Heikki to run to the door and hide by the entrance. She looked around. The street was quiet, only a drunk in the

distance talking to himself and holding a bottle. She
followed Heikki to the door of the block of flats.

'Quickly, you know what to do.'

Heikki looked at Pia, his eyes wide. They were both
tense.

'We can't trick a second person. C'mon before anybody
sees us,' she said, and added, 'Don't tell me you don't know
how to do this?'

'You're incredible,' Heikki said. He removed something
that looked like a thin silver knife from his school bag. He
pushed the implement into the lock, and wiggled it about
for a while. Pia looked down the stairwell through the glass
door. No one.

'There you are, Madam!' Heikki said triumphantly. He
opened the door for Pia and they went inside. The door
locked behind them.

This time the stairwell was quiet, and even Heikki managed
to walk noiselessly up the stone steps. Outside Anni's door
they stood for a moment and listened.

'I suppose you want me to undo this lock too?' Heikki
whispered.

Pia gave him a look. It took him a lot longer this time,
there seemed to be something slipping inside the lock.
Eventually on the third try, the mechanism caught and the
door opened.

The flat was cold. Some furniture had been removed,
like the rug, and a lamp, but it looked as it always did when
Pia came to visit. The lights were on in the hall. Why hadn't
she seen their reflection from the street? All the curtains
must be drawn, she thought. She went into the kitchen.
Heikki followed. She put the light on. This window over-

looked the inner courtyard, and she hoped, if the Russian was watching them, he wouldn't see the light from the outside. The kitchen was neat and tidy, just as it had been after the KGB left on Wednesday night. Pia looked inside cupboards, nothing seemed out of place. She walked slowly into the room where she'd been held together with Anni and her father. The small table was there, and the bed, covered with a lace bedspread. Just as she remembered it. The dusty smell of the room made her shiver.

Pia went back into the kitchen. Heikki wasn't there. She heard a door shut and followed the sound into Mr Linnon-maa's study. It was the third door on the left in the hall. She'd seen him come out of the room many times carrying a bundle of papers, but had never been inside. Pia saw Heikki bent over something. He was looking into one of the drawers of Mr Linnonmaa's large desk. A lamp on top of it was lit. Pia saw the heavy curtains were indeed drawn.

'What are you doing?' she said.

Heikki jumped up. Pia realised he hadn't heard her come in. She saw the silver thing he'd used to open the door to the apartment lying on the desk. Heikki grabbed it quickly and shut the drawer. He looked fleetingly at Pia. 'Oh, nothing, just wondered if we'd find out where they've gone.'

Pia looked at Heikki's face. He was lying. Why?

'What do you have to do with all this?'

'Nothing, I'm just helping you, remember?' Heikki put his arm around Pia. He turned off the lamp on the desk. The room descended into darkness and Heikki started kissing Pia. 'Not now, we have to make sure no one's here!' Pia said. She turned towards the thin strip of light showing under the door.

They looked into every room. The lounge looked empty

of furniture. Only a coffee table remained, but the dining room was untouched. Pia lingered a moment longer in Anni's room. Her clothes rail was half full, as if someone had grabbed a bunch of clothes and left the rest. On her desk were school books in a neat pile and make-up arranged in a tiny box. In Anni's parents' room some of her mother's dresses were hanging at one end of the rail. As with Anni's clothes, it looked as if the rest had been taken away in a hurry.

Pia sat on Anni's parents' bed. The cover was made out of quilted satin. Heikki stood in front of her. She looked up at him and said, 'I'm worried about Anni. What if the KGB have taken them somewhere horrible?' She felt like crying, but held the tears back. She must stay strong. She put her head in her hands. It was hopeless, how could she help her friend when no one told her anything. What did Anni's father have to do with a Russian defection? How had she, Pia Mäkelä, got involved in something like this?

Pia felt Heikki's arms around her.

'It's OK, baby,' he said.

'How do you know?' Pia saw Heikki's eyes flicker, just for a moment.

'Mr Linnonmaa is a celebrated diplomat. He can look after his family, I'm sure. They probably just left in a hurry and will send for the rest of the furniture and clothes later. And,' Heikki squeezed Pia harder, 'diplomats have immunity anyway, the Russians aren't allowed to touch Finnish diplomats.'

'But they did!'

'Yes, but they let them and you go. I'm sure the KGB guy just didn't know who he was dealing with.'

'Heikki,' Pia said.

'Yes?'

'What were you looking for in Mr Linnonmaa's desk?'

The front door opened and slammed shut. Footsteps echoed on the stone floor of the uncarpeted hall. Pia was glad Heikki had his hand around her. They heard the steps pass the door to Anni's parents' room. Whoever it was, had gone into Mr Linnonmaa's study.

13

Iain had his doubts about Heikki. When he saw Pia take his hand and run to the tram he swore silently to himself. What had he just told the girl? He turned away from the window and ran out of the Council.

The Colonel was far too nonchalant about the girl's safety. Iain was getting too involved, and he knew the Colonel thought so too. But damn the man, these were real, innocent people. In the tram he suddenly knew where Pia had gone. But when he stepped out of the carriage on Kasarminkatu, he started to doubt. It was late. Surely Pia would go home, so as not to arouse Maija's fears. Iain pulled the collar of his coat up and walked up Tehtaankatu. Though the street looked empty, he walked around the block and entered the Linnonmaa apartment from a different direction.

Iain had been standing in the corner of Tehtaankatu for a while, with a good view of the entrance to the block, when he saw an elderly man come out. He was wearing a bottle-green coat and a felt hat. Iain looked at the man carefully and started to sway. He picked up an empty bottle of Frascati he'd spotted by the side of the street. He started to sing a song. He'd heard one of the old puliukko sing it at the Helsinki railway station as the drunk was being led away by two policeman. He recognised it as one Virpi's father sang, when he had too much beer and vodka after a long session in the sauna. 'Minun kultani kaunis on, vaik on kaitaluinen, hei luulia illalla, vaik on kaitaluinen...' The man didn't even look in Iain's direction. He was just about to stop the singing – he only remembered the one line – when he saw Pia and Heikki come out of the door. So his hunch had been right! Thank goodness, they were now out, surely this meant they would go home. When another girl appeared, Iain swayed more. Pia looked once in his direction, but didn't seem to recognise him. At least she didn't let on. Good girl, Iain thought, and started walking slowly up the street. Then both Pia and Heikki disappeared back inside the Linnonmaa apartment block.

Iain walked up to the entrance and stopped. He looked up and down the street and used the key he'd got from Linnonmaa's file to open the door. He listened to Pia and Heikki talk in whispered tones. Then he heard a door being opened and shut.

Iain sighed.

There was a space to wait behind the spiral staircase. The stairwell was dimly lit. The only light came from the large windows on the landing between the first and ground floors. They must overlook the inner courtyard, which was lit with a single streetlight. The snow reflected light back into the hallway, so there was no need to put the light on. Iain hoped he was safe in the shadow of the spiral staircase. He crouched down. What would Pia find in the Linnonmaa flat? Presumably the family was out, and presumably the old man had interrupted Pia and Heikki trying to break in. This really was not wise, Iain thought. If Iain was caught in a compromising situation in the Finnish diplomat's home, the Colonel would probably send him straight back to London. Then who would look after Maija and Pia?

Iain didn't trust Heikki, nor was he sure Pia wasn't in danger from Vladsislas Kovtun. He'd been watching her for some reason, and if he thought the girl was an obstacle to his plans...

The entrance door to the block went again. Iain listened carefully. The steps were heavy set, a man's.

When the man had taken a few steps up the staircase, Iain moved the top of his body slowly and silently around the stone pillar. He caught sight of the man's black coat and boots. Iain would have recognised them anywhere. 'Damn, damn, damn,' he swore silently as he huddled back in the small space under the stairs. The steps stopped on the second floor, paused for a moment, and then Iain heard the door into what must be the Linnonmaa apartment open and shut.

There was no time to think. Iain moved slowly up the stairs. There were two apartments to a floor. As he walked past flats numbers one and two, his heart beat so hard he could hear the blood rushing in his ears. At the bottom of the first step leading up to the second floor, he paused and tried to steady his breath.

Iain could hear no sound from inside the flat. The whole apartment block was deadly silent. Had Kovtun already taken the two children hostage, or worse? Iain had certainly not heard a gunshot, but then the Russian had other, much quieter, means at his disposal. How would he explain the deaths, and how would he get them out of the flat without being seen? And why was he even taking a risk like this so close to his move to the West?

Iain looked at the hallway. He spotted a door in between the two apartment entrances. He took hold of the handle and pressed it slowly down. The door opened to a small cupboard. There was a mop and bucket and some old dusters hanging up on a makeshift clothesline.

Iain moved back to the Linnonmaas' door and rang the bell, then moved swiftly into the cupboard. He left the door only slightly ajar and waited.

Minutes, more like hours, passed. The Linnonmaas' door opened and the face of Vladsislas Kovtun appeared in the doorway. Leaving the door ajar, he walked up to the top of the staircase and peered down. He didn't have a gun, and was still wearing his long black overcoat. Suddenly he turned around and scanned the hallway. Iain stopped breathing. The man's eyes lingered on the cleaning cupboard. Did he know of its existence? Had he spotted the door slightly ajar? He nodded slightly towards the door, then turned on his heels and went up to the door of the apartment. Kovtun closed the door, took a key out of his pocket and double locked it from the outside. A few moments later, Iain heard the outer door of the apartment block slam shut.

Iain touched his watch. The display lit up and he waited exactly five minutes before stepping out of the cleaning cupboard. As he did so, the Linnonmaas' door opened again. He rushed to Pia and Heikki and pushed them back inside.

'Oi!' Heikki said when they were back inside.

'Quiet!' Iain took each youngster by the arm and led them into the kitchen. 'Now, you two, what are you playing at?'

Pia was looking down at the floor. She looked frightened. The boy's face was as defiant as ever.

'Pia, didn't I tell you to be careful?' Iain said.

The girl looked at him and now he saw she'd been crying. Suddenly she flung herself on Iain, taking him aback. He felt her soft breasts against him. Iain put his arms loosely around the girl, and started to pat her back. 'There, there,' he said in English. Over Pia's head he scrutinised Heikki. He did look a little pale.

'Did he see you?' Iain asked.

'No, we were in Anni's parents' room when he came in. Who was it anyway?' Heikki said. His voice was higher than usual. He was obviously frightened. Good, Iain thought.

'Now Pia, it's OK, as long as he didn't see you?'

'No,' Pia sniffled. Iain gave her a hankie from his trouser pocket. She moved away from Iain and said, 'I was so scared. Can we just get out of here?'

'Yes, but first I need to know why you're here.'

'I wanted to see Anni,' Pia said.

'So it was your idea, Pia?' Iain examined Heikki's face.

'Yes, but the man said they'd gone to Moscow.'

'What man?'

After Pia had told Iain about the neighbour, he remembered the man walking out of the block just before Pia and Heikki. He'd have to describe him to the Colonel. Just as well he'd had a good look at him.

'Did the neighbour talk to Anni or her parents?'

When Iain heard the removal men had foreign accents, he knew something was very wrong, very wrong indeed. He needed to telephone the Colonel. Or perhaps he should just go home and think it through himself and then talk to him later. But first he'd have to make sure these two youngsters had played enough heroics for one night.

'Why wouldn't Anni tell me she was moving?' Pia asked.

Iain looked at her face. Her mascara had run in dark

smudges around her eyes. She'd have to wash that off before she went back home.

'They might not have been allowed to say, I'm sure. The removal men weren't allowed to either. It's all absolutely normal in diplomatic circles to be called up at short notice.' Iain hoped he sounded calm and reassuring. The boy was looking at him sceptically. Pia seemed to believe him. Maybe she wanted to. 'But now, young lady, we've had enough antics for one night. Go and wash your face and I'll take you home.' Iain turned towards Heikki. 'Might be best if you make your way out of here first. I'll follow, then wait for Pia. OK?'

'Sure,' Heikki said. He turned towards Pia and kissed her lightly on the lips. 'See you tomorrow.'

Pia didn't feel as brave as she had done earlier. Hiding in Anni's parents' bedroom had made her feel as though she was still being held by the KGB. When she saw Iain on the landing she could have cried there and then. She could see Heikki didn't like the man. She herself should dislike him after all the lies about the drugs he'd told her mother. But Iain had apologised, and he seemed to be the only person who could and would help her find Anni. And he seemed to want to protect Pia and her mother. She felt like crying when she thought about Anni.

'Is she OK, do you think?'

Iain didn't reply for a while, but then said, 'Yes I should think so.'

Pia looked long and hard at Iain. Was he telling the truth? Would he tell her if he thought the KGB had the Linnonmaa family?

'Who was the girl you were talking to outside?' Iain asked.

'Sasha.'

'Do you know her last name?' Iain was scribbling into his notebook.

'Roche.'

'That doesn't sound like a Finnish name?'

'I think her father is French or something.'

'Hmm,' Iain was quiet for a moment. Then he looked at Pia, 'And is she friends with Heikki?'

Pia stared at Iain. His large eyes settled on Pia's for a while with a sad look. Then he looked away, as if he was a little embarrassed.

Pia remembered the way Sasha had asked Heikki in a mock whisper to call her. How they'd been standing close to one another at the smoking place, and the conversation she'd obviously interrupted outside the lockers in the entrance hall of the Lyceum. And when Pia had accused Sasha of trying to get it on with Heikki, she'd called her a 'stupid girl'.

When Pia said nothing, Iain coughed and said, 'I assume they are, hmm, friendly?'

Pia decided she might as well tell him everything.

'Pia, can you do something for me?' Iain finally said after they'd discussed all that had passed that evening. 'I'm not going to let you out of my sight. The Colonel has agreed that I will give you constant surveillance. But, and this is very, very important, Pia. Do you always wear that colourful scarf?'

'I can do,' Pia said, puzzled.

'Can you wear it from now on, or at least until I tell you not to?'

'Of course, but what...'

'Listen,' Iain said, interrupting Pia, 'if you can't see me, stop and take your scarf off. If you still don't see me, make your way here to the Council.'

'But Kovtun said I should keep away from the Council.'

Iain was quiet for a moment. Then he dug something out of his pocket. 'This will get you in quickly.'

Pia took a small brass key from Iain's hand. 'Thank you,' she said. She felt grateful towards Iain, and less alone with the awful fear she felt for Anni.

Iain smiled and said, 'And now I will take you home.' He patted Pia on her arm.

Pia said, 'Can I ask you something?'

'Of course.'

'Heikki and Sasha. Why are you so interested in them?'

Iain looked at Pia for a long time, as if judging whether she was strong enough to cope with what he was about to tell her. 'There's no reason. We're just making sure no one knows of Kovtun's plans to defect.'

Pia was glad Iain walked her home. Even though she could tell he wasn't pleased about it. All that she had learned that day was going around in her head as they walked briskly along Kasarminkatu towards her block of flats. It was dark, but the street lights and the snow made it perfectly easy to see. Pia glanced sideways at Iain. He still looked cold in his new coat and his breath froze in the air, making it seem as if he was puffing on a cigarette. Pia looked up and down the street. A tram was turning the corner. No sign of the Russian. Iain must have frightened him off.

Pia could not sleep at all that night. She knew there was a connection between the KGB and Anni's disappearance, and that connection must have something to do with the planned defection of the blond-haired Russian. If only she could talk to her mother! But Iain had warned her not to say a word about her theory to her mother. As if she would blab again, although it would be difficult not to talk to Heikki tomorrow.

14

Maija woke early. She'd spent the whole night trying to get to sleep. Now she felt exhausted. Her bedside clock showed 6.05. She put on her dressing gown and walked over to Pia's door. Silently, she opened it and peered inside. The girl was fast asleep, her head half buried inside the duvet. Maija closed the door soundlessly and went over to the telephone in the hall.

The number she dialled answered immediately.

She listened to the man's voice and said, 'I'll meet you at 7.30.'

Again she listened and said, 'Alright. Goodbye.'

Maija put the phone down and for a while stood still in the hall, staring at the receiver.

Before Maija left the flat half an hour later, she wrote a note for Pia, saying she had to get into work early. She often did overtime on Saturday mornings, so it shouldn't rouse Pia's suspicions. It was still dark outside and bitterly cold. As she waited at the tram stop, moving her feet about to keep warm, she wondered how she hadn't made the connection before. Though how that would have changed anything she didn't know. It was pure chance their two daughters were the same age, and ended up in the same class in the same school. Maija knew that by meeting the man she was entering the world she had chosen to leave eighteen years before. But now Pia was involved. She would have to do everything she could to protect her. She needed to know what he was up to. Why he wanted to see her.

Jukka Linnonmaa hadn't really aged. Even under the harsh lights of the Happy Days Café, he looked youthful. Perhaps the odd line around his mouth betrayed an age over forty, for surely he was older than Maija? He still had all of his fair hair, falling softly onto his forehead.

'You haven't changed,' she said to Mr Linnonmaa.

He stared at his cup of black coffee. He looked up, surprised, 'Neither have you, Miss Kuortamo.'

'Mrs Mäkelä, now.'

'Of course'

Neither spoke for a moment. Maija was thinking how eighteen years ago their paths had hardly touched. Mr Linnonmaa had been far above her in the Customs hierarchy. Unlike Maija, he wasn't based at the border crossing in Vaalimaa, near the town of Hamina. She'd spoken with him on the telephone most days, but only seen him a few times. Were it not for all those rumours among the staff about his true role, Maija was sure she wouldn't have remembered him. But it was the voice, his voice, after he called the second time last night that reminded her. Was that what this was all about?

'Mrs Mäkelä...' Mr Linnonmaa began.

'Maija, please.'

Linnonmaa looked up and smiled briefly, 'I'm Jukka.' He reached his hand across the table to Maija. How old-fashioned, Maija thought. She accepted Linnonmaa's gesture and shook his hand.

'Maija, I've asked to see you because I need to explain something to you.'

'Oh.'

'Has Pia told you that I'm a diplomat now?'

'Yes.' Maija recalled what her former work colleagues had said about this man. That he had special duties at the border, to do with the illegal immigrants from the Soviet Union.

Maija's degree in Russian language had always been a problem. First her mother was against it. Maija's grandfather fought the Reds in the Civil War in 1917, and her father the Russians twenty-five years later in the Winter War. His family were from Karelia.

'It was the war that killed him,' her mother said. Maija knew it was the years at the Lappeenranta paper mill that had given him lung cancer but said nothing.

Maija's aunt talked about the two evacuations from Karelia, where 400,000 had to leave their homes and livelihoods. Her home as well as the childhood home was near Viipuri, now beyond the border in the Soviet Union. Maija's aunt was a fierce woman. Her father's older sister, she had a small build, dark eyes and a temper that could take her from burst of anger to fits of laughter in seconds. Maija was a little afraid of Aunt Eija. She was the cook in the family and would turn up before parties to make her Karelian pies and complicated cinnamon pastries and cookies. Her pies had the thinnest of rye casings and the rice filling was lathered with butter. 'We didn't have any luxuries like butter after the war,' she'd tell Maija, when, as a little girl, she was ordered

to help Aunt Eija. Auntie's husband had died in the war;
how, Maija wasn't ever quite sure. She had visions of Uncle
Kaarlo in a fist fight with a tall Russian while their large
farmhouse with beautifully carved porches was in flames in
the background. Aunt Eija carried pictures of the farmhouse
they had lost as well as a black-and-white portrait of her
dead husband in her purse. She never lost an opportunity to
take the pictures out and decry the Soviet state.

'We lost our homeland, but Finland kept her independence. We didn't lose the war against Stalin's Russia, and we
were never occupied like those poor Baltic states.'

But Maija took to the Russian language easily. She even
loved the impossible alphabet. Her teacher got her a scholarship to Jyväskylä University. When she left, her mother
stayed inside the wood-panelled house, sitting with her
back to the window, refusing to wave her goodbye. The
night before Maija was due to leave, she'd cried and said,
'You'll come back a Communist, and then all the pain and
suffering your father, grandfather and uncle went through
fighting for an independent Finland will be in vain.' Maija
tried to explain how the language had been there long
before Stalin and that she'd have nothing to do with politics,
but her mother wouldn't listen.

After graduation she had several job offers. Most of her
friends were married with small children and no money
while Maija took a well-paid job with the Customs in
Hamina as a translator. Whether it was Maija's good work
prospects or the three lonely years her mother spent in the
little cottage by the lake in Lappeenranta, while Maija was
at university, when she came home her mother was finally
placated. She arranged a feast with Aunt Eija, with a long
table laden with Karelian pies, meat stew, pastries and cookies. There was even home-brewed beer, sahti, and strong

black coffee, which some of the men strengthened with large glugs of grain vodka.

The first months in Hamina were her happiest. Maija loved the translation work. She had money to buy what she wished. She went home at regular intervals to see her mother. The Customs had built a new block of flats and Maija got a small studio with an alcove kitchen. Many of her colleagues were young and lived in the same kind of flats. After a few months she was asked to interpret for a Russian man who'd crossed the border. He was unusually thin with wispy blonde hair and an untidy beard. He never stopped smiling, as his eyes darted from Antti, the Finnish Immigration Officer to Maija. After he'd given his name and occupation – carpenter – he was asked why he wanted to settle in Finland

'I am escaping Communism.'

Maija translated.

Antti lifted his head from the pad he was writing on. He leant back in his chair and looked at Maija. He coughed and said, 'Miss Kuortamo, can I have a word?'

He took Maija to a long corridor running the length of the old red-brick building.

'This is a little awkward,' Antti said.

Maija looked at his pale eyes. She'd only met Antti once before, at a drinks party thrown in the first week of Maija's new job by one of her new friends from the customs office. He was engaged to a pretty dark-haired girl who worked in the grocery shop in Hamina. The girl had been a little drunk, holding onto Antti's arm the whole of the evening, so Maija hadn't really spoken to him at all.

'Did I do something wrong?'

Maija was afraid she'd spoiled her first big chance in her new job. She preferred simultaneous translation. It gave her a thrill. There was no time to go back and correct your mistakes. You had to be right first time. Compared to interpretation, editing and re-editing long passages of translation was boring.

Antti looked down at Maija. He was a head taller than her.

'No, it's just that these Russians...' Antti paused, 'they don't know what they're saying. But if you translate everything, I have to note it down.'

'I don't understand.'

Antti looked up and down the corridor where they stood. He came closer to Maija and lowered his voice, 'If I put he's here for political reasons, we'll have to send him back. Finland's neutral, remember?' he said and winked.

Maija had been naïve, even stupid. Of course, she must be careful. She nodded. Antti followed her back to the interview room.

The carpenter had been lucky. Most of the Russians trying to cross the border were shot by Soviet marksmen before they reached Finland. The ones who got through were helped by Antti and a few others who shared his convictions, but many were marched back to the Soviet officials. 'Shipped to Siberia if they're lucky,' Antti said to Maija.

'The KGB are all powerful in Finland. They can take whoever they like and do whatever they like to them.' Antti shrugged his shoulders, 'We just do as much we can. Which isn't much.'

This was October 1961, the same year the Soviet Union closed the border between East and West Berlin and started shooting anyone trying to climb over the wall and escape to the West.

Linnonmaa had been Antti's superior. Maija thought Antti must have reported to him, and he often phoned Maija up to ask for some clarification or other on the transcripts. Maija never found out what happened to Antti. Whether he ever married the dark-haired girl or not.

Maija hung her head. She didn't want to remember how, indirectly, she had betrayed that poor man, and others like him, who thought they had reached safety in Finland. She'd believed that the immigration process was fair. It was only in the month she gave in her notice that she'd realized the Russian had not been granted refugee status in Finland. In the files she happened on accidentally, not one appeal was accepted. And there were at least a hundred names on the list she saw. The man had told Maija he'd be imprisoned, if not killed, if he was returned to the Soviet authorities.

But when she found out the truth, Maija was engaged to be married to Ilkka, and ready to start her new life in Helsinki. She hadn't wanted to get involved in politics, not with a baby growing inside her. So she never spoke to anyone about her work. But every time she saw a Russian in Helsinki, she remembered and felt ashamed she hadn't done anything. Like the tiny Finnish nation, in the face of the whole of the Soviet machinery, Maija was helpless. With bitter disappointment she realised she had little of the fighting spirit, sisu, that her father and grandfather had displayed in standing up to the Russians.

She looked over to Linnonmaa, who was stirring his coffee with a concentrated effort.

'It is rather delicate,' he said.

Maija waited.

Linnonmaa settled his pale blue eyes on Maija and continued, 'I don't want you to be alarmed, but something the girls have got involved in...something they shouldn't have.'

'Drugs? But the other night on the telephone you said they weren't into...'

'No, not drugs. It's to do with diplomatic relations with the Soviet Union.'

Maija stared at Jukka Linnonmaa. Had he heard of her snooping all those years ago? How did her work then have anything to do with Pia?

A door behind them opened, letting in a noisy group of women. A chill wind blew in and reached down the back of Maija's spine. She shivered and pulled her cardigan tighter around her.

Jukka Linnonmaa leant closer to Maija and said, 'It's Anni who's gone and...' he sighed and said, 'she is such a kind girl. She's befriended these Commies at school. It's rather difficult for me as they have contacts to the Soviet Embassy and...'

'What has this got to do with my daughter?'

'Well, Pia is friends with them too.'

'Oh.'

'Oh dear, this is rather difficult.' Linnonmaa smiled again; it was the same insincere facial expression he had made when they'd started the conversation.

'Go on,' Maija said, glancing at her wrist watch. She wasn't in a hurry, it was only half past eight, but she wanted Linnonmaa to get to the point.

'Alright, the friend I'm talking about is Heikki Tuomila.'

15

Leena spotted the man as soon as she walked out of the gym hall. It had become her little Friday treat to take the tram to Stockmann's, instead of having lunch in the dreary staff room at the Lyceum. She usually chose a luxurious tuna salad or an open rye sandwich in the café on the top floor of the store. The place was always busy and she enjoyed watching suited businessmen or well-dressed ladies enjoy their coffee and sandwiches. Afterwards she'd admire the clothes on the first floor. She rarely had the money for the expensive items, but once she'd bought a pair of French trousers; they were still the best piece of clothing in her wardrobe.

The man was standing in the exact same spot as last Monday. He had on a different coat, a little more sensible for the weather, but he still looked foreign, and come to think of it, cold. No Stockmann's lunch today. This was her chance. She'd show Vadi what a clever woman she was!

'Can I help you?'

'Hmm, sorry?' The man looked shocked. I'm not that frightening, Leena thought. Perhaps her teacher demeanour was a bit too overpowering. She'd just finished another frustrating session with the Friendship Tournament team, and Pia's lack of co-ordination was sending her over the edge.

'Actually, I wondered if you had a cigarette?' Leena tried to soften the tone of her voice.

'Hmm, no, sorry, don't smoke.' He still looked like a frightened rabbit, not at all the evil character Vadi had made him out to be. Suppose he was just following orders. Leena had to change tactics. 'Are you waiting for Pia?' Now this was bold.

'Actually yes, her mother asked me to...' The man still had the madly worried look, but he did relax a little. He wasn't that bad looking, quite tall, with wavy slightly grey hair. His ears were frozen and pink. He'd catch the death of cold here if he stood in this place for much longer. The temperatures had plummeted the night before. The thermometer outside her kitchen window had read -19°C that morning. Leena herself was wearing a fur-lined coat and a matching fur-trimmed hat. A 40th birthday present she'd bought for herself.

'Ah, she's been detained, I'm afraid.' Leena lied.

'Oh?'

'Pia has extra gym class tonight. For the Friendship Tournament, you know.' Leena wondered if this would bring a reaction from the man. She might as well get straight down to business, she thought. Besides, Leena was sure she could talk him into understanding how important a win would be for the Lyceum.

'Why don't we go and wait for her at the café? She'll be another hour yet.' Leena nodded towards the Rixi Bar. Its rickety red neon sign shimmered in the half-light of the late afternoon. She smiled at the man and took hold of his arm. Leena had to hurry. Pia could appear at any moment.

'Oh, yes, of course,' he said and started walking beside Leena.

As they moved away from the Lyceum, and crossed the road to the Rixi Bar, the man glanced backwards. As if he was waiting to see if Pia would appear after all. Leena hurried into the café. Normally she wouldn't dream of frequenting this little shit hole, where she knew most of the students spent their breaks and often lessons too. But she needed somewhere warm to talk to the man sensibly about the matter. Vadi was obviously worried about Pia, so Leena would find out if there was anything untoward about this foreigner. There was no harm in using a little initiative when the opportunity presented itself. Besides, Leena hadn't heard a word from Vadi since he left in such a hurry the night before.

There was a shock of silence when they walked into the café. She spotted three or four sixth formers smoking and drinking the low-alcohol beer establishments like this were allowed to sell. Most of the children were underage – she should really report both them and the management of this place to the authorities. But she didn't care to think about that now. She chose a table in the corner and said, 'Would you mind if I had a coffee?'

The man went and got two coffees. He started stirring his, while looking at Leena, saying nothing.

'Now, why is it you want to sabotage our chances in the Friendship Tournament?' Leena said.

Iain didn't see Pia until the afternoon when she stepped out of the Lyceum building and ran to the tram stop. He was standing on the other side of the building and the girl didn't spot him. Just as well, he didn't want to attract attention to himself. Being accosted by the gym teacher was bad enough. The Colonel would not be pleased.

Iain had to run to catch the same tram as Pia. Luckily the group of youngsters from the Lyceum had entered the long Russian tram through the front. He could hide in the back without being spotted. He queued up behind two men talking to each other about an ice-hockey match. It seemed Finland had come very close to beating Russia last night. The Russians had won in the last minute with a penalty shot. 'I suppose it would have been a diplomatic incident had we won,' the younger man said, laughing bitterly as he stepped onboard the tram. Once inside the carriage, Iain tried to see Pia. The two joined carriages were fairly full, and it was difficult to see past people standing in the aisles. But when the tram climbed the hill towards Erottaja, Iain spotted Pia's blonde hair resting against the colourful scarf. She was sitting with her back to him on a seat at the front. Next to him, the two men from the tram stop were still discussing the ice-hockey match. The younger one was convinced that the game and the winning penalty in particular, had been fixed. 'No way was that tackle a penalty! The Russians can do what they want with us, can you ever see the Finnish officials complaining to the Big Eastern Brother? Mutual co-operation and friendship my ass!' he said. The other man gave Iain a worried glance.

'Don't be stupid,' he said, his eyes on Iain while talking to his friend. 'You're just being bad a loser.' He nudged his friend and nodded towards Iain. Iain hadn't realised he was staring at the two men. They must have thought he was a Soviet informer and would report them. He tried to smile reassuringly at them and moved slightly forward in the carriage.

But as he stood there, thinking about how this country

was gripped at all levels by the necessity to keep diplomatic relations with the Soviet Union sweet, Iain suddenly thought about the Friendship Trophy.

'She came to talk to you?' The Colonel said.

'Yes.' Iain was once again standing in the urine-smelling telephone box on Kasarminkatu. Opposite, a small kiosk selling tobacco, magazines and sweets was busy with people stopping to buy the evening paper. A newspaper placard outside read, 'Charlie's Angel actress to visit Finland'. Iain was cold. He'd been walking around Maija's block since four-thirty. At six o'clock he decided to make the call.

'And our friend?' The Colonel asked.

'Not seen him, Sir.' Iain had a sudden urge to say 'all quiet on the Eastern Front' but knew the Colonel wouldn't appreciate the joke. Instead he stamped his feet while he listened to the Colonel's breathing.

'And she knew who you were?'

'No, Sir, she thought I was from the International Gymnastic Committee.'

'Hmm. The civilians all there?'

'Yes, the daughter came home at four and the mother five-thirty-six.'

'Ok. But the situation with the gym teacher is not good. She is heavily involved with our friend. They were seen in the city together. Go home and I'll let you know tomorrow how to proceed.'

'Sir, there's something else.'

As Iain made his way from Ullanlinna to the harbour, he pondered on a feeling that Kovtun was playing a game with

MI6. It had been too easy to get rid of him last night at the Linnonmaa apartment. And why had he held both Pia and the Linnonmaa family hostage for so long? As some kind of a warning to them? It didn't seem as though he'd planned to take Pia, but then told the girl to listen to Miss Joutila and even mentioned the Tournament.

As Iain saw the outline of the Geordie Gunboat, a dull grey bulky shape against the white frozen sea behind it, he knew he shouldn't visit the ship again, the Colonel had been quite clear about that. But this was urgent. He hoped the old man would see it that way too. He'd have to convince the Colonel that his theory on what Kovtun was planning was feasible. He'd use what he had found out from Miss Joutila as an indication that Pia was in grave danger during the Friendship Tournament. After listening to the two men in the tram, Iain was convinced his theory was right. At Monday's competition the cat and mouse game Kovtun had them in would come to a close.

The Colonel was puzzled, Iain could tell that much. But he didn't want Iain to see that he had no idea what Kovtun was planning. He muttered something about, 'Helsinki and Moscow, eh.' The Colonel told Iain Kovtun used the Tournament as decoy to keep his comrades at the Soviet Embassy off the scent, but Iain wasn't convinced. Neither was he convinced by the assurances from their Finnish contact that the Linnonmaas were now safe.

'It isn't for us to question our host country's word.' the Colonel said dryly.

If only Iain could talk to the Finnish contact directly. But naturally the Finns weren't able to have any detectable links to the disappearance of such a high-ranking KGB officer from Helsinki. Iain understood that. The Colonel assured him, 'There is no resistance, nor effort to stop the defection from the Finnish side. Seems they're glad to get rid of the chap.'

'How do we know Heikki and Sasha are KGB informants? From our Finnish contact?' Iain asked

The Colonel looked at Iain over his glasses, but said nothing. They were sitting in his cabin. The Colonel's supper tray stood on the table between them. The bastard, Iain thought. He knew absolutely nothing about Heikki or Sasha! 'Need to know, is it?' Iain said sarcastically. Too sarcastically.

'Look here, Collins. Sometimes we have to take a whisper, or a hint, seriously. It is quite possible...'

Iain got up. 'And what about Pia's involvement in the Tournament? Kovtun is keeping an eye on her, we know that. There must be a connection. Only a fool would not see it!' Iain shouted. He was fed up with the pretence he now saw from the Colonel. As if he knew everything and divulged just as much as he was willing to Iain. He suspected the Colonel knew almost as little as he did.

'Collins, that's enough.' The Colonel got up and was standing close to Iain. 'Your job is to see to it that the Russian is delivered to us safely. We've known about the Tournament for a while now. We know Kovtun is planning some kind of procedure during it.' The Colonel inhaled deeply.

Iain sat down. The Colonel did the same.

'This man is violent. As far as we know he's killed at least once in Stockholm. And then there's the suspicious death of his secretary at the Embassy. In Helsinki a death of a civilian, a girlfriend say, would not even be investigated, so how

many has he done away with here? This is the man we want
in the West?'

'Collins. I hope I don't have to remind you the signifi-
cance of the crypto to our navy?'

'No'

Neither man spoke for a while. Iain calmed down a little.
He'd spent a few weeks in a submarine. He hadn't enjoyed
the lack of washing facilities, the cramped conditions, nor
the hot bunking. It was strange to see the man who'd slept
in the same bunk only fleetingly as you changed shifts. The
submariners told him it was comforting to climb into a
warm space after a cold night shift on the bridge when the
sub wasn't diving. But when Iain's ship picked him up, he
knew he'd not volunteer for submarines. His time in the sub
made him admire the men who did it, tour after tour,
spending weeks, even months out at sea, much of it under
water. They had a kind of comradeship Iain had not seen
before. He knew that if Kovtun delivered the Soviet crypto-
graphic key card to MI6 the subs would be more efficient at
plotting the Soviet navy's paths. And spend less futile time
underwater.

'It'll give us the edge, old boy,' the Colonel said.

Iain sighed. He would just have to make sure Pia was
safe. He got up, but the Colonel lifted his hand to stop him.

'There is some news from the Soviet Embassy.'

Iain listened.

'The secretary mentioned in *Helsingin Sanomat*. She was
working for Kovtun.'

'And?' Had the Colonel forgotten Iain already knew this?

The Colonel snapped, 'Don't you see?'

Iain said nothing. He'd really had enough. He wasn't
going to play anymore guessing games.

The Colonel continued, 'The Finns think she knew that

Kovtun was in contact with us. So we must proceed as quickly as possible before his own side gets to him. All we can hope for is that Kovtun got to her before she reported back to Moscow.'

'So you think she found out about the crypto codes he's been passing onto us?'

The Colonel raised an eyebrow. On that first meeting at the British Embassy Iain had been told not to mention that Kovtun had been working for MI6. 'Walls have ears and all that,' he'd joked. Iain thought that since the Colonel had mentioned it now, the ship was a safe place to talk.

Eventually the Colonel nodded slowly.

Iain was silent for a moment. He was thinking that if Kovtun had killed the secretary there was no guarantee he'd got to her, as the Colonel put it, in time.

'And why is the Finnish contact so keen to help us with him?'

'Well, he's not exactly made any friends here...'

Iain risked appearing stupid, again, 'I'm not sure I follow, Sir. If they hate him so, why don't the Finns just shop Kovtun to the KGB? I presume they know about his, hmm, divided loyalties?'

The Colonel didn't say anything for a while. Surely he must have wondered this himself? Iain's anger was rising again. He was tempted to get up and just leave. Eventually the Colonel took off his glasses. 'Look, Collins, I know I haven't always been straight with you, and I cannot tell you much. All I can say is that the Finns want our man in the West.'

Iain pondered how this was going to affect Pia at the Tournament. Did it have any bearing? 'The gymnastics teacher, Miss Joutila, would she be worth talking to a little more?'

'On no account are you to approach her!'

Iain looked up. The Colonel had raised his voice.

'Is that clear? Keep away from anyone apart from the two civilians. From now on you can leave Kovtun and his girlfriends to me.' After a while he calmed down and continued, 'I have to also warn you, you are getting very close to your subjects. Personal involvement like that only hampers operations. Makes one misjudge things.' He was looking at Iain. His eyes looked naked, even vulnerable, without his glasses. 'Believe me, I know.' He was quiet for a long time. Then he put his glasses back on. He was already attending to the file on his lap. Clearly the interview was over.

16

Sunday the weather turned even colder. The snow was no longer falling, but there was a bitter wind. Did it really blow all the way from Siberia, Iain wondered. It was the lowest temperatures he had ever known. To avoid having to stand in the harsh weather for too long, he got to the corner of Kasarminkatu and Vuorim-iehenkatu only five minutes before Pia was due to emerge from her block of flats. He knew he was cutting it fine, but then he'd made Pia promise she would be at the tram stop at 9.10. Iain glanced at his watch. It was now five minutes past. When he again looked at the entrance to the flats, he saw two women emerge. Damn, he swore to himself.

Iain now had to run up to Johannes Church to the next stop in order to catch the same tram. He must not be seen by Maija. As he ran up the hill, Iain hoped that Pia was keeping her promise not to tell her mother anything. He agreed with the Colonel. The less people knew about the defection the better, especially as Kovtun was behaving so strangely and with his own side after him. A desperate man was a dangerous man. But if Pia had kept her promise, why was

Maija with her? The bank was closed on Sundays. Surely
she was not planning to attend the rehearsals with Pia this
morning?

Iain was astonished how tough Pia had been through
this affair. Having never had children, he couldn't imagine
what worry a girl like Pia could bring to her parents. The
father didn't seem to be on the scene at all, which must
make it all that much more difficult for Maija. Again, Iain
felt the pangs of guilt. He was really not cut out for the life
of an impartial agent.

Iain sighed in relief when he saw Maija climb out of the
tram on Mannerheim Street. He made his way towards the
front part of the carriage and sat down on the now empty
seat next to Pia.

The girl glanced sideways but said nothing.

Iain took a newspaper out of his pocket. It was yesterday's *Helsingin Sanomat*. He spread it out in front of him and
whispered to Pia.

'I have to go elsewhere. I'm off at the next stop. Be careful, do not step out of the tram before the school stop, and
then walk straight to school. I'll be outside, opposite the
gym hall, at lunchtime.'

Pia was tired. She'd cried herself to sleep. The thought of
Anni being held by that awful blond Russian had tortured
her all night. Iain didn't seem to know where she was.
Unless he just wasn't telling her. Poor Anni, she had been so
brave in front of the KGB men. She, Pia, had been a slob-
bering baby. Mr Linnonmaa had said the KGB would not
dare to come back, so perhaps the Linnonmaa family had
left town for their own safety? If only Pia knew!

And did Heikki have anything to do with any of this? Sasha? The thought of her and Heikki together made Pia sick. Yet Sasha was always hanging around him. Heikki didn't seem to be able or willing to stop it. Pia was glad she hadn't made any plans to meet up with him today. She wasn't sure she wanted to see him. She couldn't guarantee she'd act normally when she saw him or when he touched her. She needed to be absolutely sure Heikki loved her and no one else. She'd ask him but not until all this was over. Iain had said that by tomorrow the Russian should have gone. Pia couldn't wait.

Approaching the school building, Pia spotted two figures standing outside the entrance to the Lyceum. She recognised them immediately. Pia's throat felt dry.

Sasha was standing so close to Heikki their heads were touching. What were they doing at school on a Sunday and what were they talking about?

Pia looked around the schoolyard. She didn't want to be seen by them. She could hide by the low red-brick gymnastics hall. She stepped sideways and stood with her back to the wall. She heard Sasha's laughter. She said, 'So, how long are you going to wait?'

Pia couldn't make out Heikki's reply. He mumbled something in a low voice.

Again Sasha laughed, 'Well, I've warned you.'

Pia hurried up the staircase and into the gym hall. It was empty. None of the other girls had turned up yet. There was a light in Miss Joutila's office. Pia dropped her bag onto the floor of the changing room and took off her boots. It was cold, so she left her jumper on over her costume. She walked along the mats with her legwarmers pulled high up. There were voices coming from Miss Joutila's office. Pia felt bad eavesdropping on her teacher again. Should she go back to the changing rooms and wait there? But she couldn't help hear what was being said.

'I told you not to talk to the man! You are mad, mad woman!'

She would have recognised the voice anywhere. It was Kovtun.

'Please don't be angry,' Miss Joutila said. Her voice quivered. She was sniffling.

'Do you understand what you do! You make everything wrong.'

There was a crash. Something broke as it was flung onto the floor.

Pia was frightened but she couldn't move. Miss Joutila was weeping.

'I'm sorry, Vadi. I didn't know, I...'

But Kovtun didn't let her finish. 'I tell you what you do. You talk to this Englishman again. You tell him you sorry, very sorry. You were stupid. And you do not, hear me woman, you do not say my name!' There was a bang. Kovtun must have hit something. Pia held her breath. Then, Kovtun continued in a more gentle tone, 'Leena, dusha, you want to live in England with Vladsislas and his beautiful daughter, yes?'

'Yes.' Leena's voice was so low Pia could hardly make out what she said.

'But this man try to stop us, see?'

Leena sighed, 'OK, I'll talk to him again and tell him I was mistaken.'

Later when Pia came out of the gym hall, Heikki was waiting for her in the corridor.

'Pia,' he called when she tried to walk past him. Heikki

took hold of Pia's arm and said, 'Please, can we talk. We could go to the Rixi Bar?'

'Ok,' she said. Iain would be outside by now, and would follow them. She felt safe knowing that. 'But, instead of Rixi, we'll go to my place, OK?'

'Sure.'

Heikki seemed meek as a lamb. He followed Pia rather than taking hold of her and leading as he usually did. They walked out of the school building, picking up their coats from the lockers. Neither spoke. Outside, Pia scanned the street, but couldn't see Iain. Then she remembered what Iain had told her and took off her scarf.

'What are you doing?' Heikki asked. 'It's bloody freezing out here!'

Pia said nothing, but continued to scan the people on the street. No sign of Iain! She took Heikki's hand and ran to the tram stop. The number ten was just pulling up. Pia felt for the key in her pocket and decided she'd take Heikki with her to the Council. At least there they would be safe.

Pia and Heikki got out of the crowded tram at Erottaja.

'I thought we were going to yours?' Heikki said as their feet hit the pavement. Pia didn't reply. Her heart pounded hard against her jumper as she looked up the hill towards Ullanlinna. A few people were hurrying down the slippery street and along the tree-lined South Esplanade. The lights of the Happy Days Café seemed bright against the grey sky. Where was Iain? Without his protection Pia felt vulnerable.

Pia and Heikki were standing at the zebra crossing waiting for the lights to turn to green. Suddenly she couldn't bear it any longer. She took hold of Heikki's hand and ran against the red light. A car sounded its horn, narrowly missing them. A man, standing on the opposite side of the street caught Pia's eye.

'Why are we going there?' Heikki asked, nodding at the Council building. 'Just follow me,' Pia said and took a few steps sideways and hurried past the man. Please don't let him grab us, she thought and glanced back. The man moved towards the edge of the curb. Pia took a deep breath in and ran to the heavy door of the Council building. She took the key out of her pocket and went to open the door but it gave way. Thank God, Pia thought, it's unlocked. She glanced back. The man was now on the other side of the road, hurrying towards Stockmann's.

The woman at the reception to the Council made a phone call before she allowed Pia and Heikki inside. Pia had to show the key that Iain had given her. Heikki raised his eyebrows but said nothing. Once inside one of the outer rooms, which looked like a library, the woman asked Pia in perfect Finnish, 'Would you like a hot drink? Tea, coffee?' She smiled and looked almost friendly. Her demeanour had changed after she'd put the phone down.

'Yes, please, coffee' Pia said. Heikki nodded. Suddenly Pia was starving, and as if the woman had known this, she brought something to eat with the two cups of hot drinks. There were English sandwiches on a blue patterned plate, soft white bread filled with ham and cut into small triangles.

The woman closed the door and Pia and Heikki sat in a corner of the dark room smelling of old books, with a low table between them, and started eating. Pia picked up a sandwich and looked at Heikki. His shoulders were hunched, he didn't seem as confident as he had done the last time he was here. Pia wished Iain could see him like this. With his head bent, eating his sandwich, he glanced at Pia, but didn't say anything.

'I saw you talking to Sasha outside the school this morning.'

Heikki looked up and bit his lip.

'She warned you about me?'

'No!' Heikki nearly shouted the word. Now he'd gone bright red. Did this mean he was lying? 'Look, Sasha and I belong, belonged,' Heikki's voice got higher and for a moment he looked embarrassed rather than sad or angry, 'or rather it's our parents that really belong, to the Pioneers.'

Pia looked at Heikki. 'The Communist thing?'

'Yeah, well it's kind of fun, they do camps in the summer and discos for us older kids.'

'So, you and Sasha...?'

'We've known each other since we were babies.'

'You never said.'

'Belonging to the Pioneers isn't exactly cool at the Lyceum.'

Pia thought about what the Old Crow's reaction would have been if she'd known, and nearly smiled. 'But how did you keep it a secret? And why? I thought you lot were proud of your beliefs.' Pia couldn't believe she didn't know this about Heikki. There was a girl in the year below her who everybody knew was a Communist. She wore grey clothes and always had sweat marks under her arms. Nobody spoke to her. Pia's grandfather had fought Stalin in the war and her grandmother hated the Russians. She'd told Pia they wanted Finland to belong to the Soviet Union, to lose its hard-fought independence. If the Communists had won the civil war, or if Finns hadn't fought so hard against Stalin, she said, there'd be no Finland. The country would be like Estonia or Poland. There'd be food shortages, bad clothes and everyone would work in large factories earning little money, and live in huge, cold blocks of flats. Pia wanted to say all this to Heikki, but she wondered if it would have made any difference. 'Communism is like a disease, once you get it, you can't be cured,' her Grandmother had told Pia.

Heikki was quiet. He leant back on the low chair and ran his fingers through his hair. Normally Pia would have wanted to kiss Heikki, seeing him do that, but now she was strangely unaffected by the gesture.

'I didn't think you'd understand,' he said after a long while.

'You're right,' Pia said, 'but that's not important now. Tell me, without lying,' Pia emphasised the last word, 'what you were looking for in Anni's father's desk?'

Heikki's face was serious, 'Nothing.'

Pia considered Heikki. He looked Pia squarely in the eyes. He seemed sincere.

Maija closed the door behind her and plonked the two heavy shopping bags on the hall floor. She'd been so preoccupied this week she forgot to shop for food on Saturday and had to go all the way to Valintatalo, the only store that was open on Sundays.

'Pia!' she shouted. Her room was empty. Maija glanced at her watch. It was nearly two o'clock. The rehearsals were supposed to finish at lunchtime. Where was the girl?

Maija wished she'd accompanied Pia to the training session. They could have shopped together afterwards. She had wanted to, but didn't want to be the over-protective mother. Besides, what could possibly happen to Pia at school? But now, Maija started to wonder if Jukka Linnonmaa had been right after all. Maija dismissed his warnings about the Communist conspiracy President Kekkonen was heading. She knew he was a right-wing activist. Sitting opposite

Linnonmaa at the Happy Days Café, in the middle of a harsh Helsinki winter, Maija had felt the same fear she now knew made her leave the Customs. But surely it was highly unlikely that Pia's new boyfriend could be involved in something similar. She'd politely listened to Linnonmaa for a while and then told him she had to get to work.

Maija decided to meet Pia at the school and re-entered the slippery street outside the block of flats. The sun was high up in the sky, but covered by a thin blanket of clouds. The tram was empty and it gave Maija an eerie feeling that something was amiss. When the tram stopped at Erottaja, Maija was leaning against the back window of the carriage. She saw a man in a grey coat running through the Esplanade Park towards the vehicle. Suddenly, he turned and crossed the street without looking at the traffic lights. Maija looked closer and saw it was Iain. He entered an office building on the other side of Erottaja. When the tram started to move, Maija thought how different Pia had been since Iain had falsely accused her of using drugs. More grown-up somehow. She'd also talked less to Maija about her problems. But perhaps it was Heikki's influence. Maija saw how fond Pia was of the boy when he came over the other night. Maija sighed. Perhaps there was something in what Mr Linnonmaa had told her. Perhaps he'd been trying to protect Pia after all? Where could the girl be now? With Heikki? Maija decided to go after Iain. Perhaps he could make sense of it all.

Maija got off the tram outside Stockmann's. The store was shut up and there was no one else on the street. She walked back up to Erottaja and made her way to the building Iain had disappeared into. Inside the gleaming entrance hall, she looked at a blackboard of office names.

There was a dentist, a solicitor's office, debt collectors. Then she saw it, 'British Council 4th Floor'.

Iain was panting when he walked through the door, 'Thank God you're alright!' He came over and put his hand on Pia's shoulder. 'Good girl,' he said in English. 'You did exactly the right thing coming here.' He was standing between Pia and Heikki, surveying the two from a height. He took his coat off and pulled up a chair and sat down. 'Heikki, are you alright?' he asked. His breath was still quick and as he spoke to Heikki, he placed his hand on Heikki's arm.

Pia looked at Iain with astonishment. She didn't think he liked Heikki.

The receptionist came in with a teapot and a cup. 'Thought you'd like a cup of tea, Sir,' she said to Iain in English. 'Ah, you're a dear, Mrs Cooper,' Iain said and smiled at the woman. He got up and took the tray from Mrs Cooper. 'Thank you so very much. It's good of you to come in on a Sunday.'

'Oh, you're welcome,' Mrs Cooper cooed. She started clearing up the table, removing Heikki's and Pia's empty cups.

'It's alright, you can leave those,' Iain said in English, glancing at Pia. He leant back in his chair and said to Heikki, 'Now young man, isn't it about time you told me what you're up to?'

Heikki looked sideways at Pia and started talking to Iain.

'I was just telling Pia about the Pioneers. It's a youth group. We meet every Thursday at The Workers' Hall in Töölö.' Heikki was fiddling with his hair. 'A few times we'd get a Comrade from the East to come in to talk about life in the Soviet Union.' Heikki's eyes now met Pia's. 'They've got such a good education system, you know, and jobs for everyone after school. Not like here where you're unemployed however many qualifications you've got!'

'Yeah, yeah,' Pia said.

Iain gave Pia a stern look. 'What?' Pia said, 'you're on their side now are you?'

'It's alright, we just want to hear what Heikki has to say,' Iain said, then turned to Heikki. 'Go on'.

'This one guy came in a few months ago, his talk was brilliant. He had slides and everything. Both Sash and I wanted to go and visit his town, Minsk. Anyway, we got talking to him afterwards and he said he could arrange a scholarship for us to go and study there. We were so excited! The week after, when we were playing pool, he came in again. By that stage we'd both thought he'd just been all talk, we'd not heard from him though he said he was going to write to our parents. He'd taken our addresses and everything. My Mum was so excited when I told her!'

'Did this man tell you his name?'

'Yeah, Vladsislas Kovtun.'

Pia gasped and put her hand to her mouth. Iain looked at Pia and shook his head. Heikki was watching both of them intently. 'I know, that's why I've been trying to find out what's he up to, haven't I?' he said.

'And when was this?'

'Oh, just after Christmas.'

'Go on, Heikki,' Iain said.

'Anyway, he came back and started talking to me and Sash. We were playing pool and she was beating me so I was glad of an interruption,' Heikki grinned at both Iain and Pia. She glared at him.

'He said he could arrange a scholarship at a university in Minsk for both of us.' Heikki looked pleadingly at Pia, 'You know how difficult it is to get into a university here, especially with the results I'm going to get.' Heikki paused for a moment. Pia didn't feel at all sorry for him, if he was so worried about his studies, why didn't he work a bit harder? Heikki continued, 'Anyway then the guy started talking about Anni.'

'What did he say?'

Heikki looked down at his hands. 'He wanted us to find out about Anni and her dad. Just ordinary stuff, you know.' Heikki's head was hanging and he was looking at Pia and Iain from under his eyebrows. 'Next time the Comrade came to the meeting we told him all we knew. He told us our scholarships were a certainty. Sash and I started talking about going to the USSR when we'd finished the Baccalaureate, but then weeks went by and we heard nothing. Then at last week's meeting we had another Comrade in, and after his talk about the Moscow children's homes, he came straight up to us as if he knew Sash and me and started asking questions.'

'What was his name?' Pia noticed that Iain was leaning closer to Heikki as if afraid he might miss a word he said, just like he and the Colonel had done when Pia came into the Council before. Where was the Colonel, Pia wondered. Shouldn't he be here listening to Heikki too?

'He didn't tell us his name.'

'Shame, but go on,' Iain said.

'This guy seemed to be very interested in what Vladsislas had promised us and he knew all about the scholarships, though he still wanted us to tell him exactly what the first Comrade had said. And he asked a lot of questions about Anni.'

'Who was he? Did he tell you who he worked for?'

'No.

'The next Monday when I saw Vladsislas at school and Anni was behaving so oddly...both Sash and I were shit scared that it had something to do with this scholarship and the other bloke.'

'Apart from spying for the Russians, what else have you been up to?' Pia's throat was dry. She could hardly bring out the words.

Iain coughed, 'I don't think that's quite fair.'

Pia shot an angry look at him.

'Nothing, really,' Heikki said. 'I thought you knew something about it, so I followed you around for a bit.' Heikki was looking at Pia.

Pia's heart was pounding. She looked down and fought the tears filling her eyes. She wasn't going to show Heikki how much he meant to her.

But Heikki just carried on looking at Pia with that sheepish look. 'Pia, I've always really liked you and...'

'If you say so,' Pia said. Her voice was high, too high.

Heikki was quiet.

Pia straightened up and trying to steady her voice said, 'And what were you really looking for in Mr Linnonmaa's study?'

Heikki looked up at Pia. Leaning closer to her, he said earnestly, 'I was desperate to find out what was going on, if Mr Linnonmaa knew about Kovtun's visits to the Pioneers, and me...'

'Just trying to save your own skin, that figures.' Pia said. She looked away from Heikki.

'Pia, please!' Heikki tried to take hold of Pia's hand across the table.

The Admiral coughed, and said, 'You two will have to sort that out later. Let's go back to Kovtun. Did he mention Miss Joutila to you?'

Heikki looked surprised, 'No, why?'

'What about the Friendship Tournament? Did he talk about that?'

Heikki thought for a moment, 'No, he just talked about all the good the Comrades were trying to do for the Finnish youth, you know to enable the continuing of...'

'The friendship and mutual co-operation,' Pia finished the expression all politicians were always harping on about. 'More like exploitation of a weaker country!' she said more forcefully.

'No, it's not like that at all!' Heikki had got up but seeing Pia's face he sat down again. 'I knew you wouldn't understand,' he said.

'You're right!' Pia said.

When the lift doors opened Maija saw a woman in a smart suit standing behind a reception desk.

'Can I help you,' she said.

'I'm looking for Iain Collins.'

'I'm afraid we're shut today.'

'But Mr Collins is here, I saw him come in. And the door was open.' Maija didn't like the woman's superior attitude. As she spoke she looked Maija up and down, as if assessing the cost and age of her coat.

'I'm sorry, you must be mistaken.'

'But he's English!'

The woman laughed. It sounded more like a cough. She looked pityingly at Maija. 'I'm sorry,' she said.

Iain, followed by Pia and Heikki appeared at a door behind the woman.

'Pia!' Maija shouted. 'And Iain!' she said, looking pointedly at the receptionist.

'I'm sorry,' the woman said to Iain in English. Iain looked at Maija, and then the woman. He came across and gave Maija a peck on the cheek. 'What a nice surprise!' he said unconvincingly.

'What's going on?' Maija said looking straight at Iain.

'Nothing, Mum, I've just come to the Council to borrow some books,' Pia said. 'And Iain happened to be here at the same time! Isn't that a coincidence?'

'I thought you were shut.' Maija turned her head towards the arrogant woman.

'The young lady was...' The woman began, but Maija lifted her hand to stop her and said to Iain, 'I think I'll hear it from you. What's Pia doing here?' She stared at Iain who was not returning her gaze.

'Let's go home, Pia,' she said, touching Pia's arm, and turned on her heels. Pia stood motionless for a moment, her eyes on Heikki. She nodded to him and eventually followed Maija into the lift.

17

Iain stood in the reception for a while listening to Mrs Cooper's apologies. 'I'm so sorry, Sir, I didn't hear you come in and she was just about to go.' She was speaking in her perfectly accented English. Iain looked at Mrs Cooper's well made-up face. She treated her job at the Council with the utmost professionalism. 'Serious people, these Finns, even those we work with,' the Colonel had remarked about her. Iain wondered how much she knew about Kovtun.

'Not to worry, Mrs Cooper.' He pulled on his coat. He needed first to talk to the Colonel and then he must make sure Maija and Pia were safely at home.

'I'm off,' Heikki said. He stood next to the lift with his hands in his pockets.

Iain had forgotten about the boy. 'Hold on,' he said. He turned back to Mrs Cooper and asked for a piece of paper. He wrote: 'Make sure the boy is followed until safely at home, phone the Colonel if need be,' and handed the note to Mrs Cooper. She read it, nodded and smiled.

'Heikki, I want you to wait here until Mrs Cooper has made a phone call. Can you do that for me?'

'Yeah, sure, but can't I come with you? I'm really good at following people, and I can undo locks, remember?' The young man's face lit up.

Iain glanced at Mrs Cooper. 'No. I'm not, I mean, sorry, that's not possible. Stay here until Mrs Cooper tells you otherwise, and go straight home. OK?'

Heikki hung his head, but nodded in agreement. He walked slowly to a chair in the lobby and sat down with a flourish. He looked like a bag of bones settling into an empty basket. At least the boy is well out of the mess now, Iain thought.

The walk down the Esplanade seemed to be getting colder each time. The afternoon light was just starting to fade. Iain looked at the grey sky above him. At least it wasn't snowing.

'Well, well,' the Colonel said after Iain had run through what the youngsters had told him at the Council.

Iain waited as long as he could, while the Colonel stared at the carpet of his cabin.

'Kovtun is getting very close to these youngsters, don't you think, Sir?'

'Hmm.'

'I think I should...'

'No, Collins.' The Colonel gave Iain a stern look. It was a warning. Iain dropped his gaze.

The Colonel spoke, 'The ship's company are preparing for the Open Day tomorrow. The Finnish public will be admitted between the hours of 15.00–19.00. Kovtun will arrive, with the crypto card, a few minutes before seven o'clock. We will sail at 21.00.'

'Of course Sir, I understand.'

The Colonel looked at Iain for a long time. He got up and went to fetch something out of a drawer. He came back and gave Iain a heavy black case. Iain looked at the Colonel and lifted the lid.

'You did pass your firearms training?' the Colonel said.

'Yes, Sir,' Iain said. He tried not to show that his hands were trembling as he placed the gun carefully into the inside pocket of his coat. The Colonel nodded towards a set of cartridges and Iain placed them inside another pocket. The Colonel gave him a set of car keys. 'It's a moss green Opel Kadett parked in bay 229 in the car park underneath Erottaja. You know the air shelter?'

'Yes, Sir.' Iain thought how much easier his task would have been if he'd had a car all along but said nothing.

'Now, what you need to do is to make sure both Pia and Maija are safely at home.' The Colonel gave Iain a consoling smile, 'And then go home, have a beer or two and watch the ice hockey on television. There's bound to be a match on!' The Colonel laughed. A short, efficient barking sound that came out of his mouth and made his eyes briefly crease in the corners. 'Take the night off; tomorrow could be a long day.'

The coat felt heavy on him as he walked out of the ship and into the cold Helsinki night. He scanned the dark jetty and wondered why he felt no fear. He pulled his coat tighter around him and decided the person who would know most about Kovtun was Leena Joutila.

.   .   .

Maija sat with her hands on the kitchen table, thinking. Pia's make-up was smudged and her hair a mess. Maija could hardly believe what the girl had been through on her own.

'C'mon darling, let's get you cleaned up.' Maija pulled Pia up and together they went into the little bathroom. 'Why didn't you tell me all of this before?' Maija handed Pia a clean towel.

The girl sniffled and said, 'Iain told me I shouldn't. Anni is still missing, and he said as few people as possible must know in case that put her in danger.' Her face, now scrubbed clean of make-up looked like a frightened child's.

'But I'm your mother!' Maija said. She felt a surge of anger towards Iain. He had most certainly used her, but more importantly he had used her daughter. He had lied to both of them and all for what? Maija still couldn't believe that the unassuming Englishman she knew was some kind of a spy. Was his job at the British Council just a cover? And was his story of his failed marriage to a Finn a lie? How had he learned Finnish? What about the recent increase in his feelings for Maija, were they false and made up for the sake of his other secret life too? The intense kisses, the loving words - all lies? Maija pushed her own disappointment aside and looked at her daughter, tearful and obviously in shock. She stood shivering in front of the mirror, not even looking at her sad face. Maija would not let any man do this to Pia! From now on she would be more vigilant and protect her daughter, as she had protected her from her father's absence.

'I'll make us some coffee,' she said and put her arm around Pia, leading her back to the kitchen. Her daughter was already a little taller than her, but Maija felt stronger. She would sort this mess out. She would speak to the police, to Mrs Härmänmaa, she would take Pia out of school, she would take leave, unpaid if need be, and they would go and stay with her mother in Lappeenranta. A few days skiing by the lake, eating home-made rye bread fresh from the oven and drinking hot berry cordial would do them both good. Iain and this Heikki boy could go to hell as far as Maija was concerned!

The doorbell rang.

Pia and Maija looked at each other. Pia glanced towards the door and said, 'Don't open it, it could be the KGB!'

'Nonsense!' Maija said. A doubt registered fleetingly in her mind, but she brushed it away. It was 1979, not 1939 and they lived in a free country, not behind the iron curtain! Maija looked through the spy hole. 'It's Anni!' she said and opened the door.

The two girls hugged each other as soon as Anni was inside the flat. Maija placed the chain on the door. At least now Pia wouldn't have to worry about Anni anymore. She was glad she didn't have to tell Pia how she knew the Linnonmaas were safe.

'Mrs Mäkelä,' Anni said when Maija walked into the kitchen. 'I am so sorry about all the trouble you've had. My father sends his regards and says not to worry, everything will be sorted soon.'

Maija smiled, but regarded Anni carefully. It didn't seem as if she knew about Maija and her father's shared past. She looked even thinner than she had last time Maija had seen her. She was wearing a tight pair of white jeans, with boots and a loose woollen jumper.

'I would like to talk to your father,' Maija said.

Anni was quiet. She regarded Maija, as if judging if she could trust her.

'I think we've got a right to know what's really going on, don't you?' Maija said, trying to control her anger.

'It's not Anni's fault, none of it is!' Pia said.

Anni touched Pia's arm. 'It's OK, your mum's right. It's a bloody mess and innocent people are getting caught up in it.'

'I wouldn't call being held, threatened and followed by the KGB, as being "caught up"!' Maija said.

'Anni's eyes flashed, 'Followed? What do you mean, followed?'

'Oh, Anni, Iain told me everything about Kovtun. That he's about to defect, and that you might be in danger.' Pia said.

'You mean the Admiral? You know he works for the British Intelligence?'

'Yes, of course we do,' Maija said and continued, 'Do your parents really know you're here?'

'Not exactly.'

Maija sat down. She felt tired. The coffee-maker was making gurgling noises and she got up again, mechanically, to get three cups out. She poured the hot coffee and said, 'Right, Anni, now it's your turn to tell us what you – or your father – thinks is going on. Perhaps then we can get back to normal. Agreed?'

'Of course, though I don't have much time,' Anni replied.

'Are you back in your flat?' Pia asked.

'No, we are kept in a Finnish SAPO safe house in Kirkkonummi. I've to get the bus from the station at 18.30, otherwise they'll notice I'm gone. I was only supposed to go out for a walk.'

'I don't understand. Is the Finnish secret police involved in the defection of this Kovtun type?' Maija asked.

'Yes, they want to get rid of him. That's what my father

told me. He was joking that the Brits don't know what kind
of paskiainen they're getting.'

Maija was quiet. They agreed on that score. The man
could easily be described as a bastard, though she herself
would not have used such language. Then she had a
thought.

'But isn't it dangerous for the Finnish state to be involved
in a defection? I thought we were neutral. Certainly we can't
help the West, can we? Doesn't Big Brother mind?'

Anni looked coy. She gave a sideways smile and said, 'Of
course the Finns don't know anything about it – officially!'

'I see,' Maija said. She tried not to panic. It was obvious
the girl didn't understand the severity of the situation. How
foolish Jukka Linnonmaa was to tell her such secrets!

'And your father doesn't know you're here?'

Anni didn't answer. She looked at Maija with her clear
blue eyes, but Maija could not tell from her expression what
she was thinking. Maija saw the time was approaching six
o'clock. Anni too looked at her watch.

'Do you have to go back?' Pia said. She looked miserable.

'Listen, both of you. The reason I came was to warn you.
We think, or at least Dad does, that Kovtun is planning
something involving one of the girls in the team.' Anni was
silent for a moment.

Maija sat back down, 'Why do the Finns want to get rid
of Kovtun so much? Surely all the Soviet Embassy staff are
the same? They're all Russians and Communists, aren't
they?' she asked.

Anni looked very serious. 'My father says this Kovtun is
worse than the others.' Anni paused for a moment and
looked down at her hands. 'He thinks he's the King of
Helsinki! But he's been present at Kekkonen's talks with the
Soviets, even with Brezhnev. You know their secret talks?'

Anni looked at Maija and Pia in turn. Maija had no idea what the girl was talking about, but nodded. She wanted to hear all that Anni had to say. 'Kovtun has been present at these talks as the only other person. He's been acting as interpreter. He knows what Kekkonen has promised the Russians on our behalf. If Kovtun gets to the West, he will tell all, and then everyone will know what Kekkonen is really up to!'

Maija stared at Anni. This was far more serious than she had thought. This is what Linnonmaa was involved in – treason! Although Maija didn't support Kekkonen, and had never voted for him as she regarded him as far too soft on Russia, he was still the elected President of the Republic! Maija also believed that without Kekkonen, Finland could now be part of the Eastern Bloc. It was his diplomacy that had kept Finland independent when other European countries such as Hungary and Czechoslovakia were time and time again pulled back behind the iron curtain. And unlike many right-wing people in Finland, Maija didn't believe that the West would come to Finland's aid if Russia decided to invade. Finland was simply not important enough.

Maija regarded Anni. Her eyes were wide. Pia was staring at her friend too. 'So it's really important to let the Brits have him! Important for Finland!' Anni said.

'But what if this Kovtun does speak about Kekkonen and the Finns vote Kekkonen out and replace him with a right-wing politician? Will that not force the Russians to invade?' Maija said. She gave the girl a stern look. 'Besides, this is not something any of us should be involved in. What your father does is up to him and his conscience...'

'What do you mean?' Anni's eyes flashed at Maija.

'Perhaps I've misunderstood,' Maija said.

'Yes, I think you have. My fat her is a Finnish diplomat and he always acts in the best interest of the fatherland.'

Maija thought that sounded like a phrase this girl had heard often. 'Well, I'm not sure I understand any of it,' Maija put her hand on Anni's arm, 'but what is it we can do to keep ourselves out of all this? That is why you've come, isn't it?'

'Yes,' the girl said keenly, 'Pia, you must keep your ears and eyes open at the Tournament, and keep an eye on the little girls. I just wanted to warn you that something is going to happen at the competition tomorrow. I couldn't let you go without warning you.' Anni looked at Pia, and squeezed her hand.

'Shouldn't she stay away from the Tournament, if it's dangerous?' Maija said. She had crossed her arms over her chest. Anni said nothing.

Pia ignored her too. 'I'm so glad you're alright!' she said with tears in her eyes, hugging Anni again.

Maija got up. 'I'm going to phone the police. I'm sure they can sort this out. There must be a procedure...' she was on her way to the telephone in the hall.

Anni got up too and blocked her way. She looked Maija in the eyes and said, 'The police will not be able to do anything. Besides, they won't believe you!'

Maija regarded Anni. Again she seemed so authoritative. 'Please, Mrs Mäkelä, phone my father, if you like. He'll say the same as me!' Anni scribbled a number on a piece of paper and handed it to Maija, 'Ask for Mr Laine.'

Maija took the piece of paper and stared at it for a moment. 'Please Mrs Mäkelä. My father really does know what he's doing, and this is for the best. For Finland!'

Anni glanced at her wrist watch. 'I need to get back.'

'I'll take the tram with you into town and then we can talk on the way,' Pia said.

'No way, girls. Anni, I'm afraid you are going to have to make your own way back. I cannot let Pia get into more danger.' Maija thought, if need be, she would physically detain Pia.

'Mum!' Pia protested, keeping hold of Anni's arm.

Anni freed herself from Pia's grip and said, 'Your mum's right, Pia. I'll be OK, nobody knows I'm here. I'll give you a ring when we're back in Helsinki.' She picked up her down coat, and hugged Pia hard. Then she was out of the door. Maija and Pia went back into the kitchen. They peered out of the window out into the darkened street, lit only by the faint glow of the street lamps. After a short while, they saw Anni step onto the street. They watched in silence as Anni's long blonde hair disappeared around the corner.

'Mum, is she going to be alright? What if the Russian follows her, and...?' Pia burst into tears and Maija took her daughter into her arms once more. She looked at the number Anni had written on the piece of paper in her hand. Would speaking with Jukka again plunge her and her daughter deeper into the world of intrigue and danger? Maija needed time to think before she spoke to anyone.

18

Leena was waiting for Vadi. He was over an hour late. The rage that she had started to feel after the first half hour was now subsiding. Instead she was worried. What if something had happened to him? Perhaps it had something to do with the Englishman. Leena hadn't yet tried to contact him. She didn't really know how. But Vadi had been in such a rage, she hadn't told him that at the school that morning. Leena decided not to think the worst; the man was probably just working late. She looked at the small table she had set with two plates and two glasses. The lace tablecloth she had bought from a large Gypsy woman who had called at her door. She should never have bought anything; now the same woman was there almost weekly, though Leena did not open the door when she spotted her wide black skirt through the spy hole.

Now she was going up to the spy hole every time she heard the lift move in the hallway. But there was no one outside her door. No sign of Vadi. Leena looked at her watch; it was past seven o'clock and he'd promised to be there by six.

Leena had been quite upset about Vadi shouting at her. Luckily no one had been around, but even so, right in her office at school.

After she had left the Rixi Bar, she felt exhilarated at her ability to bluff the Englishman. Back in her office, before Vadi's unannounced appearance, she guessed it was because some of what she'd told him was the truth. She did want to win the Tournament. It was important for her as well as the Lyceum. And Pia. Though she couldn't understand why Vadi wanted the Finns to win. How did that further his cause? The way he was behaving towards her lately, she'd decided it wasn't any sort of reward for her either. If Vadi was worried about keeping Leena on his side, he was going about it in a strange way. But by now Leena had learned that Vadi was not one to explain things in too much detail.

Leena heard the lift move again. She pressed her eye to the spy hole and waited. It stopped somewhere further up. Leena could hear a woman laughing, and then the lift descended and stopped at the ground floor.

Where was Vadi? It was nearing half past seven. The cabbage rolls she'd bought from the corner shop would be stone cold now. She'd need to reheat them. At least the *Koskenkorva* was chilled.

Just then her telephone rang.

'Hello, can I speak with Leena Joutila?'

'Speaking' Leena was disappointed. It wasn't Vadi.

'Hello, it's Iain Collins. We met yesterday.'

'Hello' was all Leena could think to say. How had the man found her number? She wasn't in the book, mainly to stop the students finding out where she lived. Besides, the man had been in a hurry to leave Leena, so much so, that he'd left his coffee untouched.

'I wondered if we could meet?'

Leena was thinking hard. If she said no, he'd certainly suspect something was up.

'Yes, why not,' she heard herself reply.

The man suggested the bar at the InterContinental Hotel. Leena had been there once with a friend who'd gone to teach in the USA for a year and had come back engaged to an American. The wedding reception at the hotel had been a grand affair. Leena wondered what she should wear there on a Sunday night, and decided on a pair of flared black pants and a colourful top. Shoes, as always, were a problem. Nothing less than her thick-lined winter boots would negotiate the walk to the tram stop. Usually on an evening out, she took a pair of indoor shoes to change into, but somehow that seemed wrong tonight, as if she was expecting to go dancing with the foreigner. Leena decided to take a pair of black patent shoes with her anyway, and see when she got there whether she'd have an opportunity to change into them unnoticed.

Vadi, too, was a problem. What if he turned up while she was away? When she was ready to leave, it was already eight o'clock. He was now two hours late. Then Leena had a thought. Her not being there – if, and when, he turned up – would teach him a lesson. Why did he assume that she didn't have better offers? That she didn't constantly refuse other men to be with him? She was sticking her neck on the line for him, the least he could do was to keep a date they'd arranged.

The bus dropped Leena off at Töölö Square, and she walked down the hill to the main entrance of the hotel on Mannerheimintie. It looked even grander than she remembered, but Leena took a deep breath and walked confidently in through the large revolving doors. She looked around the lobby and suddenly stopped. She only saw the man's back, but she would have recognised him anywhere.

Vadi stood with his arm around a woman's waist. They were talking to a receptionist at the desk. On the floor next to him was a holdall. The receptionist laughed at something Vadi said. She caught Leena's eye. Leena ducked sideways and hid behind a pillar. Then she saw a sign, 'Toilets.' She walked briskly towards a set of doors to the left of the lobby and went inside. There was no one inside. She opened a door to a cubicle and sat down on top of the toilet pan. Her hands were shaking as she took her boots off and placed the high-heeled shoes on her feet.

Although she hadn't seen his face, Leena was sure the man was Vadi. She recognised his long coat, his black boots and his blond hair. The way he stood, the way he waved his hand while talking to the receptionist, were the same. She even thought she had heard him laugh. The woman standing next to him had looked as if she did it all the time. They were very comfortable together.

When Leena saw Iain Collins, she was relieved, though a little disappointed by his appearance. He looked unshaven, and his jacket was scruffy, as were his boots. Still, he got up when he spotted Leena and offered her a drink.

'Cuba Libre,' Leena said immediately. She had decided what she was going to ask for while in the bus, and now she was glad. That way she appeared confident and would have the air of a woman of the world. She knew she'd get nervous and now after seeing Vadi with the woman her heart was racing as if she'd just run five kilometres. In the bus here, it had occurred to her that if this man was an enemy of sorts to Vladsislas, he would probably harm her too. But now, with Vladsislas here with another woman, the situation was even more terrifying. What Leena really wanted to do was go home and cry into her pillow. Everything was lost – Vadi, the Tournament, her pride. But, in the small cubicle of the ladies' room, she decided that she would pull herself together. She would make the best of if. If Vadi had been unfaithful to her all these months, so what! Leena could get over him as she had got over other men she'd fallen for before. Not having to be involved in Vadi's scheme would be a relief. If the foreign man started acting funny, she would simply say her farewells and leave. They were in a public place after all. What harm would come to her in front of all these people? She looked around the room. As she remembered, there was a long bar to one side, a dance floor in the middle, and tables arranged around it. Each table had a small lamp, giving a red glow to the people sitting there. But the rest of the room was so dark that Leena could barely make out the features of the people on the bar stools from where they were standing. When the barman brought Leena's drink, Iain Collins took it and led Leena further down the dimly-lit room. The place was half full, but Leena spotted a free table in the corner and said, 'Can we sit there?'

'Of course,' he replied.

Leena slid awkwardly onto the sofa. The fabric of her trousers rubbed against the velvet upholstery and it took her time to settle down. All the while the Englishman stood watching her, with his hand on the chair opposite. Then he seemed to change his mind and said, 'Do you mind if I sit next to you?'

Leena was glad of the red glow, it hid her blush.

'Of course.'

They were both now sitting diagonally opposite each other, with their knees touching under the table.

'Sorry,' the man said, 'but I want to see the bar. I'm looking for a friend.'

'Oh,' Leena said. Why was she here, what did he want with her? She'd have the one drink and then go home for a good night's sleep so that she could give her full support to the girls at tomorrow's competition. She would forget about Vadi and any chances of winning the competition. The Helsinki Lyceum girls would do their best, and she would tell them to hold their heads high and be proud of their achievements when the inevitable loss of the trophy was announced.

'Well, cheers,' the man said in English, lifting his glass and smiling at Leena.

'Cheers,' Leena said and felt a little more comfortable. She took a closer look at the man. Iain, he had called himself. He was tall, and quite slim, with square shoulders and a kind face. His wavy hair was very dark and there was a lot of it. Foreigners always had such good hair, Leena thought.

'Leena, may I call you Leena? I'm Iain,' the man said.

'Yes, of course...Iain,' Leena replied and smiled. Such politeness, so rare these days!

'I know this may sound wrong, or strange, but I believe you have been cheated.' The man's eyes were steady on Leena, looking gravely at her. 'Your friend at the, hmm, Embassy,' the man leant closer to Leena and whispered the last words, 'he's not what you think he is.'

'I know that!' Leena said, a little too loudly.

'You do?' Iain said, surprised.

'Yes, I saw him, just now, with her. I don't know, but...'

'You saw Vladsislas Kovtun here?' The man's eyes had widened and he was leaning even closer to Leena.

'Yes, just before I came into the bar, he was in the lobby!'

Iain scanned the bar, and leant back in the seat, taking a large gulp of his drink.

'You're sure it was him?'

'Yes,' Leena said. Of course she was sure!

'We need to leave,' Iain said.

The Englishman got up and took hold of her arm. 'We need to be quick.' He pulled her towards the other end of the bar, and through a side door into the lobby. The reception was now empty. Iain smiled at the girls at the desk and said, 'Good Evening,' in English. He nodded towards a set of stairs at the side and led Leena to the top of them.

'What about my coat and boots!' Leena said when they were standing outside. The hotel was built into a hill, between Töölö Square and Mannerheimintie. Leena didn't know there was another entrance on the Töölö Square side. She was shivering, looking at the cold night and the snow-covered street just beyond the doorway they were huddled in.

'What?' the man said, and looked down at Leena's feet, 'Where are they?'

'In the cloakroom!' Leena dug out the ticket she'd been handed by a girl.

'Ah', Iain said. He took the ticket and opened the door. They were once again inside the hotel, in a long corridor. 'You wait here,' he said and disappeared down the stairs.

Leena was still cold. Her slacks were made out of very thin fabric, and the weather outside must have been nearly -15°C. Typical of a foreigner not to think about things like this, Leena thought. She looked around. There were several rooms either side of the corridor, and a lift at the end.

Suddenly she heard voices. A door opened further down and two people, a man and a woman, stepped out of a room. Leena froze. It was Vadi and the woman from the lobby. He had his arm around her. The woman was now wearing a black, body-hugging dress. She looked about the same age as Leena, she guessed, but she was more slender, perhaps even taller than her. Leena was transfixed. The woman saw her and smiled and said, 'Hello,' in English. This caused Vladsislas to turn his head too. He saw Leena, smiled, as if he didn't know her, and nodded. He placed his hand under the woman's elbow and led her towards the lift. Leena wanted to run the length of the corridor and take hold of Vadi and scream at him, but she wasn't able to move. As if in a dream, she watched the two step inside the lift. Vadi turned and held her gaze. Leena stood still, his confident look bending her to his will, as the doors closed.

What on earth was Kovtun playing at? Iain ran down the stairs and back into the lobby, trying to think straight. Miss Joutila had said he was here with a woman. The Colonel had specifically told Iain the transfer was going to be solely Kovtun, that he had no family. He must find out more from Miss Joutila, or Leena, see if she might have been mistaken. The Colonel could find out from the hotel if Kovtun had indeed checked into the InterContinental. Of course, he'd use a false name, but MI6 had a good man inside the hotel. Obviously unknown to the KGB! Iain smiled to himself as he made his way to the public phone booth in the lobby.

Iain was relieved to see Leena still at the top of the stairs when he returned. She had a surprised look on her face, as if she hadn't expected Iain to succeed in retrieving her coat and boots. He smiled at her.

'Here we go, sorry about that.' Iain must be gentle. Obviously it had distressed Miss Joutila to see Kovtun with another woman. Iain wondered if she had started to suspect Kovtun. Goodness knows what he had promised her in addition to a win at the Friendship Tournament. A promise Iain guessed Kovtun had done absolutely nothing about. Iain hoped that Leena's involvement had been accidental. He couldn't believe that Kovtun would have been able to make her do his dirty work for him.

'Look,' Iain said, 'I'd like to talk to you, but not here.'

'No, not here,' the woman agreed, 'I live fairly near. Do you want to come over to my place?'

This took Iain by surprise. He watched as she unzipped her fur-lined boots and placed her shoes in the nylon bag. Her tone was matter-of-fact, but still...

Miss Joutila caught Iain's expression and said, 'I mean to talk, and just that,' she said firmly.

'Of course, that's very kind of you.'

The gym teacher's flat was smaller than Maija's, about the same type and size as the one Iain was renting. When she showed Iain into the living room, he noticed a low coffee table laid out for dinner: two plates, two tall wine glasses. No guesses who Miss Joutila had been expecting for dinner. She walked into the room and saw Iain looking at the table.

'Yes, he was supposed to come over tonight!' Leena gathered the crockery and glasses together and took them to the kitchen. 'What would you like to drink? I have coffee.' Before Iain was able to reply, Leena popped her head out of the doorway and added, 'Or if you prefer, *Koskenkorva*.'

'Hm, vodka I think, please.' Iain said and sat down. He wondered how much he would be forced to tell Leena about himself to get her to talk. The less she knew the better. Things were going well so far, she didn't seem hostile. He just had to be careful not to push too hard.

As soon as Leena sat down opposite Iain, she started to talk. Even if he'd wanted, Iain couldn't have stopped her.

'I want what's best for my students,' she began. She paused for a moment, taking a sip of her drink. 'So when I met this lovely man in Moscow and he started, well, courting me, and then said he could arrange that we would win the trophy, well, I could not say no, could I? How was I to know he was, well, that he had someone already?' The gym teacher's face was turned towards Iain, her eyes open wide.

'No, of course you couldn't know.' Kovtun's philandering is the least of his crimes, Iain thought but said nothing.

'I feel so stupid. The woman seemed innocent. She looked so nice, smiled at me even when I saw them again...'

'What do you mean you saw them again, where?'

'They came out of one of the rooms when I was waiting at the top of the stairs.'

'I'm so sorry,' Iain said

'Of course, I knew about the daughter, Vadi talked about her often. That's why I...' Leena put her head in her hands.

'The daughter?'

'Yes, Leena said, looking up at Iain, 'he said Pia reminded him of her.'

'And where is this daughter now? Moscow?'

'No, she lives in Minsk. But she's coming over for the Tournament.'

Iain stared at Leena.

The gym teacher got up and poured herself another large glass of vodka. She paced up and down the small flat, then sat on the chair and started sobbing.

Iain put his arms around the woman. She was slightly built, but her body felt muscular under the flimsy fabric of her blouse. She was wearing a strong perfume. Iain waited. Gradually Leena's sobs lessened. Iain got up and sat down opposite her. She looked at Iain with red, smudged eyes and said, 'I've been a fool.'

19

Pia woke up in the middle of the night to a bad dream. She'd been on the ship again. This time the Gestapo man had been Heikki. She'd seen a glimpse of his face and then confronted him. She woke up before she heard Heikki's reply. She couldn't get to sleep again. All she could see in front of her was the image of his laughing face beneath a shiny black cap and his buttoned-up dark uniform.

Pia crept into the kitchen to find her mother sitting and drinking tea in the dark.

'I've decided you are not to take part in the Friendship Tournament today,' she said.

'But I want to win! You know how much this means to me. And I can't let everyone down! Anni said...'

'Anni said a lot of things.'

'Have you spoken with Mr Linnonmaa?' Pia asked.

'No,' her mother said. She looked tired. Pia wondered if she'd slept at all.

'What about Iain?' Pia said. You said you'd do nothing until you'd spoken with him.'

Maija sighed and walked to the hall.

'It's four o'clock in the morning, you can't call him now!' Pia said.

Her mother had already lifted the receiver. She'd done that at least a dozen times during the night, every ten minutes it seemed she was trying Iain's number. By midnight she'd given up and told Pia to go to bed. They hadn't discussed Anni's father. Pia had a feeling her mother didn't trust either Anni or Mr Linnonmaa.

Pia's mother now turned around and said, 'Why not?' and started to dial the number.

Pia put her head into her hands. She was so incredibly tired. All she wanted to do was go to sleep. She felt her mother's arms around her. 'No answer,' she said. She kissed Pia on the forehead and said, 'I don't use these very often but I think you should take one.' She handed Pia a small white pill and got her a glass of water. 'Sleeping pill,' she said.

Pia woke to voices coming from somewhere in the flat. She felt groggy. When she was a child Pia spent all her summers at her grandmother's place. Sometimes she'd wake up with her eyes glued together. Grandmother would fetch a bowlful of warm water and slowly remove the 'sleep' from her eyes, as she used to call it. The woozy feeling she now had was exactly the same but her eyes were clear when she opened them. Pia listened to the voices. It was a man and a woman arguing. She pulled on her jeans quickly and found a jumper on the floor of her bedroom.

The lights in the kitchen were bright. It was still dark outside. When Pia stepped into the room both Iain and Maija stopped talking. Pia looked at them. They'd been arguing. Her mother was wearing her pale blue dressing gown and her hair was a mess around her shoulders. Iain looked dishevelled too. He was unshaven, his trousers looked creased and there was no tie. He looked old.

'What time is it?' Pia said and slumped into a chair.

'Half past six. You should go back to bed.' Pia's mother said. Giving Iain a quick glance, she came over and put her hand under Pia's arm and started leading her out of the kitchen. As if she was a sickly child, Pia thought.

Pia pulled her arm away and said, 'No, I want to hear what's going on. Did you get to talk to Miss Joutila?' Pia was looking directly at Iain, who sat down opposite her.

'Yes.'

'He spent the night with her,' Maija said. She was measuring coffee into the machine, with her back to them. Iain lifted his eyes up to Pia, but said nothing.

'What did she say?' Pia said.

'She's been very badly treated.'

'She has? And what about us?' Pia's mother turned around to face Iain.

Iain looked from Pia to Maija.

No one said anything for a while.

'Did you tell him about Anni?' Pia asked.

Pia's mother stood with her arms crossed over her chest. 'No, why should I tell him anything after the way he has treated us.'

Iain sighed heavily. 'Look, I know it wasn't right and I feel awful about the whole business. But, it's my job, at least for now...'

'What do you mean for now?' Pia asked. She looked at her mother and saw her features soften.

'Oh, it doesn't matter. We haven't got time for that now. Tell me about Anni.'

Pia's mother sighed.

'Please tell me – what about Anni?' Iain pleaded.

Pia recounted what Anni had told her about the Finns wanting to get rid of Kovtun

'That makes sense,' Iain said. 'Of course, we know he's a trusted interpreter.' Iain looked up, 'It's hard to get hold of Finnish Russian translators. Strange, but very few Finns want to learn the language.'

Maija lowered her eyes. 'Were you aware of Mr Linnonmaa's involvement?' she asked.

'Of course,' Iain said.

'But you said Anni was in danger.' Pia was watching Iain carefully.

Iain took Pia's hand and said, 'She was, and is, in danger. How do you think the Russians will react to a Finn getting involved with a defection to the West? Not to mention the Finns. Anni's father is playing a dangerous game. In my opinion...' Iain hesitated.

'So you knew about Jukka's plan all along?' Pia's mother had moved closer to the table.

Both Pia and Iain looked at her. Pia didn't understand who her mother was talking about, but Iain said, 'Jukka?'

Pia's mother's mouth was slightly open. She was staring at Iain, as if she couldn't understand what he was saying.

'Maija?' Iain said.

Finally her mother seemed to come out of her trance, 'Mr Linnonmaa and I exchanged Christian names on the telephone after Pia's little accident...' She coughed and continued, 'But the point is you knew what he was planning?'

Now it was Iain's turn to look uncomfortable, 'Well no, not exactly, but we did have information that Mr Linnonmaa was involved somehow...'

Again there was a long silence. Iain was still watching Maija. She turned around and started to busy herself with washing up cups and saucers left in the sink.

Finally Iain said, 'I'm glad you two are OK.'

Maija stopped washing up and faced Pia and Iain again. Her arms were folded over her chest but she smiled.

Iain got up and said, 'What time are you planning to leave here?'

'I'm not sure we're going yet.' Maija said.

Iain said, 'Look, I'll be there all the time keeping an eye on Pia.'

'Mum, it'll be fine,' Pia said 'You'll be there too, and all those people. What could possibly happen to me in the middle of all that? It's a huge hall, it can seat at least 1,000 people and Miss Joutila has been going on about how many people there will be watching us. Then there are the other schools and their trainers and parents. Finnish and Russian officials, the police will be there, isn't that right?' Pia turned to Iain, who just nodded, then said, 'Look Maija, it's up to you. If you don't want Pia to go, don't let her.'

Pia let her hands drop, 'I'm supposed to attend the final training session at ten, and then we're all transported to the Myllypuro hall in a bus. The competition is due to start at one o'clock.' Pia looked at her mother but she averted her eyes.

'Ok, I'll be there whatever you decide,' Iain said.

Standing side by side, the two women watched as Iain walked wearily out of the kitchen and out of the flat.

The morning was beautiful. When Pia woke for the second time that Monday, she couldn't believe the strength of the light filtering through her closed Venetian blinds.

Maija was already dressed. She had even put on her make-up and looked polished in her work suit.

'I'm coming with you to the rehearsals and then the Tournament,' she said.

Pia ran up to her mother and hugged her hard. 'I knew you'd understand!' She gave her mother a light kiss on the cheek, careful not to disturb her make-up.

'But what about your job?'

'I've phoned in sick.'

Pia looked at her mother. She was glad she'd told her everything.

'It's quarter past nine, so we haven't got that long.' Maija handed Pia a cup of coffee. 'I've also spoken with Iain. He'll be at the Myllypuro hall waiting for us. Hopefully that'll be enough.' She sighed.

'Did Iain say anything about Anni?'

Maija paused briefly before replying, 'No, but we spoke only a few words.' She added, 'C'mon, Pia, you only have half an hour!'

Pia had an unreal feeling. It was strange being at home this late on a Monday morning. She'd been given the day off for the Tournament while the rest of the class would already be listening to another boring lecture from the Old Crow. She looked out of the window. The street was quiet. The sun reflecting on the newly fallen snow was blinding. How could anything be dangerous on a bright and beautiful day like this? She started eating the rye bread and cheese her mother had laid out for breakfast. Pia wasn't in the least bit hungry, but knew she needed to eat in order to have the strength to carry through the programme.

. . .

Leena woke after a sleepless night. Iain and she had talked until the early hours. Had she made a mistake telling Iain everything? She peered at the large window in her living room and saw the sun was shining through the long thin curtains. It was in this room that Vadi had confessed his love for his daughter. Leena remembered how touched she had been.

'My daughter, Leena, my daughter crying in sleep every night. I must do something, I must get her out!'

Leena now wondered if any of what Vadi had told her was true. If this Alyona even was his daughter. Iain knew about the defection, but not that he was going to be accompanied by his daughter. But why would Vadi make up such an elaborate lie? The whole forced schooling of talented gymnasts, how Alyona was made to train even when ill with exhaustion or injured. How the Tournament proved the perfect opportunity to get Alyona over the border to Finland and then to London. He had even told Leena he'd send for her when they had both settled in England. Or had Leena just been fooling herself? Thinking about it now, she couldn't remember when he had actually said she would join them in London. Leena put her head in her hands. She looked at her watch by the bed. Just before nine. This won't do! She got up to have a hot shower.

The girls looked nervous. The gym hall was bathed in strips of bright light from the windows near the high ceiling. Pia Mäkelä had come with her mother. Leena went over and shook her hand. She was a copy of Pia, just a little older.

'Miss Joutila,' she said and there was a chill in her voice. But Leena didn't have time to think about that now. She needed to concentrate on preparing her girls for the Tournament.

The group of five girls looked smart in their sky-blue competition costumes. The cuffs and collar had thin white edgings on them. Leena had designed the costumes herself to reflect the colours of the Finnish flag. 'Helsinki Lyceum' was discreetly embroidered over the top left breast of each girl's suit. The three girls with long hair had it up in a tight ponytail, just as Leena had told them to. Leena frowned at Pia's leg warmers. They looked shabby. She'd have to remove them before the routine. All that was left now was to get through the programme as well as possible.

Leena clapped her hands together and shouted, 'From the top, start with the front roll, on my signal!'

When they had run though the whole of the ten-minute programme the third time, there was clapping from behind Leena. Other parents must also have decided to come to the rehearsals. Leena turned around to see who was being so enthusiastic.

The man clapping and whooping loudly was Vladsislas. He was now walking towards Leena, with a big grin on his face. He was wearing the long black coat and boots.

'Vadi,' Leena whispered. She felt the eyes of the girls and Pia's mother drill into her as Vadi took her hand and shook it.

'Vladsislas Kovtun, I am from the Friendship Committee. We met in Moscow some time ago.'

'Yes, yes, I remember,' Leena said. His touch made the hairs on the back of her neck stand up. She was afraid he'd notice her body shaking with the fury she felt. She needed to keep breathing. She must stay calm.

'I am here to offer you our best wishes.'

'Oh, yes, of course.' Leena was thinking hard. Why had

he come? And why the elaborate pretence? Surely he remembered Pia had seen them together in the classroom only a week ago? Was the man losing his mind? Leena saw Pia and her mother exchange looks. They had moved closer together and Mrs Mäkelä was holding Pia's hand.

'Are you not going to introduce me to all the ladies?' Vadi said, smiling. He turned around and started walking towards Pia and her mother, who were now standing apart from the group of girls, near the exit of the gym hall. Pia's mother had her arm around Pia, as if to protect her from the Russian. Vadi offered his hand. For a painfully long moment Pia and Mrs Mäkelä stared down at Vladsislas' hand, refusing to touch it. Leena walked over to the group and said, 'I'm sorry, Mr Kovtun. We are in the middle of rehearsals. Perhaps you'd like to sit down and honour us with your opinion of the routine?' Leena pointed to a slatted bench. Vadi let his hand drop, and with a forced laugh, said, 'Yes, of course.'

Leena checked her watch and saw they'd only have time to practise the whole programme two more times. They needed it. Pia had been slow in the start and they had overrun by thirty seconds. They couldn't afford to do that in the competition.

'C'mon girls, let's carry on!'

When Pia entered into her front roll, Vladsislas came close to Leena and whispered. 'I talk you in private?'

Leena felt the man's warm breath on her neck. She felt sick, but made herself turn her face towards the Russian and say, 'Yes, of course.' She watched Pia finish at the end of the mat and move into the correct position for a back flip. She looked at the large clock on the far wall of the hall and gestured with her head towards her office by the changing rooms. As she walked, she could hear her heart pounding in her ears. She hoped the man following her didn't notice how nervous she was. Be strong, you can do it, she repeated to herself.

Once inside the small office, Vladsislas pulled violently at Leena's arm and said, 'I warn you!'

'What are you talking about?' Leena forced herself to look puzzled.

'Yesterday at hotel, I warn you, not say word!'

Leena freed her arm and sat down. She crossed her legs slowly. She had dressed carefully that morning. Just because she was the gymnastic teacher didn't mean she had to wear her normal tracksuit. She'd finally chosen a short, black skirt and matching suit jacket with a simple white shirt. She was also wearing her best high-heeled Palmrooth boots. She noticed Vadi's eyes wander from her heels to the top of her thighs.

'Oh, that,' Leena said, and smiled, 'Of course I knew about you and that woman. It was just a bit of a surprise to see you and her there.'

The man was gawping at her. Leena wanted to laugh, 'I wasn't alone, you see,' she said and got up. She touched Vadi on the lapels of his coat and said, 'Don't worry, I won't say anything if you don't. Now I must return to those girls, if we are to win, don't you think?'

When Leena returned to the gym hall, the girls were standing around panting, with their hands on their hips, at the end of the programme. All were watching Leena. She was shaking, but pulled her back straight and lifted her chin, 'Right, all begin stretching, first quads, then hamstrings, arms and hips.' None of the girls moved. They were all staring at Vladsislas, who was marching furiously past them all, towards the back door.

'Do svidanja!' he shouted from the door and waved his hand in Leena's direction.

Leena looked down at her boots. She felt her cheeks redden and hoped she wasn't blushing too visibly. Leena coughed and said, 'Come along, girls, we mustn't let you cool down now! A quick stretch, and then one last time from the top!'

Pia's mother was staring at Leena. For a moment she thought the woman was going to come over and hit her. Instead, she sat down on one of the benches by the climbing ropes and watched as once again Pia pushed up her hands in preparation of the first front roll.

20

Iain watched Kovtun come out of the gym hall and walk into the centre of the schoolyard. He'd got to the spot in good time. He parked up opposite the main entrance, behind a corner where he still had a perfectly good view of the door to the gym hall. After the initial rush of children arriving for school, the yard was empty. During his wait the car had got cold and his breath was visible against the windscreen. To warm up, he'd run the engine for a while but turned it off just before Kovtun reappeared. Iain wore a felt hat, which he'd bought from a stall at the Market Square on his first day in Helsinki. He'd found it in the corner of the hall that morning and on the spur of the moment thought it might come in handy. As long as Kovtun didn't walk past him, the Russian wouldn't spot him. Iain checked his watch: 11.02. Half an hour before the Lyceum girls were due to leave for the Stadium.

Iain crouched down a little further. Why had Kovtun come to the school? To see Leena? Or Pia? Iain watched the Russian walk up road and disappear behind the sports hall. Iain lifted his head in order to see a little better. He felt in his pocket for the gun. On the other side of the road two men came out from behind the tram stop opposite and walked along the street in the same direction as Kovtun. Iain hadn't seen them before, but their clothing gave them away. It was one of the few useful things the Colonel had told Iain: 'The middle ranking KGB all wear standard issue Finnish Tiklas overcoats and fur Cossack hats.' Iain shook his head. He wondered if Kovtun knew he was being followed.

Twenty minutes later the door to the hall opened and Miss Joutila, followed by five girls and Maija, holding tightly onto Pia, walked from the gym hall towards the waiting bus.

Miss Joutila stepped determinedly inside the bus. All the girls apart from Pia followed. She was detained by Maija, who was saying something to her. Pia shook her head almost imperceptibly, and the two women ascended the bus.

When the bus had left the school car park, Iain waited fifteen minutes. Just in case Kovtun reappeared.

The drive to Myllypuro took over half an hour. It was in the far northeast corner of Helsinki. On the map it had looked a simple enough journey. All along the way, Iain tried to spot the bus.

Finally Iain came to what looked like a country lane. A small sign, marked Myllypuro Jäähalli convinced him he was on the right track. There were snow-covered fields all around, just an occasional two-storey wooden house. It was hard to believe he was still inside Helsinki's city limits. The road was bumpy too. Iain had to slow right down to avoid the pot-holes.

Finally he saw the modern low-slung building, with Finnish and Russian flags fluttering at the front entrance. Several cars were parked at the front, including a Russian plated bus. It had blacked-out windows, and for a moment Iain wondered how they could have driven the children all the way from Moscow in it. According to Council staff, Finnish tourists venturing over the Eastern border were also transported in buses with blacked out windows. 'In case we happen to see the true extent of the poverty over there,' Mrs Cooper had told Iain.

When Iain passed the ice-hockey hall, he saw the yellow and blue bus parked at the front. 'Thank God, they're here!' Iain said out loud in English.

He drove to the other side of the hall where there were steps leading down to a door. The car slid as Iain tried to stop too fast. For a moment he felt the vehicle was out of his control. He took his foot of the brake and found the first gear, while he pulled on the steering wheel and turned the car to face a large refuse bin. The car slowed down as Iain gently squeezed the brake and eventually came to halt.

When Iain opened the car door, he caught sight of something. He pulled himself down, and feeling inside his pocket for the gun, made his way slowly to two large bins standing at the far corner of the building. One was for refuse and one for sand. They should have used the sand on the car park, Iain thought. He could feel his heart pounding from the near accident he'd had. Or was it because of the puffs of smoke he could see slowly drifting up into the cold air from behind the bins? Iain ran doubled over and placed his back against one of the bins. He could now see the car exhaust and hear the low burr of the engine. Somebody was keeping the car warm. Iain didn't risk checking who; he could guess. He made his way to a set of stairs leading down to the back door of the building. With a little flick knife, Iain managed to open the door; suddenly he was inside a dark corridor. There was loud music and the sound of people walking in the arena on top of him.

Pia was so nervous she couldn't help join in the giggling of the younger girls. They were sitting in the cold changing rooms waiting for Miss Joutila to speak. They were one of several groups of girls of different ages. Some were still getting changed, some were practising their routines. Miss Joutila stood in front of them, looking down at her hands. They were shaking. Pia grew serious, 'Miss, can I...' she began but was interrupted by the gym teacher.

'Quiet, please.' Miss Joutila put her hand up and gave them a deadly serious look. 'You have a great routine and you have worked hard to perfect it. All you must do is go out there and perform. Enjoy the music, smile and give everything you have!' Miss Joutila ran through the procedure of the competition again, about when they were to enter the stage, when to leave, what to do at the end of the routine. She'd done it so many times before, Pia and the other girls knew it by heart.

When the gym teacher finished speaking, the younger girls jumped up and down and clapped. Without really wanting to, Pia joined them. She wanted to win so badly she felt sick.

Miss Joutila led them through the long corridor towards the arena. As they approached the steel stairs, Pia heard the Russian girls' prattle from further down the corridor. Just like them, the five girls were walking in an orderly line, with the smallest one in front. She was amazed at the size of the first girl. She could only have been six years old at the most. The tallest girl looked confident. Something about her was familiar. Her brown hair was tied in a ponytail with a bright red ribbon. The sickle and hammer on her costume made Pia shiver. She caught Pia's look and smiled. Her face, though kind, looked sad. Did she not want to compete? Or was she homesick?

'C'mon Pia.' Miss Joutila guided her by the arm. The teacher's face was contorted, her mouth in a straight line. Pia couldn't understand why Miss Joutila was so nervous. She should be used to competitions like this. It was Pia and the other girls who should be nervous and Miss Joutila, if she were a proper teacher, should calm them down by example. Perhaps she'd had another fight with Kovtun. He'd looked fed up with her at the gymnasium earlier. Well, it was her own stupid fault to fall for a violent man like that. Miss Joutila should have known better.

The lights of the vast hall blinded Pia as she followed Miss Joutila and the girls onto the stage. As if in a trance she curtseyed to the audience and then to the judges as Miss Joutila had told them to.

Maija was reluctant to let Pia out of her sight, but Pia convinced her that she must go alone into the changing rooms with Miss Joutila and the other girls. The teacher grabbed hold of Maija's arm and said, 'She'll be fine. I promise.' Maija watched as the girls walked around the building. People were milling around the entrance to the ice-hockey hall. Another larger group of girls alighted from a bus and, giggling, went the same way as Pia and Miss Joutila. A blue and white Finnish flag fluttered next to the red flag of the USSR in the slight breeze. The sun was low and hidden behind grey clouds. Maija couldn't decide what to do. Should she go after Pia? Iain had told her not to get involved, but to act as normally as possible. Maija shook her head. None of this was normal.

Maija found a seat right at the front, only three rows from the edge of the rink. The hall was full. She saw a few familiar faces from the school. No Anni or Mr Linnonmaa, though. The stage was decorated with the two flags at the far end. Maija wondered why the Russian one seemed much larger than the Finnish one. Was that a trick of the eye or had the Soviets brought a bigger flag with them? She wouldn't be surprised if they had. There was a large blue mat in the middle, and a long table with a row of chairs behind it facing the mat. The table was covered with a piece of felt that reached the floor. The judges, five women and two men, were sitting at the table chatting to each other in low voices. One woman in the middle wore black-rimmed glasses and her lips were painted bright pink. While the others chatted across her, she occasionally glanced at the large clock on the side of the hall and then at her wrist watch. She surveyed the hall as people drifted in and were seated. She seemed to be in charge. Suddenly she raised her arm. This silenced the people around her and most of the spectators.

The woman spoke in Russian and seemed to be addressing a cordoned off area on the opposite side of the hall. It was mostly made up of men dressed in dark suits.

Next a Finnish man spoke, but Maija wasn't paying any attention to what he said. Instead she was scanning the hall, trying to spot Iain. He had promised to be there to keep an eye out for Pia. Perhaps he'd gone down to the dressing rooms? Would they let him in?

When at last the Finnish man had finished talking, all the people at the table got up and started clapping. The group of dignitaries in the hall did the same. Slowly the

spectators realised they too should stand up and clap.
Finally a group of girls with red costumes and ribbons in
their hair ran out into the middle of the mat. The Russian
girls stood in a row, the tallest one first and the smallest last,
reminding Maija of the Sound of Music children. They curtseyed first to the judges then turned around and did the
same to the men in dark suits. Maija noticed a stout looking
woman with grey hair pulled into a bun watching the girls
from the sidelines and clapping enthusiastically. She must
be the trainer, Maija thought. She didn't look anything like
Miss Joutila. Once again the audience was on its feet clapping politely. When the smallest of the girls started running
back towards their trainer, the tallest one looked back into
the hall searching for someone. She was the same age as Pia,
and she had the same long dark hair. Suddenly her narrow
face lit up and she waved towards a man standing in the box
of dignitaries. The girl did a small skip and a jump, making
her brown ponytail bounce, and caught up with the rest of
the girls. Maija stretched to see who she'd been waving to.

She couldn't believe her eyes.

The man the girl had waved and smiled to so sweetly
was Kovtun. A shiver ran down Maija's spine and she
wanted to get up and go to Pia when the Lyceum girls ran to
the centre of the stage and started curtseying and waving to
the audience. Maija felt a lump in her throat when she saw
Pia in her smart blue costume, smiling up to the hall. How
confident and tall she was! And how beautiful! Maija's heart
was filled with pride. The feeling was almost unbearable.
She even wished Pia's father had been there.

Maija clapped so hard her hands were hurting. Before
the Lyceum girls disappeared and Pia ran away, she smiled
briefly in her direction, and blew a kiss to her daughter. She
looked over to where the Russian was standing. He was

clapping politely, showing no recognition of Pia. Maija sighed and once again scanned the audience.

No Iain.

Four other teams were introduced, two each from Finnish and Soviet schools. The severe looking Russian trainer seemed to be in charge of all the Russian children, whereas the Finns had a different teacher for each school.

Everyone sat down as the lights dimmed. The first Russian team of girls ran towards the blue mat. They stood still at the edge for a moment, and then broke into fast rolls and jumps, one girl imitating the next in rapid succession. Even Maija, who knew very little about the sport, could see how talented the Russian girls were. Their supple bodies were able to bend in ways that seemed impossible. When they jumped it seemed that they had springs on the bottom of their feet. Something made Maija look up to the top of the hall and she saw a familiar grey head. Iain was here after all! Maija smiled and turned her head away, relieved.

When the music stopped, all eyes were on the judges who had their heads down, making notes. After a few minutes, the woman in black glasses lifted her head up and glanced along the line of the table, first left then right. She nodded to Miss Joutila, who had appeared at the side of the hall. Miss Joutila opened the door, and with Pia leading, the Lyceum girls ran to the edge of the mat. The music started, and this time Maija recognised it. A piece from Sibelius' Karelia Suite filled the hall.

Maija had tears in her eyes as she watched the competent, but clearly inferior gymnastic display of the Finnish team. Now Maija felt even more anger at Miss Joutila. She had let the KGB agent into Pia's life and been telling the Lyceum girls that they had a good chance of winning the Tournament. The teacher must have known how brilliant the Russian girls were. Maija looked for Miss Joutila, but now she couldn't see her. Perhaps she was too embarrassed to stay.

Maija sat motionless and watched the other teams perform. Each time the Russians were much better. A small girl who performed an individual routine looked as if she was double-jointed as she performed her splits and handstands with a serious expression on her face. The taller, much older Finnish competitor in the individual category moved a couple of beats slower and achieved less complicated positions. Maija wondered what the point of the competition was. The teams were obviously at totally different levels.

After each performance finished to rapturous applause, the judges deliberated in silence. When it was over, all eyes were on them. The woman in the black-rimmed glasses wrote furiously. Then she lifted her pen and appeared to reread what she had written. Maija saw her turn the page and examine her previous notes. She lifted her head and looked across to the group of dignitaries. She nodded and turned her head right and left, waiting for each of the judges to lift their heads up and nod to her.

Again she spoke in Russian thanking the town and people of Helsinki for hosting the tournament. The woman sat down and a few people in the hall clapped. Now it was the turn of the Finnish speaker. Maija and the rest of the hall listened in total silence as he announced the winners.

21

The Russians are good, Iain thought. He was crouching behind a low wall at the top of the hall. There was a reasonable view of the stage through the banisters. Iain watched the movements of the tallest Russian girl. There was something about her, but Iain could not think what it was. He racked his brain as the hall filled with Russian balalaika music.

Earlier, Iain had spotted Maija settling into a seat at the front. He'd seen her look upwards, but he didn't think she'd seen him. That was good. He knew his time was running out. The performances would soon end and the Colonel would welcome Kovtun onboard. The ship's company was ready to sail that evening.

The music stopped. During the silence Iain moved closer to the stairs. If someone had spotted him, it was best to move about as much as possible.

The Lyceum girls entered the stage, led by Pia.

Suddenly Iain saw the connection.

Iain opened the door very carefully and glanced behind him. No one was watching him. The whole of the hall was holding their breath, willing the Finnish girls to do well. Iain shook his head and started running down the stairs. He hoped the music in the hall would conceal the rattle of his footsteps on the steel staircase.

When Iain reached the corridor once more, a door further down opened. A matronly woman came out and locked her hard eyes on him.

'Hello,' Iain said in Finnish.

The woman didn't reply. She folded her arms over her considerable frame and surveyed Iain. The door she'd come through was left ajar. Iain heard someone talking in Russian. There were giggles, and a man's raised voice. The corridor smelt strongly of sweat and disinfectant. The woman moved to call to someone inside the room, when a door close to Iain opened. It was Leena, 'Here you are!' she said and smiled. She nodded to the woman and said 'Zdravstvuite' in Russian, and then in Finnish, 'my husband.' She motioned to Iain. Once inside, Leena locked the door behind them.

'What are you doing here? You're not allowed come into the girls' changing rooms!' Leena hissed. 'That was the Russian trainer!'

'I'm sorry, I needed to talk to you,' Iain said.

Leena surveyed him, 'And how did you know where the girls' changing rooms are?'

'Aren't you supposed to be up there watching the girls – watching Pia?'

Leena looked down at her hands, 'I'm too nervous.'

'Ok,' Iain looked at his watch. He had no time for female logic. The Open Day was due to start in one hour fifteen minutes. It would take half an hour to drive back to Helsinki from here.

'Leena, could you go back up to the hall.'

'Why?'

'I think Pia is in grave danger. We must stop Kovtun.'

Leena was staring at Iain, 'I don't understand. What are you talking about?'

'Miss Joutila, this looks bad, I know, but trust me.' Iain took a deep breath and continued to hold Leena's gaze. 'I have Pia's best interest at heart and I believe she's in danger, in grave danger.'

Leena continued to look at him.

'Please, Leena, believe me, I've only told you what you need to know. Kovtun is a dangerous man. He has already killed a secretary at the Soviet Embassy and an innocent young woman in Stockholm.' Iain bit his lips. He was taking a big risk telling Leena all this.

'I don't understand,' Leena was shaking her head, 'I knew he was a liar, but...if what you say about him is true, how can you alone stop him?'

'Don't worry, I can do it. Now, you must go!'

Leena's eyes darted from Iain to her hands and back.

'I'd better get to the girls,' she said finally.

'Please, Miss Joutila, Leena, bring the girls down here and wait for me.'

'What are you saying – that Vadi is planning to hurt Pia? But why?'

The music stopped, and they heard the start of the enthusiastic clapping from upstairs.

'There's no time to explain, just make sure you bring Pia back here.' Iain nearly pushed Leena out of the changing rooms.

The corridor was empty again. Iain tiptoed past the doorway where the Russian woman had stood, walked to

the end and then out into the cold. The sun had set while
they'd been inside the hall and it was dark. There were no
street lamps at the back of the ice hockey hall. Iain climbed
the steps slowly, all the time keeping an eye on the bins to
his left. Following the brick wall of the building, he made
his way slowly to the bins. Some of the snow had frozen in
clumps and made a crunching noise as Iain stepped on it.
He cursed silently and stopped each time it happened.

He didn't see evidence of the car until he came right up
to the container wall. First he smelled the exhaust, and then
he saw the floating puffs of smoke. Iain froze when he heard
voices. He moved forward and knelt beside the container. A
man and woman were arguing in Russian. Iain hid in the
shadows between the lights from the ice hockey hall
windows and a street lamp on the edge of the car park. He
heard a car door slam, then the muffled sound of steps on
the snowy car park. He crawled between the wall of the hall
and the container. From here he had a clear view of the
headlights of the car. Iain heard the steps go past the
container, then recede. If Kovtun was going to go back to the
changing rooms, he'd catch sight of Iain crouching in the
snow as he descended the steps. Iain crawled towards the
headlights of the car. He got back on his feet and, staying
close to the wall, made his way towards the second
container, trying to walk normally. As he passed the car, he
caught sight of a frightened woman's face inside the
passenger seat. She was alone in the car, her face turned
away from him. Iain turned the corner out of sight and
stood for a while, catching his breath. His feet felt weak and
his hands were trembling. He now had a clear view of the
main car park at the front of the hall. The Russian bus with
its covered windows had started its engine.

Iain tried to think. If Kovtun was about to use Pia, how

would he get her? Was he mad enough to think it would work? He had to get back to Pia. He started running towards the front of the sports hall. He slipped in the poorly sanded back car park and landed on his hands. It stung. He heard steps behind him.

As Iain tried to scramble to his feet, a hand grabbed his collar and pushed him back onto the ground. His mouth filled with snow and ice. He tried to kick but the weight of the man was on his back. He tried to lift himself up and turn around, push away whoever was on top of him, but his back was punched. Iain tried to shout out, but a gloved hand grabbed his jaw.

'Silent, or I will kill you.'

Kovtun, Iain thought as the Russian pulled him up and started walking towards the girls' changing rooms. He felt the gun against the back of his neck. Iain's blood was rushing in his ears. He tried to keep calm as Kovtun pushed him into an empty changing room. Iain stumbled, nearly losing his balance, but managed to turn around. He tried to punch Kovtun's face but instead saw the raised hand with the butt of the gun pointing towards him before he fell down.

Pia was grabbed so quickly she didn't even have time to scream. When she tried, no sound came out of her mouth. It was as if her throat had dried up. She'd seen surprise in Miss Joutila's face and then she was grabbed. Next she was dragged along the corridor. She'd seen Kovtun's dark eyes staring at her briefly before he'd pushed her face against the rough brick wall, pulling her left arm high up to her back. It hurt and she let out a whine. The rough wall was scraping her cheek. There was a burning sensation on her face. The

Russian pulled Pia's other arm to join the left and pushed her whole body harder against the wall. Pia managed to scream. Now the Russian's lips were behind Pia, close to her, whispering in her ear, 'Quiet now, little Miss.' He smelled of vodka just as he had done at the Linnonmaas' flat. Pia tried to kick him from behind but the Russian was strong. He pushed his leg up against Pia's knees to stop her from moving, and stuffed something damp into her mouth. She tried to bite the hand, but couldn't through the foul-smelling cloth. It was wet and tasted sweet. The rope against her wrists was hurting, but at least her face was released from the rough wall. Now the Russian got hold of her waist and hoisted her up, while holding the cloth up to her mouth. She had a heavy feeling in her head. The brick walls of the corridor whisked by. She tried to struggle, but Kovtun pulled tighter on her wrists and pushed the cloth deeper into her mouth. Pia thought she was going to suffocate. She tried to kick again, but her legs felt heavy, as if she had weights around her ankles. The Russian eased his grip on her mouth and Pia saw her chance to scream, but when she tried she could not summon the energy. She managed to keep her eyes open, but couldn't make out anything. It was dark and cold. She felt like crying. Now there was cold air on her sore cheeks and she realised they were outside. She tried another shout but couldn't find the energy to open her mouth. Then she realised it was already open but had something in it. Pia bit into the strange-tasting cloth. She saw a bright light and they were moving towards it. Next, she was propped up inside a warm place. She tried to focus, but all she could make out were vague shapes. People? Who? She felt a sensation that they were moving, that she was no longer being held in the Russian's grip. Then everything went black.

. . .

Leena ushered the girls into the changing rooms and shut the door. She was out of breath, and panting hard.

'What's happened, where's Pia?' one of the girls asked.

She glanced over her shoulder at the four girls huddled in a corner of the changing room. Leena turned around and smoothed her skirt over her boots. She said, 'Girls, it's time to get dressed!' Leena tried to keep her voice steady. The girls looked up but didn't move. 'It's OK, she's just gone to see her mother.'

Leena felt a lump in her throat. She should protect these children against the monster she had befriended and...loved?

'You must wait here!' Leena told the girls. She grabbed her long coat.

The corridor was very dark. Only a faint light was filtering through from the arena upstairs. Leena could hear the Soviet anthem playing. She paused.

The Russians had won.

Of course, it had always been a lost cause.

Leena started running towards the end of the corridor.

As she passed the Russian girls' changing rooms, she paused for a moment. It was quiet. They must be upstairs collecting the trophy, Leena thought. Would the Lyceum team be missed? It would cause alarm, Leena hoped.

There was the door at the end of the long corridor.

Leena pushed the door open. A cold gust of wind made her wrap her arms tight around her long coat. The sky was pitch black above Leena. The lights from the hall reflected onto the snow beyond the small car park. Leena could just about see the shapes of two bins. There was something behind them. Leena walked over and saw from between the two bins the shape of a car. Suddenly she heard the car door open and shut. Leena took a quick intake of breath. Her heart started racing as she heard heavy footsteps scraping against the compacted snow. A tall figure in a long coat came into her view from the far side of the other bin.

'I think I'm owed an explanation!' Leena shouted.

The figure stopped. When he turned, Leena could see he was carrying a bundle. Pia! Leena ran towards the man, but he was quick. He went back to where he'd come from and pushed the bundle inside the car. He shut the door and turned to look at Leena. She was now standing so close to Vadi she could smell the vodka on his breath. His blond hair was tussled, and he had a hurried look about his eyes.

'What?'

'Bastard!'

Vadi didn't expect the blow, Leena could see that. She surprised herself with the force she was able to put into it. She'd never punched anyone in the face before. Her knuckles hurt a bit, but she didn't care. He deserved every bit of it!

The car door opened on the other side and the woman Leena had seen at the InterContinental Hotel last night stepped out. She screamed when she saw Vadi on the ground.

Vadi had lost his balance and was holding onto his face. Leena ignored the woman's screams and took advantage of Vadi's momentary lack of concentration and kicked him between the legs. She aimed her heel where she knew it would hurt the most. The effort of the kick was so great she too fell to the ground. When she looked up, she saw Vadi was doubled over, on the floor next to the front wheel of the car. The woman was holding onto him. Leena stood up quickly and went to open the passenger side door.

'Pia?'

The girl was hunched up, wrapped up in a blanket in the corner of the car. Her eyes were closed.

'What has he done to you?'

Vadi was moaning loudly. His eyes flashed angrily at Leena. The woman was trying to help him up. Leena was thinking fast. She looked at the dark forest that surrounded them. The black tree trunks stuck out from the white snow, at least a metre high. To escape there with the girl was impossible. There was no one in the car park, and she could not carry the girl even the short distance to the other side of the sand bins and the door of the changing rooms. She decided to flee alone and try to get help. But as she turned around, Vadi had regained his composure and was upon her. He pushed his face into Leena's and opened up his coat. Leena saw a flash of metal. She looked into Vadi's eyes and wondered how she could have fallen for this man. His eyes were cold and his teeth looked yellow when he spoke. She felt tears well up inside her. Vadi grabbed her chin with his gloved hand and said, 'Quiet, enough games Leena?' His warm breath was sour. Leena forced her face away from Vadi. She could no longer stand the sight of him.

22

M aija couldn't understand why the Lyceum girls didn't return to applaud the Russians when they were presented with their medals. She surveyed the dark entrance where the competitors had emerged, searching for Pia, or Miss Joutila, or one of the smaller girls. But no one stood in the shadows. Neither the judges, nor the dignitaries in the boxed area seemed to notice the absence of the girls. Where were they? Maija looked around the hall, trying to spot Iain. She left her seat as soon as the Russian anthem finished.

Suddenly there was a throng of people, all trying to get out of the hall at the same time. Maija tried to look above the heads of the crowd, to see if she could spot either Pia or Iain. When she got to the top of the staircase leading out onto the exit, she saw the Russian in the long black coat. He had his arm around a girl.

'Pia, Pia!' Maija shouted. Several people turned around, but the Russian carried on walking out of the ice-hockey hall. Maija pushed past people and shouted 'Mr Kovtun, Pia!'

At last the man turned around. Maija was now standing so close to the girl she could touch her shoulder, 'Pia, where have you been?' She'd recognise Pia's white down jacket anywhere.

The girl turned around, but it wasn't Pia. The Russian smiled at Maija and said, 'Goodbye, Mrs Mäkelä.' He put his arm around the girl and led her towards the glass doors. The girl said nothing, just allowed herself to be led by Kovtun. It was the same girl who had smiled so sweetly at the man before the performance. Something about the way she looked now didn't seem right.

Kovtun and the girl disappeared somewhere into the shadows of the car park. Maija guessed they'd got onto the Russian bus. It looked menacingly dark with its black windows. A row of other Russian girls, led by their masculine trainer, walked past Maija. The trainer had a clipboard as she counted the girls out of the hall. There were at least thirty gymnasts and staff. Maija couldn't help but feel sorry for the Russians. She had heard awful things about the Soviet Union. There were food shortages, imprisonment for the tiniest criticism of their leaders, and severe poverty. She wondered if these talented gymnasts had it any better. Did their families benefit from their successes abroad? Did they strive for perfection so they could leave the Soviet Union? Like the ballet dancer, Nureyev?

Maija watched as the Russian bus was loaded up with bags by two men in shiny black jackets. The Finnish yellow and blue bus, parked next to the Russian one, was locked up. There was no driver and no lights on.

The Russians looked ready to leave. Kovtun had reappeared and was discussing something with the trainer with the clipboard outside the open doors of the bus. Kovtun was waving his arms about, and finally they both stepped inside the bus. Kovtun came out just before the doors of the Russian bus closed and it turned away from the ice-hockey hall. Kovtun then walked into the dark car park and Maija lost sight of him. Maija felt relief when she saw the Russian was gone. She went inside the hall again. She must find Pia.

Leena woke with a start. She felt for her hands, but she wasn't able to move them. Her ankles were also tied together. She lifted her head slowly and looked around. She was in the back seat of the car, alone. The fabric of the seat smelled stale. Leena struggled to lift her body into a sitting position. Where was Pia? She saw there was someone sitting in the driver's seat. Or was there? It was dark, but she could make out the shape of a head with long hair. Suddenly a set of headlights of another car lit the space and Leena saw briefly the eyes of Vadi's woman in the rear-view mirror. But the eyes had looked different from the way they had the night before. Where was Vadi? Why was this woman holding her prisoner? And where was Iain? She needed to know Pia was safe. A glimmer of hope entered her mind. Perhaps Iain had rescued Pia from the car and taken Vadi to the police. But in that case, why hadn't he also freed her. No, it was hopeless. Leena's head hurt and her mouth was dry.

She leant over towards the front seat and said, 'Please,' in English.

Another flash of light from a car leaving the ice-hockey hall revealed the woman was gripping the steering wheel hard. She was no longer looking at Leena, but staring out of the window into the empty woods.

The front door of the car opened, startling both Leena and the woman. No lights came on inside the car, but a cold gust of wind hit Leena's face. She winced; it made her face sting. A girl with long brown hair sat down in the passenger seat. She glanced briefly behind her, with an expressionless face. Leena recognised her, Vadi's daughter. Leena shivered.

At that moment the back door on Leena's side was flung open. Leena saw Vadi's boots and the hem of his coat. He bent down and looked at Leena, grinning. He was holding the gun, casually pointing it at Leena. He motioned for Leena to move and sat next to her. Leena was too slow and was half crushed. He shoved the gun onto Leena's ribs and said, 'Not a sound!' Vadi made a gesture with his other hand, and the woman put the car in gear and drove slowly away.

'What are you going to do to me? Where are we going?' Leena said.

But the Russian didn't reply. Instead he took hold of Leena's shoulders and tied a rag around her mouth. Then he pushed her down to the floor. Leena hit her head hard against the seat in front of her, but she was too afraid to make a sound. She sat silently, trying to think.

Iain came to as the door hit his back He tried to lift himself up, but felt an intense pain in his temples as well as his back. Suddenly he remembered and got to his feet. The door to the large shower room was open and a boy was standing in the doorway gawping at him.

'Mr Collins?'

'Good God,' Iain said, 'Help me up, Heikki, we haven't got much time.'

Iain motioned for the boy to follow him. They ran through the corridor. Iain banged on the door of the Finnish girls' dressing room. A small face peered at him. Iain forced himself to appear calm and friendly when he asked, 'Is Miss Joutila there?'

'No,' the little girl whispered. Her thin hair was limp on her shoulders.

'Pia?' Iain said, 'is Pia inside?'

'No, she already went with her mother, and Miss Joutila went after her. She told us not to open the door to anyone, but we're frightened.'

'What's going on?' Heikki said.

'I'm not sure.'

Iain ran along the eerily quiet corridor and back through the equally deserted arena. Heikki followed, then overtook him and was in the main hall before Iain. He saw a lonely female figure waiting in the middle of the vast space.

'Maija,' Iain shouted.

'Where's Pia?' Maija asked.

'She's not with you?' Iain said.

Maija's face turned white. She looked at Heikki, and then back at Iain. 'Where is she?' she whispered.

'We have to find her,' Iain said and grabbed Maija's hand. Followed by Heikki, they ran through the cold car park to the back of the building. 'Get into the car!' Iain threw the keys towards Heikki.

Iain ran to the bins and looked behind them. The Russian's car was gone. He flung himself onto the driver's seat, next to Maija.

'What's going on? Where's Pia?' Maija asked. Iain swerved dangerously out of the car park. Damned ice, there's no grip. He forced his voice to calm, 'Don't worry, Maija.'

Iain was now on the narrow lane with the pot-holes. It was dark, and impossible to avoid them. Iain pushed his foot down onto the floor of the car and wished it could go faster.

'Where are we going?' Heikki said from the back seat.

Iain half turned to say something to the boy but saw Maija was holding onto the dashboard. Her eyes were wide with fear. He decided not to tell them what he feared had happened to Pia. The next moment, he misjudged the sharpness of a bend in the road and the front wheels hit the edge. Snow was billowing in front of them. All Iain could see was white.

Maija screamed.

Iain turned on his windscreen wipers. He could see the main road a few metres ahead. Without stopping he turned right. There was a slow car in front of them. 'Hold on,' he said to Maija and went to overtake. He narrowly missed an oncoming lorry.

'What are you doing?' Maija shouted.

'We have to get to Pia. I think she's on her way to Moscow.'

'What?' Heikki said. Maija was quiet, too quiet.

'With Kovtun?' she said.

'No, I don't think so,' Iain said. 'I think Kovtun is on his way to a ship with his daughter.'

'The ship?'

'Yes,' Iain said.

'What's Kovtun's daughter got to do with Pia?' Heikki said. He was leaning towards the front, in between the back seats.

'I don't understand...?' Maija said.

'Look Maija, you've got to trust me – and you too, Heikki,' Iain glanced at the boy through the rear-view mirror. 'I think the Russians have taken Pia instead of Kovtun's daughter. If I'm right, Pia is at this moment in the Russian bus, somehow disguised as Kovtun's daughter.'

'Oh my God!' Maija put her hand over her mouth. 'I saw him, with the girl, and she had Pia's coat on. I thought she must have the same kind of coat.' She was quiet for a moment, and then said, 'I could have stopped him.'

Iain pressed his foot hard on the accelerator.

Maija was quiet for a while, then she said, 'And what happened to you?'

Iain touched his face. It hurt and he was ashamed, but he forced himself to tell Maija how he had been attacked and shut into the Russian girls' changing rooms.

Iain drove on, feeling the warmth of Maija's presence next to him. She was a good woman, he thought. If he'd be in her situation, he doubted whether he'd have the kindness of heart to be friendly.

Iain overtook a few more cars, but otherwise the road towards the Russian border was quiet. Maija had told her she'd seen the bus leave about 25 minutes before Iain found her. But it could easily have been more than that, Iain thought. He looked at the speed they were making, nearly 120 kilometres per hour. They were now on the outskirts of Hamina. He'd seen a sign as they were approaching the small seaside town, saying the border at Vaalimaa was 48 kilometres away. Assuming the bus was also breaking the speed limits, Iain knew there was little hope of reaching the border before the Russians. Iain looked over to Maija. With her hands on her lap, she was staring out of the window. She'd been like that for the past hour, quiet, despondent. But as they came into the centre of the town, she pointed to a small church.

'That's where Ilkka and I were married.'

Iain looked at the small neoclassical church. 'So you know this area?'

'Yes, I was born northeast of here, a small place called Juvakkala, near Lappeenranta,' she said, sounding absent-minded, as if none of her past mattered.

Iain was thinking.

'Isn't that on the Russian border?'

Maija turned to look at Iain, 'Yes, very close.'

'But...'

'Look Iain, it's less than half an hour to the border from here, if you're right and Pia is on that bus, we must hurry!' Maija's voice was quivering. She was holding back tears.

'It's alright, Mrs Mäkelä, I'm sure we'll get to Pia,' Heikki said.

Iain glanced at the boy. He too looked pale and miserable. Iain blamed himself for being such a fool to allow Pia to take part in the tournament and then get himself knocked out by the Russian. Now here he was, on a wild goose chase after a bus that by now could be closer to Moscow than the border.

They left Hamina and the street lights came to an end. Iain drove as fast as the little car could go on the deserted country road. Suddenly the road widened and became straight, with generous curbs on either side. There was a sign 'Vaalimaa Border Crossing'.

There was still no sign of the Russian bus.

Suddenly Heikki shouted, 'Look, there are lights ahead!'

'Yes, I can see them too. Iain drive faster!' Maija put her hand on Iain's knee again.

Iain skidded as he pushed the car to its limits. But he got to the coach just as it reached a sign saying 'Border Control Ahead 1 km'. Iain overtook the coach, then turned the car so that it came to a halt in front of it. The Russian coach swerved, but stopped just short of Iain's car, diagonally blocking the road. Maija looked at Iain. 'Thank God!' She stumbled out of the car, but Heikki had pushed past her and was in front, running. Heikki was already at the door of the coach and was banging hard on it when Maija and Iain got there.

'Why aren't they letting us in?' Maija said. She was standing a little behind Iain, in the headlights of the Russian coach. The fumes from its exhaust filled the air. Iain looked further along the road, at the lights of the Customs building in the distance. Would they see what was going on? If the Russians didn't let Pia go, would the Finnish border police come and help? The Colonel would not like this, Iain thought. He pushed Heikki aside and banged the glass with his fist, harder. Suddenly he heard the noise of a lever being released and the door swung open. A man in a black shiny jacket stood on the steps.

'Can you help us?' Iain said in English. He took a step into the coach, but the man would not let him pass. Iain shouted, this time in Finnish, 'You are holding one of the Finnish gymnasts!'

'Pia!' Maija came up behind Iain and was trying to force herself past Iain into the bus. The man's face registered surprise and he looked behind him. The Russian trainer had come to the door and stood in front of the guard. She was at least a foot taller than him.

Maija stood close to the woman and started talking in Russian.

Iain stared at Maija, but she continued talking, waving her arms about. Once, she turned around and said something about Iain, pointing to his face. Iain touched his cheek.

For a long while, the Russian woman stood and contemplated.

Heikki stepped forward and said something in Russian.

Everyone is speaking Russian all of a sudden, Iain thought.

Without saying a word, the trainer stepped back and let Maija into the coach. 'You stay here,' Iain said to Heikki. The boy hesitated, but stood still when Iain stepped inside.

Maija ran along the isle of the coach and shouted, 'Pia, Pia!'

Iain walked behind Maija, past two serious-looking muscular men, one of them the man who'd opened the door. They sat at the front, and behind them, along rows of seats were the frightened, upturned faces of the Russian girls. Iain looked closely at their faces. No Pia.

The back of the coach was nearly empty.

Iain heard the trainer say something in Russian behind him, but then Maija screamed, 'Pia, what have they done to you?'

Iain ran to the last but one row of seats and looked down at Maija, who had her arms around an unconscious girl. She was wrapped in a blanket, and when Iain pulled it away to reveal her face, he saw Maija was right. Pia's eyes were half-open, and she looked drowsy. She was dressed in a white jogging suit, with the Soviet hammer, sickle and star sewn onto its chest. 'Mum,' she muttered and put her head in Maija's lap. Iain turned around to face the Russian trainer. She had her hand covering her mouth, staring at Maija and Pia. Behind her, the two men looked equally astounded. 'As I thought,' Iain said. Addressing Maija, he said, 'I'll carry her out of here, follow me.'

As they left, Heikki nodded to the trainer, but said nothing.

23

When Leena came to, she realised she was hunched up on the floor of the car. There were angry voices. She saw Vadi was leaning towards the front, his body filling the middle space between the two front seats. Leena didn't understand a word of the Russian Vadi and the woman were speaking, but she could tell it was bad. While her father was arguing the girl was very quiet. Leena wasn't sure but she guessed they were arguing about her, because every now and then Vadi glanced angrily at Leena. She tried to pray, but it wasn't helping. She couldn't for the life of her remember the words of the Lord's Prayer, even though she'd learned it as a child and always followed the pastor word for word in church. Leena leant her head against the seat in front of her, and suddenly she remembered. 'Isä meidän joka olet taivaassa...'

The slap came as a surprise. 'Quiet!' Vadi hissed. His eyes were blacker than Leena had ever seen them. Leena tried to crouch further into the corner of the floor and continued praying silently.

Suddenly the car came to a halt. Vadi got out. Leena was

shivering. She tried to be silent, but kept hearing a noise. She realised it was her own whimpering. Vadi opened the door to her side and took hold of Leena's arm. 'No, no,' she whispered. Vadi held the gun close to Leena's head. Leena stopped breathing and felt her bladder weaken. She sobbed as she felt the warm liquid flow between her legs. Vadi said something in Russian and sniffed the air, disgusted. The woman and the girl in the front seat looked behind them. Their eyes were wide and still.

Vadi pulled her out of the car and flung her onto the ground. Leena felt cold snow hit her face. She tried to sit up. She was surrounded by darkness, broken only by the bright headlights of the car. Leena saw how Vadi brought his daughter gently out of the car. He hugged her and placed something over her mouth. The girl went limp in his arms. Hurriedly, he laid the girl in the back seat and closed the door. Leena could hear the woman shouting loudly in Russian. She got out of the car and started screaming, and hitting Vadi. But Vadi punched her hard in the face, and threw her down on the ground. Her limp body landed on Leena's stomach. Vadi was holding a gun, pointing it at Leena and the woman. Leena shut her eyes, and continued her prayer, 'tapahtukoon Sinun tahtosi ...

'Are you just going to let them get away with it?' Heikki said when Iain had been driving for a while. They'd not waited to see whether the border police were alerted. Iain wanted to get away. He hoped the Colonel would not get to know how close they'd come to involving the Finnish police.

Heikki and Maija had changed seats in the car. Heikki was now next to Iain while Maija was sitting in the back seat, clutching her daughter.

'No,' Iain said, keeping his eye on the road. 'I'm not going to let him get away with it!' He glanced at Maija in the mirror, 'Is she waking up?'

'No, but she's breathing normally. What has he given her?' Maija's voice was trembling.

'Maija, I need you to trust me.' Iain turned half around and took hold of Maija's hand. She looked at him, with tears running down her face. 'We need to get to Kovtun before he reaches the West. He needs to pay for this,' Iain said.

Maija nodded.

Iain thought about the Russian Maija had been speaking. Then he remembered how Maija had called Linnonmaa by his first name.

'I didn't know you spoke Russian,' Iain said.

Maija was staring at him through the rear-view mirror.

'I was a Russian translator at the Vaalimaa border before Pia was born.'

Iain nodded to himself, 'And Linnonmaa?'

'He worked there, too, but not with me. He was some kind of Internal Affairs official.'

Iain glanced at Heikki. The boy had been unusually quiet.

'You know anything about this?' Iain said.

The boy shook his head.

'Iain, my work for the Customs has nothing to do with this!' Maija said. Iain glanced at the mirror again and saw Maija had tears in her eyes.

'Maija, it's OK.'

Maija nodded. 'I don't think the Russians will report any of this.'

'Why?' Iain tried to keep his eyes on the road while watching Maija's face through the rear-view mirror. She looked pale and spoke quickly.

'They were very embarrassed. The two men said no one was to know and the trainer agreed. They just wanted to cross the border as soon possible. I guess she'll pay for it when they reach Moscow. Poor woman.'

Iain sighed and turned to Heikki, 'And you, how come you're here?' The boy looked at Iain. 'Though I'm glad you are. Goodness knows how long I would have been lying there, unconscious...'

Heikki's face was earnest when he spoke. 'I was in the audience. When I saw Kovtun leave and then couldn't see you anymore, I came to investigate. I was worried when I didn't see the Lyceum team turn up at the prize giving.'

'Good lad,' Iain said, and tapped Heikki's shoulder.

Just before they reached Töölö, Iain heard Pia stir. Maija spoke to her in hushed tones. Iain overheard Pia tell her mother about being tied up, and the smell of the cloth that Kovtun had put against her mouth. Chloroform? That would wear off in time, but still the girl should be looked at by a doctor tomorrow morning. You never know with the Russians, they could be using something new. Iain looked at the clock on the dashboard. They only had an hour before *Newcastle* was due to sail back to the UK.

Pia felt incredibly cold. Iain had insisted she wear his new winter coat, but underneath she had only her jogging suit over the gym costume. Heikki too had offered her his leather jacket, but Pia had turned him down. She was ignoring him. In the car Heikki had asked how she was feeling. Pia wanted to say 'What's it to you,' but hadn't had the energy. She'd just closed her eyes.

Iain pulled the car up to the jetty. There were a number of cars parked up by the ship. 'Can you walk?' he said. Pia nodded.

Iain hurried Maija, Heikki and Pia along the dark jetty towards the ship. The upper deck lights of the frigate were shining brightly against the Helsinki night.

As they climbed the narrow gangway up to the flight deck, Pia wondered what she must look like with the large coat on. She put her hands inside the pockets and felt something heavy and cold against her fingers. She pulled her hand away quickly and looked at Iain. He was speaking to a man who touched his cap in a rigid salute when they stepped onboard the ship. There was a breeze coming from the sea.

'Welcome onboard, Sir' the officer said. He led them through a doorway and they were inside the ship.

The Colonel didn't look pleased to see them. Iain stammered when he introduced Maija to the Colonel. The Colonel ignored Pia and Heikki when he offered his hand to Pia's mother and said, in English 'How do you do, so glad to meet you.' He wasn't glad at all, Pia was sure of it. But he asked them all to sit down in the small cabin. Iain, Heikki and Pia had to perch on a bunk, while the Colonel and Maija had seats opposite.

'Sir,' Iain began, 'Kovtun tried to kidnap Pia today.'

'What?' The Colonel said.

Iain told him everything, how the Russian had drugged Pia, and then wrapped her in a blanket and smuggled her into the Russian coach. 'If we hadn't got to her she'd be on her way to Moscow by now, Sir,' Iain said.

It felt to Pia as if they were talking about somebody else completely. She put her hands around the gun inside the pocket of Iain's coat. She watched Iain and the Colonel intently as they argued about the Russian while ignoring the others. Heikki adjusted himself on the narrow bunk, but his face was fixed on Iain and the Colonel. Slowly Pia lifted the gun out and placed it inside the waistband of her trousers.

'I believe he was planning to swap the two girls, so that he can take his daughter to the West. The Russians wouldn't have noticed the swap until they were safely over the border. And, I believe, by then they would have been too embarrassed to admit to the error.'

The Colonel sat with his hands over his belly. He didn't seem at all surprised. 'I think it's best we show the ladies, and this young man, into the wardroom, or perhaps the captain's sea cabin if it's free,' he said.

Pia looked at Iain. 'I'm sorry,' she said.

Iain looked at her with a puzzled face, 'It's alright, Pia.'

The officer, who'd shown them in, appeared in the doorway again and led them out of the Colonel's cabin.

'But Sir, surely you must see that he is a psychopath!' Iain stood before the older man. He knew he had raised his voice and tried to calm down. He could see from the Colonel's expression that his mind was set. Iain sat down and started to explain, again, 'Sir.'

The Colonel put his hand up to silence him.

'Collins, calm down. He's already here, with his daughter.'

Iain shook his head

A tall man in a civilian dress came to the door. He ducked his bald head as he stepped over the bulkhead. Seeing Iain, he raised an eyebrow. 'Sir' he said to the Colonel.

The Colonel rose from his seat. 'You stay here, Collins.

Do not move, do you hear?'

Iain didn't reply. He watched as the Colonel got his cap and followed the man out of the cabin. It's going to be a crowded passage home, he thought. There must be more than one MI6 officer onboard for the debriefing. Then there's Kovtun's daughter and the woman from the Inter-Continental. Who was she? Iain remembered seeing her in the driver's seat in Kovtun's car. He'd forgotten to tell the Colonel about her.

Iain picked up his coat, which Pia had discarded on the bed, and checked for the gun. It wasn't in his pocket. He checked all the pockets of the coat. Iain looked underneath the bunk, the small desk and the two chairs. He opened a couple of drawers. Perhaps the Colonel had taken it while he saw the women and Heikki out of the cabin. But one drawer was full of the Colonel's personal stuff, and the other one was locked. Iain cursed under his breath.

The Colonel would be back soon and then he would not be able to do anything. It would be over. Kovtun's defection would be hailed as a great coup against the Soviets by MI6. At least they now had the crypto key. But Iain would get the sack. Back to Whitehall, if he was lucky. He had to get away.

Iain looked along the gangway. An older couple were being shown off the ship by a proud-looking sailor. They were on their way up the ladder. When their feet disappeared from view, Iain headed in the opposite direction, below.

The quarterdeck was deserted. Iain listened to the distant voices of the ship's company getting ready to sail. He estimated he had around fifteen minutes before he needed to find Maija and Pia, and Heikki, if they were all still onboard. He assumed they'd been taken off the ship, and he hoped the Colonel had ordered them a taxi.

Iain walked on the slippery surface of the quarterdeck in the semi-darkness. It was bitterly cold down here, too, even though it was sheltered by the flight deck above. A chill, icy breeze was blowing from the sea, which was frozen solid, nearly touching the ship's sides. Iain wondered how long it would take for the ship to be engulfed by the relentless ice and snow.

Iain saw that the low guardrail at the edge of the deck was also frozen. And there was a section missing. They must have had a ship alongside, and forgotten to replace the rail. Someone would be told off for it, he thought. He went to stand by the missing section of the rail, and regarded the icy water below. Once again, he realised how much he missed being at sea, being part of the camaraderie, having a defined set of duties, being confident in his position.

Iain sighed and walked slowly back. He stopped and stood with his back to the bulkhead, in the shadow between the two doors running on either side of the ship. This was his last resort, a mere chance. He would soon be discovered, once the Colonel realised he was missing. But there was a possibility that the debriefed man would come for a break here, for a swig from his flask of vodka, or a cigarette. Iain settled against the bulkhead and waited.

Iain's knowledge of the ship and of Kovtun's habits paid off.

The Russian, in his long black coat and boots, walked loudly and confidently along the starboard side. Iain watched his back. He went to stand by the guardrail, almost exactly where Iain had stood a moment before. He coughed and dug something out of his pocket. Iain stopped breathing. Kovtun took his right hand glove off and lit a cigarette with a match. He inhaled deeply and without turning around said, 'How long are you going to stand there hiding, British agent?'

It took a moment for Iain to recompose himself. The bastard still had to show off and make Iain feel small and incompetent as a spy.

Kovtun turned around with a short, sharp laugh. 'You not going to speak with me? We on same side, comrade.'

Iain walked closer to Kovtun. He needed to see the man's eyes. 'We saved Pia, you know,' he said.

Kovtun was quiet for a moment. 'What she to you? You not worried about the gymnast teacher!'

Iain couldn't bring himself to speak. His mind was racing, 'Why?' he said in spite of himself.

'She was a very good, how do you say it, at fucking, very nice body, but...'

Now Iain understood what the man was telling him. 'What have you done to Miss Joutila?'

'Aah, you English, you are so polite, Miss this, Mrs that. I knew her only as Leena. The Finnish women, as I am sure you yourself know, are very easy. They are like little peasants, simple and very grateful. But she got difficult. She had to be...' again the Russian hesitated, 'taken care of.' Kovtun flicked his cigarette over the side. He regarded Iain, and continued, 'But, you, you are English, you must soon leave this cold place in hell, eh, and go back to London, and we can have drinks, yes? No woman fucking good enough to stay here, eh?'

'You disgusting Russian pig!'

Iain turned around and saw Pia walk slowly towards Kovtun. She was holding Iain's gun and pointing it at the Russian. 'No, Pia, don't!' Iain shouted. Pia squeezed the gun.

Nothing happened.

Kovtun leaned back against the guardrail and took hold

of it. 'Crazy, you are all crazy.' Then he started laughing, knocking his head back.

Pia was crying. Iain was now by Pia's side and had taken the gun out of her hand. He saw the safety catch was still on.

'Throw it overboard,' Kovtun said.

The Russian was fumbling in his pocket. Bloody hell, didn't they take away his gun, Iain thought. He threw his own gun away and pulled Pia down to the deck. He covered the girl's head and his own underneath his arms and waited for the shot.

Instead Iain heard a strange moan. He looked up. Kovtun was struggling with his left hand. It had stuck to the frozen guardrail. He was swearing in Russian, pulling at his left wrist and waving the gun in his right hand. His eyes darted from the frozen hand to Iain and Pia. He raised the gun again to aim at them. Iain saw Kovtun's foot was inside the loop of a rope that reached up to Iain. He leapt up and pulled at it. The Russian lost his balance. He toppled slowly and the gun flew out of his hand into the air. The heavy bulk of Kovtun's body started to lean over the side of the ship and his frame disappeared unto the dark. There was a loud splash.

Suddenly the quarterdeck was quiet and empty.

'Did you kill him?' Pia whispered.

Iain looked around him. Faint voices came from around the ship but no one had come down to the quarterdeck. He picked up his own gun and walked slowly up to the missing section of the guardrail. A frozen piece of flesh stuck to the rail. The dark water below looked deep and undisturbed.

'They're going to find him.' Iain said, almost to himself.

Pia put her hand in his and said, 'Not until the ice melts in the spring, and by then he might have drifted back to Russia.'

24

Next morning the weather turned. The temperature was just below freezing and Pia left her hat and scarf at home. She'd decided to go to school even though her mother tried to convince her to stay away for a day. 'After everything you've been through, you need a day's rest!' But Pia wanted to get back to normal and her mother didn't insist. Unusually, she didn't mention the absence of the hat and scarf either.

The world looked different when Pia stepped out of the flat. The snow had started to melt, and there were dark brown puddles of slosh and sand on the pavements as she walked up to the tram stop alone. Maija took another day off work. Iain had stayed the night with them. He was still in bed when Pia and Maija were drinking coffee in the kitchen. That was another reason Pia wanted to go to school. She didn't need to be there when Maija and Iain 'discussed things'. Pia realised she'd stopped worrying about what he meant to her mother. If her mother wanted to marry, that was her affair. Soon Pia would be going to university and moving away from home anyway. She'd talk to Anni about that today. Of course, Pia wanted to see Heikki too. Though what she'd say to him she didn't know.

The classroom was quiet when Pia walked in. Everybody watched her. She looked past the staring eyes of her classmates to the back of the room. When she saw Anni's smiling face, she ran up to her and hugged her.

'I've got so much to tell you,' she whispered.

'Later,' Anni replied.

Pia sat down at her desk and turned around. Heikki was sitting with his legs up on the desk in front of him, balancing the chair against the back wall. He grinned stupidly at Pia. She nodded and turned back to face the front of the classroom. She was leaning over to Anni to ask her where they'd go after the class, when the Old Crow walked in.

The teacher looked deadly serious. Pia glanced behind her and saw how Heikki brought his chair back to the ground with a loud bang.

'I have some sad news to tell you this morning. Miss Joutila, one of our most respected physical education teachers has been severely injured and is in hospital. I would like you each to write to Miss Joutila, to cheer her up.'

As Pia and Anni walked out of the classroom, Heikki ran after them. 'Can I come with you?'

Pia looked at Anni. She nodded. Their next class would have been with Miss Joutila, so they had a free period followed by lunch.

'Sure,' Pia said.

The hospital was a few tram stops further up into Töölö. Heikki and Anni were reading the names of the wards on a huge sign. But Pia went straight up to a desk and said, 'My aunt is here, a Leena Joutila, can I see her?' A nurse in a white uniform took them to the lifts and showed them down a long corridor.

Miss Joutila was sitting up in bed in a large room on her own. A window overlooked the hospital car park and a row of flats. She had bandages on her arms and a funny-looking neck brace. Her face looked red and sore. Pia shivered. What had the Russian done to her?

At first Pia didn't think Miss Joutila recognized them. She looked at the nurse blankly when she said her niece had come to visit her. But as Pia, Anni and Heikki moved closer, Miss Joutila waved her free arm at the nurse and pulled her face into a faint smile. The gesture seemed to hurt and she grimaced instead.

Pia sat on a chair close to Miss Joutila's bed, 'Can you talk?'

'You're a good girl, Pia.' Miss Joutila took hold of Pia's hand and Pia saw how tears started running down her face.

'It's alright, Miss Joutila. He's not coming back.'

Miss Joutila was silent for a long time. Her face was pale, apart from a couple of red patches on her cheeks and forehead. There was a deep gash on her jaw.

Heikki and Anni said, almost at the same time, 'What do you mean?'

Pia looked over to the door and got up to shut it.

'Kovtun has gone. I saw him fall overboard on the ship before it sailed,' she whispered when back at her seat by Miss Joutila's bed.

Everybody stared at Pia.

'He killed that poor woman...' Miss Joutila started sobbing, 'and it's my fault.'

Pia thought how brave Miss Joutila had been after all. Iain had told her she'd tried to save Pia when Kovtun had drugged her, only to be beaten up by the Russian herself. She was only saved by a passing car, which had disturbed Kovtun enough for him to leave Leena to die in the cold. It was a miracle she'd been able drag herself to the main road where the police had found her.

The door opened and the nurse came in. She went to wipe Miss Joutila's eyes and face with a white cloth.

'Now, now,' she said and turned to give Pia a stern look, 'this won't do. You mustn't upset your aunt so!' Her severe dark eyes met each of them in turn. 'I think you'd better go.'

Pia looked at Miss Joutila and said, 'I'm really glad to see you, Leena.'

Miss Joutila tried to smile and squeezed Pia's hand. Pia wanted to hug her, but was afraid the nurse would tell her off, or that she would hurt Miss Joutila.

'Get better soon,' Pia shouted from the door, 'I need to practise my back flip!' Pia heard a gurgling sound from the room as she closed it after her. What do you know, the gym teacher had a sense of humour too! She took hold of Anni's arm and walked up to Heikki.

'Rixi Bar?' she said.

They sat in a corner table at the coffee place. Anni bought cinnamon buns. While Pia watched Heikki eat two in quick succession, Anni spoke in a low voice.

'My Dad says the Soviet Embassy hasn't said a word about Kovtun. Just that they're making some routine staff changes.'

'What does that mean?' Heikki said with his mouth full of food.

'They're sending the current people to Siberia and replacing them with more reliable ones.'

'Is that good or bad for Finland?' Pia asked.

Anni shrugged her shoulders. 'They're all bad.'

Pia looked at her friend. She wanted to tell her how worried she'd been about her, but something stopped her. Perhaps Anni would always be alright and Pia should instead worry about herself. She was the only person who could make her own dreams come true. She smiled at Heikki who was reaching for the last of the cinnamon buns.

'Hey, I think that's mine,' she said and leant over and kissed Heikki lightly on the mouth.

'What was that for?' Heikki said smiling.

'Nothing.' Pia linked arms with Anni and got up. 'We're going to be late for the Old Crow.'

A FREE BOOK!

Want to read more from Helena Halme? Sign up for her Readers' Group mailing list and get a free novella, *The Young Heart*, a prequel to *The Nordic Heart* series.

She's just 14. He's 21 and a grown man. Is she too young to fall in love?

Kaisa is the new girl in town – again. When a messy divorce forces Kaisa's mother to move to a small flat in an island suburb of Helsinki, Kaisa isn't looking forward to another new school. But in Lauttasaari she meets Vappu Noren, and begins to spend all her days in Vappu's large, chaotic house, filled with her three unruly siblings and their friends. Kaisa doesn't notice that she is being quietly observed by the friend of Vappu's brother, a much older, serious boy, called Matti.

Matti loves Kaisa at first sight. She is just the kind of innocent girl he's been looking for. Matti makes careful plans to seduce Kaisa on Midsummer's Eve. But is Kaisa too young to fall in love?

The Young Heart is a prequel novella to *The Nordic Heart* series of contemporary novels.

If you like an honest and intimate story of a young woman's coming of age, you will adore this 'Finnish Lolita' by Helena Halme.

Go to helenahalme.com and pick up a free copy of *The Young Heart* to discover this addictive Nordic contemporary fiction series today!

DID YOU ENJOY THE RED KING OF HELSINKI?

I'd be delighted if you could let everyone know and post a review here. Many thanks!

ACKNOWLEDGMENTS

I am in greatest debt to my family, particularly to David, but also to Markus and Monika. If it hadn't been for their patience and encouragement, I'd be no kind of writer at all. Thanks must also go to Sadie Walters, Pauline Masurel and Robin Pridy, for reading many early drafts of this novel. I am also grateful for my editor Dorothy Stannard for her impeccable eye for detail.

ALSO BY HELENA HALME

ABOUT THE AUTHOR

Helena Halme grew up in Finland and moved to the UK via Stockholm and Helsinki at a very tender and impressionable age. She's a former BBC journalist and has also worked as a magazine editor, a bookseller and ran a Finnish/British cultural association in London.

Since gaining an MA in Creative Writing at Bath Spa University, Helena has published 14 fiction titles, including six in *The Nordic Heart* and five in *Love on the Island* series.

Helena lives in North London with her ex-Navy husband. She loves Nordic Noir and sings along to Abba when no one is around.

Find Helena Halme online
www.helenahalme.com
hello@helenahalme.com

Made in United States
North Haven, CT
22 May 2022

19419208R00155